THEY HAD ALWAYS HAD
THE BEST OF EVERYTHING.

KATE, JAY JAY, DANIEL, AND ROBBIE—four beautiful, bright, gifted young people. Their families had given them everything the American Dream could offer—but they cast it aside for a darker dream. Together they created a world of invented terrors, breathtaking adventure, and glittering treasure. Alone, each stepped into the darkest part of his mind to discover forbidden places and learn terrifying truths.

MAZES AND MONSTERS

"A terrifying thriller and a story of love."
—*Pittsburgh Press*

"These four people . . . fascinate us, touch our emotions, and assault our senses. . . . A chilling novel of suspense . . . it weaves such a spell . . . that one shivers, hesitant to read on in the middle of the night. . . . Low-keyed and sophisticated, convincing and terrifying . . . a novel you won't forget." —*Winston-Salem Journal*

BY RONA JAFFE

MAZES
AND
MONSTERS

RONA JAFFE

A DELL BOOK

Published by
Dell Publishing Co., Inc.
1 Dag Hammarskjold Plaza
New York, New York 10017

For information address Delacorte Press,
New York, New York.
Dell ® TM 681510, Dell Publishing Co., Inc.

ISBN: 0-440-15699-8

Reprinted by arrangement with Delacorte Press
Printed in the United States of America
First Dell printing—August 1982

FOR ZEKE

PROLOGUE:

THE GAME
Spring 1980

In the spring of 1980 a bright, gifted student at Grant University in Pequod, Pennsylvania, mysteriously disappeared. Vanishing students were not unheard of, particularly during the stressful period before final exam time, but it soon became apparent that this case was different. When the police were finally called in, it was revealed that the missing student was one of a group at Grant who were involved in a fantasy role-playing game called Mazes and Monsters.

Played with nothing more than a vivid imagination, dice, pencils, graph paper, and an instruction manual, Mazes and Monsters is a war game with a medieval background, in which each player creates a character who may be a fearless Fighter, a treasure-hunting Sprite, a magic-using Holy Man, or a wily Charlatan. The point of the game is to amass a fortune and keep from getting killed. The characters are plunged into an adventure in a series of mazes, tunnels, and secret rooms run by another player, the Maze Controller, a sort of referee. The mazes are filled with frightful and violent dangers—monsters who can kill, maim, paralyze, and enchant the players. But if the players can kill, maim, trick, or stop their assailants they can take the fabulous treasure that awaits hidden in the maze.

What made the student's disappearance so ominous was that the police discovered this particular group of players had begun to act out their fantasies in a real environment, taking the game to the underground caverns near the university campus.

The caverns had been banned by the university as off limits in 1947, when two students, amateur spelunkers, were lost there and died. Their bones were found three years later. Now, in 1980, the police cautiously began inspecting the dangerous caverns again, but stated they were quite sure that no one who was lost in there could still be alive.

None of the other students would come forward to say they were part of the group that had played the game with the missing student. As the tension-filled days wore on, the Mazes and Monsters case became both a cause célèbre and an embarrassment around Grant University. Reporters came to interview students and professors, trying to understand what was now revealed as an obsession with a game—an obsession that had turned into something sinister.

"It's a perfectly harmless *game*," one student protested. "I mean, people who think that stuff is real are just nuts."

But often a defense seemed eerily ambiguous: "It's a game that doesn't require anything more than imagination," one student said. "It's inside everybody. You just have to tap it."

One student wrote a letter to the university newspaper, *The Grant Gazette:*

I know Mazes and Monsters is a very popular

game on this campus. I played it for two years. But last summer I destroyed all my $100 worth of equipment. The game takes control of your life. You change. I strongly warn anybody who is thinking of starting to stop, and anyone who is playing it to quit before it's too late.

Perhaps what was most disturbing about this case was something that was on every parent's mind. These players, the ones who had gone too far and the one who had disappeared, could be anybody's kids; bright young college students sent out to prepare for life, given the American Dream and rejecting it to live in a fantasy world of invented terrors. Why did they do it? What went wrong?

But for the friends of the missing student, the ones who would not come forward to reveal themselves, such a question seemed trivial and meaningless. This was their *friend*. They knew what had happened. They knew it had, in different ways, happened to each of them. And they knew that no matter what anyone said, what had really happened was much, much worse.

PART ONE:

THE THROW OF THE DICE

Fall, the year before

CHAPTER ONE

Jay Jay Brockway was the first of his friends to arrive back at college after summer vacation. He was always the first to show up anyplace and the first to leave—a combination of his need to be properly prepared and his fear of being left by someone else. Small and lithe, with a pointed face and a halo of golden curls, a sixteen-year-old Sophomore with an IQ of 190, an undisputed genius, the son of rich, rather famous, successful parents in New York, he knew he was exactly the kind of person the other kids at Grant would think was weird. And so, being not only intelligent but a survivor, he had turned everything that could have been a disadvantage into an advantage. He was different? Good, he would be eccentric. He was too young and too small? Good, he would become adorable. He was out of step with the masses? Perfect, that kind of person is meant to be a leader.

Jay Jay's ambition was to be a movie or television star, or if that failed, at least an actor. He knew he was meant to do comedy. He had chosen Grant because it had a good acting school, but more importantly to spite his parents. With his marks he could have gone to Harvard or Yale. But he had chosen a relatively unprestigious university which none of his parents' friends had ever heard of, whose good acting school had not turned out one famous star, and then he had proceeded to major in English. He had picked English even though it was the one thing that pleased his parents—his father, Justin Brockway, was a brilliant young publisher and editor in New York and everyone knew Jay Jay could get a job in publishing after he graduated if he wanted to. Jay Jay thought he'd rather stick his hand over a lit match than ask the fecalite for a job. He had a love-hate relationship with his father: missing him because they'd never had any rapport since the day he was born, and then his parents split up when he was seven and he went to live with his mother; and trying to imitate him in some ways, like copying his father's preppie way of dressing.

"Justy," his father, the boy wonder in cashmere crew-neck sweaters and chino pants when all the other executives wore business suits and ties. Jay Jay, the boy wonder son who had an even dozen cashmere crew-neck sweaters to wear with his designer jeans when everyone else in his school wore plaid shirts with holes or T-shirts with slogans on them. Justy, at the top of his profession at thirty-five. Jay Jay, a college Sophomore at sixteen. Justy, funny, brilliant, eccentric, and admired. Jay Jay, ditto. And they had nothing to say to each other. Never had.

His parents had lived together when they were in college, a rather unusual thing to do in the early Sixties, and then his mother had gotten pregnant and they'd gotten married, which was what people *did* do. They were both nineteen when Jay Jay was born. He didn't remember much of those early years of his life: an apartment with cracked walls, always filled with people, nobody telling him he had to go to bed, a home where he learned how to make sandwiches and drink wine when he was four, where people treated him as a sort of pet—something cute until it wanted too much attention and then they said, "Sit!" They'd had a real pet too, a large fluffy dog his mother had rescued from the pound, but everyone said the dog was neurotic and his father had finally given it away to one of his authors who lived in the country. After that Jay Jay always had the vague feeling his father might give him away too, because Justy never really seemed to like him any more than he had the dog.

"We were married too young," his mother said afterward, explaining the divorce, perhaps explaining how they felt about him. "We were nineteen. A very *young* nineteen. We weren't ready for any of it."

He had been born when his parents were just three years older than he was now. He couldn't imagine such a weight of responsibility. It gave him a chill. No wonder they had felt trapped. But he didn't like thinking about his parents being nearly his age and being reckless and romantic and frightened. He preferred thinking about his friends and his life here at college, and his image, and the game they would be playing again this fall. And, of course, he had to think about the big problem. They needed a fourth player. Michael had flunked out last spring after final exams, and that had made it necessary to replan their entire strategy.

Jay Jay began to unpack as he thought about what they were going to do. First he took the cover off Merlin's cage. His beloved mynah bird, whom he'd named Merlin "because he brought a little magic into my life."

"Good morning, Merlin," Jay Jay said.

Merlin blinked his goofy little eyes and began to whistle "Toot, toot, tootsie, good-bye."

"Oh, I love you," Jay Jay said. "I love you the best and the most. Talk to me."

"Birds can't talk," Merlin said sternly, just the way Jay Jay had taught him to.

Jay Jay laughed and filled Merlin's bowls with mynah bird mixture and water, and then he plugged in the electric heater that kept the room warm enough for his tropical bird.

He folded his dozen cashmere sweaters and put them into the dresser drawer along with his two dozen preppie-looking shirts. He lined up his collection of funny hats along the dresser top: the Alpine hat, the hard hat, the cowboy hat, the sombrero, the Snoopy aviator cap, the World War I German helmet, and the Mickey Mouse Club beanie with the ears. Shiny loafers were neatly lined up inside the closet, under his jackets and raincoat and down coat for the hateful winters. He unrolled his posters of W. C. Fields, Harpo Marx, Charlie Chaplin, and his true love, Brigitte Bardot, and taped them on the walls. Jay Jay was crazy about older women. He blew Bardot a kiss. Stereo components assembled and plugged in, tra la. Books and records neatly placed in the bookcase. A nice bottle of Mai Tai mix in case the occasion arose. A bottle of vodka in case it didn't. Six cartons of thin brown cigarettes that looked like little cigars, in the back of the closet because people in the dorm stole things. A little bag of Acapulco Gold—the pot of gold at the end of the rainbow—under the mattress. And, saving the best for last, the maps he had made of every Mazes and Monsters game the four of them had ever played, plus his dice, his new graph paper, his already memorized *Encyclopedia of Monsters,* and his Creature Compendium Advanced Edition III.

Now he was ready to go downstairs, wait for his friends to arrive, and figure out how to replace Michael.

Last year the four of them had been perfect. Daniel had been the Maze Controller because he was a computer genius with a wild imagination. Also Daniel was calm, and he was never arbitrary. If he said the King of the Gray Rats had bitten off your arm, he was indisputably right. If you were dead, well then you were dead. Kate, Michael, and Jay Jay had been the players. Kate was the bravest, Jay Jay the cleverest, and Michael—well, forget him, he was scooping ice cream at Baskin-Robbins now. At the end of last year they had decided that this year they would all get single rooms, but Michael would room with Daniel and they would use the extra room *just to play the game.* It would be sacred. Every room had a lock on its door. They would have their own fantasy world just for themselves and no one would know. But the dummy had been so involved in the game that he stopped going to classes, stopped studying, and blew it.

Nobody would room with Jay Jay; he was too crazy, and he kept his room so warm for Merlin that nobody could stand it. Kate and Daniel couldn't room together; there was nothing romantic between them, which was just as well. If you went together and then broke up it would mess up everything to do with living arrangements. Jay Jay wondered briefly what it would be like to go with Kate, and he smiled ruefully. There were some people you just knew you could never have, no matter how much you charmed everyone else.

He remembered the first time he'd ever seen her—a year ago at Freshman Orientation Week. She had just parked her car, a little red Rabbit with California plates, in front of the dorm, and was unloading it. He couldn't believe a Freshman girl had driven all the way across country all by herself. She was just his height; which made her five feet five; and slender, and she had shiny shoulder-length brown hair, big chocolate-brown eyes, and little freckles—but what was so marvelous was her smile. It lit up her whole face and made you want to laugh. Jay Jay fell in love with her at first sight, and actually offered to help her lug her things up the stairs, a considerable task as she had everything you could think of including skis. It seemed about ten minutes later that she'd found a boyfriend, and it wasn't him. But she remained his friend. It was sad when he thought of what would never be, because he was always right about these things and he *knew* he and Kate would never be, but he also knew he was the only person who understood her. She was small and tough and fearless and inde-pendent. Nobody messed with Kate. It was typical that when they chose which characters they would be, Kate had made herself Glacia the Fighter.

Jay Jay had been Freelik the Frenetic of Glossamir, a Sprite. They planned to continue being these char-acters this year, forever in fact, unless they got killed. He was the Sprite with his flighty but wily ways, the scamp, the trickster. Can't catch me, can't hurt me, can't leave me because I'll disappear. Couldn't hurt a Fighter either. But secretly Jay Jay knew that he and

Kate were just the same. For under that armor she wore for the world, he had seen what no one else had been able to see: seen it and loved it and loved her for it—her frightened, vulnerable, wildly beating heart.

He stood now on the front steps of the large, plain red-brick dorm, watching the golden sun fall down behind the identical dorm across the street, counting what must be the hundredth car that drove up and dropped people off in front of what would be their homes for the next year. The campus, in some awful way, looked like a housing project; big and crowded and impersonal, with sad-looking trees on stingy lawns. It was getting dark, and in the distance he could see the lights coming on in the town of Pequod, illuminating the fast-food joints and gas stations, the few cheap restaurants, and the giant billboards advertising exotic liquors and airplane escapes to Las Vegas or Chicago. He wondered if this university was like most universities, and if the town was like most other college towns; a small oasis of learning in the middle of larger towns that were all alike, surrounded by superhighways that led to similar towns and communities, where people led boring lives and looked out their car windows at billboard paintings that promised adventure. He felt much older than sixteen; he felt he had discovered a truth, and all of a sudden he felt lonely.

Then he saw Kate. She was driving her brave little car, and when she saw him her face lit up in that enormous grin. She screeched to a stop, jumped out, and hugged him.

"Jay Jay!"

"Carry your bags, lady?"

"I was going to drive right up the steps. Wouldn't you have just shit?"

"No, but you'd have ripped your tires."

"I think you grew," she said.

"You want a knuckle sandwich?"

"A *what*?"

"I think you're deficient in old movies. What did you waste your time on all summer?"

"Is Daniel back yet?"

"Nope," Jay Jay said. "We're the first."

"Oh, Jay Jay," Kate said, glowing with joy, "I really missed you guys. I'm glad to be back."

CHAPTER TWO

Kate Finch surveyed her new single room and decided she would like living alone. Last year she'd had a roommate, and had thought they'd share things, just like sisters, but her roommate had been withdrawn and cool, hiding her own troubles under an impenetrable mask, and now Kate was glad she wouldn't have to raise any expectations about things that weren't there. She'd done that too often in her life, and she'd learned. She unpacked her things hastily, in a disorganized way, because she was not the neatest person in the world, and made her bed with the sheets and antique patchwork quilt her mother had sent from home. A couple of family photos on the dresser and she was set.

A Polaroid shot of her mother, smiling, and her fifteen-year-old sister, Belinda, squinting against the sun; their arms filled with their three cats and a dog, all mixed breeds, all named after the Marx Brothers; the garden of their large, airy house in the background—that was one picture. Her father, in his new incarnation as a swinging single—his hair grown long, aviator sunglasses, a Perrier T-shirt a size too large that still didn't hide his little pot belly—was in a photo by himself. His snapshot was several years old and he wasn't single anymore, but Kate really wasn't up to installing *that* family picture yet. Her father dumped them—her mother, sister, and herself—when he turned forty. He had been a normal, rather stodgy stockbroker, and suddenly he skidded into delayed adolescence, announced that his life was half over and he was going to die without ever having found out who he was, and went off to live in Mill Valley, where people were reputed to have a good time in their hot tubs and to partake of a free and energetic sex life.

"*I'll* tell you who you are," her mother had called after him as he left. "You're an asshole!"

Then she had cried. Kate did not cry at all. She knew someone had to be strong in that family, and it certainly wasn't her father, who had fled, or her mother, who was like some helpless, bewildered animal shot for sport, or her sister, who was only a kid at the time and had wailed for a week.

"There goes Mr. Right," her mother said, her eyes misting over.

"Mr. Thinks-He's-Right," Kate said.

How could he throw it all away? So what if her mother wasn't a sex object? She was a little overweight and she never bothered with makeup and she wore kind of old-lady clothes, but she was smart and warm-hearted and poetic and she was a terrific mother. She would always listen and she never intruded. Kate didn't want a young, sexy mother who tried to act like one of her children. She wanted just the one she had. But now Kate realized that all the years she'd thought she was having a perfect childhood it had been a lie.

Her father wasn't a sex object either, but he was

the one who left and found adventure. She understood intellectually why her father wanted a new life,
she really did, but she would never be able to understand it in her heart. She felt betrayed. She never intended to get married. She wanted to be a famous
writer.

She was majoring in creative writing, but in the
middle of last year after her first great love left her,
and The Incident in the Laundry Room happened,
and things started piling up on her, she began to get
writer's block. Now she was thinking of changing her
major to English lit so she wouldn't flunk out. She
had tried and tried to analyze her problem, and she
had finally decided it came from the fact that she
really hadn't lived yet. How could you write about
things you didn't know? She was only eighteen. She
had a drawer full of lugubrious half-finished stories
with titles like "City of Heartbreak" and "Children of
Pain," which she was ashamed to show to anybody.
She couldn't reveal herself in real life, but worse, she
couldn't even reveal her feelings in her stories. How
could she ever be a writer if she wasn't willing to get
hurt by criticism and rejection? Half the time she
didn't know what she felt, and the other half of the
time she wondered who would care anyway. She felt
ignorant of all the secrets of real life. Being young
was like being in a trap: you could try as hard as you
could, but you couldn't get out There—where the real
action was—because you weren't strong enough. Something had to develop, like a muscle, and she thought
what that was, was maturity.

That was one of the reasons she had fallen into the
game so easily, embracing the fantasy of the mazes
and her own character of Glacia the Fighter with en-

thusiasm. It was like really being *in* a story. And you weren't on trial, because you didn't have to write it down to get a good mark. You had to be cautious every minute to save your life, to advance in the unknown places, to risk and seize and fight—and it made her feel exuberant.

She looked at her watch. It was three hours earlier home in San Francisco, so her mother would just be getting back from law school. She'd made Kate promise to call as soon as she arrived safely at her dorm. Kate didn't know any other mother who would let her daughter drive across country all by herself, and in truth she had been terrified the entire way, which was why she had done it. Kate always did things that frightened her, so she would get over them. Windows up, doors locked, radio on, eyes boring straight ahead, remembering that she was very good in karate in case she needed to defend herself; teeth clenched so tightly her jaws cramped, and not even aware of it until she saw the sign that said WELCOME TO PEQUOD. KEEP OUR CITY CLEAN and she realized she could hardly open her mouth.

The phone she'd ordered had been installed. She hoped nobody had been there before her and run up a bill; you never knew what people would do. She dialed home.

"Hi, Mom! I'm here."

"Hi!" Her mother was sounding really happy these days, ever since she'd gotten her head together and gone to law school to make her own life. "How was the trip?"

"Fine," Kate said casually.

"You *did* have enough money for the motels?"

"Oh, sure."

"I knew you would. I don't want you to be so cheap with yourself, Kate. I ought to be glad; I'm lucky. Most kids your age are spendthrifts. But I worry if you don't eat decently and I want you to have a good time. Your father is not going to cut off the alimony until I get a job."

"That's what he *says*."

Her mother chuckled. "Don't you worry. By then I'll be a lawyer and I'll take him to court. Listen, did you know you forgot your skis?"

"Yeah. I left them on purpose."

"Why?"

"I didn't have much time to ski last year. This year will be worse. Tell Belinda she can use them."

"Kate, are you saving me money again?"

"No, I just don't feel like skiing this year." How could she explain to her mother about the game, how it took so much time? It was just too complicated. Her mother would start to worry that she was neglecting her studies.

"When I think how much you wanted those skis, and how much they meant to you . . ."

"Mom, just be glad I didn't have my heart set on a horse."

"I'd kill you," her mother said, laughing.

"Listen, I've got to go now, this is long-distance. I'll call you soon. Love you. Good-bye."

She hung up, and after carefully locking her room went down the hall to find out if Daniel had arrived yet.

His door was open and she poked her head around the sill. He looked up and smiled, happy to see her. Kate thought how much Daniel looked like John Travolta—he was probably the best-looking guy in the dorm and he wasn't even conceited. Six feet tall, a great body, bright blue eyes, dark hair, an incredibly sexy mouth, and besides that he was a computer genius who would probably make a million dollars when he graduated, working for one of the companies that would be competing for him. She had never been able to figure out why Daniel had decided to come to a school like Grant when he could have gone to Stanford or M.I.T. Maybe he wanted to be a big fish in a small pond. He got all A's without any seeming effort, as if he was just treading water here. Women were crazy about him, but that didn't make him conceited either. She was lucky to have him for a friend—she wasn't sure she could handle him any other way.

"Hey!" he said. "When did you get here?"

"Just now." She walked in and looked around Daniel's new room. He was putting his things away. He had already taped up four gorgeous ecology posters from the Sierra Club, and they did a lot to brighten the dingy beige walls. On the floor was a row of brand-new track lighting waiting to be installed, and he had even brought a large plant. Jay Jay was sitting on the bed reading *Playboy*.

"Ah, come on, Jay Jay," Kate said, "are you *reading* that degrading shit?" She made a grab at his magazine and he pulled it away from her.

"You bet I am," Jay Jay said.

"Naked women," Kate said. "Exploitation."

"I am into voluntary celibacy this year," Jay Jay said. "I just want to remember what I'm missing."

"Well, you won't see anybody who looks like that at *this* school," Daniel said.

"Come on," Kate said. "You're an ingrate."

"I think I'm going to join Jay Jay," Daniel said. "Voluntary celibacy. I want to be a virgin when I get married."

"You're about two hundred times too late," Kate said tartly. She wondered why her tone had come out more hostile than she'd meant it to be. Daniel was her friend, not her lover, and she didn't care what he did. She looked at him carefully to make sure he wasn't offended, but he wasn't. He wasn't flattered either; he just accepted it as part of the teasing they all gave each other.

"Enough of this filthy, disgusting sex talk," Daniel said. "Sit down and let's get to serious business. We need a new player."

"I know," Kate said glumly. She sat next to Jay Jay on the bed.

"Maybe we should put up a notice on the bulletin board," Jay Jay said. "Along with the gay rights meetings and the science club. Wanted: a Mazes and Monsters freak who can play at the third level and promises neither to fink out nor flunk out."

"I hate to get a stranger," Kate said. "Who's going to room with a stranger?"

The other two nodded. The rooms were small; big enough for one person, but apt to be unpleasantly crowded for two. With two beds and two desks and two dressers and two chairs in one of these rooms the occupants would have to pick their way around the furniture or suffer bruised shins. They had decided to keep the bookcases in their game room, but it wouldn't be much help.

"First let's get the player and then we'll worry about living arrangements," said Daniel. "I spent the whole summer working out the new maze. It is without a doubt the most stupendous, mystifying, horrifying maze ever invented, and what's in it will blow your mind."

Kate shivered. She could see it already: the dark tunnels that so terrified her, the creatures that could be friend or foe . . .

"Is it okay if I put up a notice?" Jay Jay asked.

"Why not?" Daniel said. "Maybe somebody's bored with the game they're in and wants to seek new thrills with a new band of adventurers."

CHAPTER THREE

Daniel Goldsmith, of all of them, was the one with
the most normal, happiest home life. If anyone was
loved and admired by doting parents it was he. He
had grown up in the comfortable suburb of Brookline, Massachusetts; his father was a professor of political science at Harvard, in nearby Cambridge, and
his mother did art therapy with emotionally disturbed children at Mass General Hospital. It was an
intellectual family, where bookshelves were overflow-
ing with all kinds of books, good art hung on the
walls, and classical music was always playing. On Friday nights his mother, who took being Jewish seriously, lit the candles before supper and said a prayer,
and his father, who was not religious, tolerated it with
a sort of wry fondness. Religion meant Family to his
mother; the two were one: stability, the most important thing you could believe in. Besides security, his
parents loved a good argument. Their house was often filled with friends having endless, spirited discus-
sions about everything from politics to psychology,
while his mother served coffee from a restaurant-size
urn.

Daniel was their joy, their hope. He was the bright
one, the son with the wonderful future. His older

brother, Andy, a handsome, easygoing young man, had chosen to be a gym teacher, and it was typical of their parents that they were just as proud of Andy as they were of Daniel, only in a different way.

"Andy keeps kids out of trouble," his mother said proudly, as if by teaching basketball in a middle-class suburban public high school he was single-handedly saving a flock of future juvenile delinquents. Andy shared an apartment with his girl friend, a pretty social worker named Beth, and his mother acted as if they were both in the same profession.

Ah, but Daniel, he was extraordinary. He was the computer genius who would save the world. Goodness knows, the world was rotten and needed saving. What Daniel really wanted to do was make up games for computers. His parents thought that would be a nice hobby, something he could do on the side. They tried not to pressure him. After all, they knew that pressure causes rebellion.

The only time they made a fuss was when he announced he was not going to M.I.T., but to Grant. They were horrified. To turn down M.I.T.?

"I want to go away from home," he said. "I need space."

"We give you space," his mother said. "You can live in the dorm. We've been saving money for your education since you were born—you can live in the dorm or even have your own apartment if you like."

"Space is an overused concept of the Seventies," his father said. "Space exists inside your own head."

"I don't want to be in Cambridge, that's all."

"If I see you coming out of the subway I promise not to say hello," his mother said. She gave him a look of disgust and went into the kitchen.

Daniel followed her. "Mom . . . I just don't know what I want to be."

"Of course you know."

"It's too soon. Everybody always knew, but I'm not so sure. I want to put my life on hold for a while."

"Terrific," she said angrily. "And then you'll come out of that Grant University and look for a job and they'll say, 'Sorry, we want someone from M.I.T.' "

"You always said money was far less important than personal satisfaction."

She had a long, wicked-looking knife in her hand and was hacking at the fat on a roast of beef, making a mess. "It's a rat race out there," she said, without looking up.

"I can always transfer," he said weakly. He felt as if she were strangling him. His parents had always given him advice but never orders, and there had never been anything he hadn't been allowed to do. Except fail. Or be ordinary. He suddenly envied his brother Andy for doing something simple that he loved, for never being hassled, for not having to be special.

"I truly don't understand, Daniel," his mother said. She looked up at him, finally, and he saw that her eyes were full of tears. "I thought you were different from other kids. You always had such a sense of purpose. Did *we* fail you somehow? Did we do something wrong?"

"No," he said. He went over and put his arms around her. Her bones felt very small. "People don't always run away from something bad. Sometimes people have to run away from perfection."

"We're far from perfect," she said, surprised, but he saw with relief that the tears in her eyes were gone.

So he had gone to Grant. And now he was starting

his Junior year, nineteen years old, comfortable with his work and his friends, involved in the game he had discovered at college, spending all his free time making up new and more devious versions. He also ran. He liked running down the long empty streets of Pequod at dawn, out to the suburbs that reminded him of Brookline, looping back past the shopping mall just as the giant produce trucks came pulling up; all the time planning strategies for the game. This was exactly what he had wanted to do with his life.

Sometimes he varied the route of his early-morning run, several times going out to the forbidden caverns that lay to the east. They didn't look so ominous from the outside. If it weren't for the iron chain that had been bolted into the stones outside the main entrance, and the green and white sign that said DANGEROUS CAVERNS. KEEP OUT, you would think they were just some picturesque caves under a hill. They looked like a tourist attraction. But he had heard they extended for miles under the ground, and were filled with bottomless lakes and black pools, stalactites and stalagmites, endless turns, and tiny, hidden rooms where a person could be lost forever. Worst of all, they were pitch-dark. Sometimes, running by, Daniel had a little thrill of curiosity; just to *see*. He supposed everybody had that feeling once in a while. It was probably what had inspired those two students to explore the caves so long ago, the students who had died.

He simply had no concept of death. Sometimes, driving in a car when he knew he'd had too much to drink at a party, he was aware of danger, but it never occurred to him that he might be killed, even though people often were. You got killed in a war. Everybody knew that. Or someday, when you were middle-aged, the pollution of foul chemicals could give you cancer. But not now. Now he felt immortal. All the terrors of disease and unexpected death were for later, for other people.

CHAPTER FOUR

Feeling very new, young, frightened, and shy, Robbie Wheeling began his first day as an entering Freshman at Grant University. Back home in Greenwich, Connecticut, he'd been a star of sorts: captain of the high school swimming team, managing editor of the yearbook, popular and secure. Now he was a stranger in a strange place. The dorm he'd been assigned to, Hollis East, seemed huge, and his single room was bare and ugly. There was a lumpy single bed, a scratched wooden desk with a matching chair, a lamp that looked like it came from the Salvation Army, and a wooden bookshelf with graffiti on it. One closet. He'd been issued a key to the lock on his door, to guard all these possessions and whatever he'd brought from home. He dropped the last of his things: his duffel bag and the large carton containing his stereo equipment, and went to look out the window. Being a Freshman, the lowliest of the low, he was assigned a room at the rear of the dorm that looked out on a parking lot. There was his little tan Fiat Spider convertible, his graduation present from his parents, parked along with an assortment of cars belonging to the people he hoped he'd eventually meet, one small motorcycle, and a jumble of bicycles, all carefully chained and locked. Behind him, through his partly open door, he could hear girls' voices and the stamp of feet along the hall. He wondered what it would be like to live in a coed dorm. Was there a lot of sex, or what? The thought of endless adventures cheered him up a little, and he began to unpack.

He was eighteen years old, six feet tall, with the long, smooth muscles of a swimmer, and a face that was so handsome it was almost beautiful. Green eyes with a thick fringe of dark lashes, fair hair, and dimples. He'd never had any problem getting girls, but he thought now, here in this strange place, that he would like to find one person, fall in love, have a real relationship. He'd never had that, and it seemed to be time. Maybe he could make it last for his entire Freshman year, or at least through the winter. He thought of a girl sitting on his bed, studying, snow falling cozily outside the window, and the room didn't look so grim anymore. *Women.* He would have to remember to call them women. They were in college now.

Robbie was glad to be away from home at last. There was nothing there at all for him, never had been, particularly ever since that night his brother ran away again and never came back. After that night Robbie could never look up at the stars without wondering where his brother was and if he was looking at them too, and if they looked the same where he was ... or if he was still alive.

His parents were victims of history. Strangers when they married each other way back in the Fifties; his mother just out of Vassar, his father all excited about his first job in an architectural firm; his older brother, Hall junior, born just ten months later—they

were a whole family before his parents even got to
know each other. His mother had told him that story
a million times. In those days people didn't live together before they got married. Other people's
parents, whom Robbie knew, had gotten married the
same way, and had kids, and they got along fine. But
his parents fought and yelled, when they spoke to
each other at all; endlessly recriminating each other
about the past, their wasted lives, their unfulfilled
dreams. Yet they would never leave each other. Something held them together, some need "to make it
work." Make what work? His mother had been an alcoholic as long as he could remember. In the suburbs
alcoholics have one of two choices: drive their kids to
the things they have to do and risk getting killed, or
become housebound and trapped. When his mother
stopped driving him Robbie was relieved.

Now his father was the head of his own architectural firm, with a big office in New York, and his
designs were featured in international magazines. As
a symbol of his success, his father had had a different
Cartier watch for every day of the week, until his
mother got mad and smashed them all, the night his
brother left. She's smashed ten thousand dollars'
worth of watches in one night. That wasn't the only
thing that had been smashed in one night—their lives
had, all of their lives . . . but he wasn't going to
think about that now.

Three weeks after he'd started at college Robbie
was enjoying himself more than he'd anticipated, and
almost as much as he'd hoped. He still didn't know
what he wanted to major in, or what he wanted to do
with his future, so he had registered for the manda-

tory courses to get them over with and had tried out for and gotten on the swimming team. He'd met quite a few people in his dorm and some in his classes, and gone to bed with a few Freshman girls who seemed overwhelmed with the headiness of living in a coed dorm and didn't seem to care if they never saw him aagin. At first he thought it was because he hadn't done something right, but then he realized they had just been let out of some uptight all-girls school, or some strict home, and were making up for lost time. Some of the guys were the same way. They all seemed to be Freshmen. The upperclassmen had already gotten over the novelty of living in a candy store and were leading normal lives. He had written only one letter to his parents, and it had taken him an hour to think of anything to say. He supposed his mother would be too drunk to read it and his father wouldn't care what he said as long as he wasn't in trouble.

Meals were served in the dorm dining room, which was like an enormous cafeteria. First you went into the kitchen, where you stood on line and served yourself from a bewildering array of food to suit any fad or dietary cult. Most of it turned out to be greasy junk anyway. Then you went into the dining room and sat at a table with people you knew, if you could find them, or else with strangers. You were really aware of how big the dorm was when you saw the crowd at mealtime. Some of the people just propped up books in front of their plates and didn't talk to anyone at all. Because of swimming practice, Robbie usually arrived at dinner late and had to sit wherever there was still room. It forced him to speak to people

he didn't know, which was scaring him less now that
he was beginning to know his way around.

Tonight, holding his filled tray and trying to
maneuver through the narrow spaces between the
long tables, he found an empty seat next to a really
weird kid. He was wearing a black leather aviator's
cap like Robbie had seen in old war movies on TV,
and around his neck was a pair of goggles and a long
white silk scarf. He had a little pointy face with a
mischievous look on it, and he looked about fourteen.

"Jay Jay Brockway," the kid said, holding out his
hand.

"I'm Robbie Wheeling."

"I've seen you before. Tan Fiat Spider."

"Right . . ."

"I had one," Jay Jay said. "Mine was red. The
fecalite gave it to me for my birthday, neglecting to
notice I was still too young to get my license, and I
sold it to bug him and bought my mynah bird and a
motorbike. Mynah birds cost a fortune if you want a
good one."

"The what?" Robbie said.

"What what?"

"Who's, what's a fecalite?"

"My father. It's a petrified dinosaur turd. Sorry, am
I ruining your dinner? He's ruined many of mine."

Robbie had never heard anybody talk that way
about their parents before, or indeed about anything
so bizarre, to a total stranger. He supposed the outfit
Jay Jay was wearing had to do with his motorbike,
but why hadn't he taken it off before he came to dinner?

"Do you like Brigitte Bardot?" Jay Jay continued.

He took a long, thin brown cigarette from a pack and lit it, then offered the pack to Robbie.

"No, thanks, I don't smoke."

"Because I'm giving a party tomorrow night for Brigitte Bardot's birthday, and if you would like to attend, it's any time after eight, second floor, the room with the noise."

"Thank you," Robbie said. Brigitte Bardot was some old movie actress, he remembered now. "Is she *here*?"

"Who?"

"Who you're giving the party for."

"Are you stoned?" Jay Jay asked, peering at him anxiously. He was beginning to look as if he regretted extending the invitation.

"No."

"Of course she's not here. Why would she come to this dump?"

"I don't know," Robbie said. He thought fast. "Elizabeth Taylor went to Harvard once."

"So she did . . ." Jay Jay said thoughtfully. His face lit up. "Maybe next year I'll *invite* B. B." He pushed back his chair and stood up. He was very short. "See you tomorrow night. Bring booze, and no more than two friends, preferably interesting."

Mynah bird? Robbie thought, looking after him. His first party at Grant! He could hardly wait.

At half past eight, when Robbie went looking for the party, he saw that it was already in full swing. People had spilled out of Jay Jay's room into the hall, and into other rooms, and music was blasting. If anyone had planned to study tonight it was obviously hopeless, but no one seemed to care. There must have been at least a hundred people milling around, drinking beer or wine, smoking, talking, dancing, and making noise. Carrying a bottle of red wine he'd bought he pushed his way through the crowd to find his host. He finally saw him, almost hidden in the sea of people, wearing a tuxedo and a hard hat, and looking very happy. Next to him was one of the prettiest girls Robbie had ever seen. She had shiny brown hair and huge dark eyes, and her lips turned up at the corners even when she wasn't smiling. Jay Jay's stereo was playing Donna Summer singing "MacArthur Park."

"Jay Jay!" Robbie shouted, holding up his bottle of wine.

Jay Jay steered him in like a ship to port. "This is Kate Finch," he said. "Robbie Wheeling."

"Hi," she said, and smiled, and held out her surprisingly hard little hand for him to shake.

After all the loves in my life, you'll still be the one, the record played. Donna singing, the beat of the music rocking through the room. Every time you fall in love you notice what song is playing, and you always remember it. Robbie looked at Kate Finch and knew that she would always be the record of Donna Summer singing "MacArthur Park." He looked into her eyes and couldn't think of a thing to say to her.

"Well, I guess you want a corkscrew," she said.

"I guess so."

She reached behind her and produced one, and two plastic glasses. He busied himself with opening the bottle so he wouldn't have to think of something to say. Jay Jay had disappeared into the crowd again. Robbie poured wine into the two glasses, although he really didn't much like wine, and handed one to her.

"You live in Hollis?" she asked pleasantly.

"Yes. Do you?"

"Right down the hall."

"Does he really have a mynah bird?"

"Right over there."

A black bird with a yellow beak was looking at him from a large silver cage. "Isn't it frightened?"

She shrugged and smiled. "With Jay Jay you get used to anything."

He wanted to say something wonderful so she would be impressed, so she would remember him, and he had never felt so stupid in his life. He looked at his still-full glass.

"What's the matter?" she said.

"I wish we could start in the middle. I wish we'd known each other for two weeks and we knew everything about each other, and we liked each other a lot, and I wouldn't be so nervous."

She laughed. Her laugh was just as good as her smile. "Are you scared of me?"

"I'm *not* usually like this," Robbie said.

"I like it," she said gently.

"I'm really interesting when you get to know me," he blurted.

She took his hand and led him out of the party and down the hall to her room. She unlocked the door and led him inside, then she closed the door. He was terrified. He didn't know what she wanted, but since she hadn't locked the door . . .

She sat on top of her desk, hooked her feet over the edge, put her arms around her knees, and looked at him with big eyes filled with amusement and tolerance and genuine friendliness. "Talk," she said.

After a while it wasn't so bad, and soon he began to feel comfortable with her. She actually seemed to care what he had to say, no matter how dumb it was, like how he didn't know what he wanted to do after college and how it made his parents concerned, but worried him even more. He didn't tell her about his brother, but he did tell her anything interesting he could think of about when he was in high school, and the things he'd liked, even about his Senior year, when he'd played Mazes and Monsters so often that between that and the swimming and the yearbook he was lucky he got into any college at all.

"You play M and M?" Her eyes lit up.

"Used to."

"What level?"

"I was up to third when everybody left for college."

"Wow! So are we. Didn't you see our notice downstairs on the bulletin board?"

"I never looked."

"Jay Jay and Daniel and I . . . Come on, you'll meet Daniel." She hopped off the desk and grabbed his hand again. Before he knew it she had pushed him out of her room and was dragging him back to the party, where she introduced him to a very good-looking guy who looked disturbingly familiar. "This is Robbie Wheeling. Daniel Goldsmith, our Maze Controller. Robbie might play with us."

For a moment Robbie panicked. He was going to do badly in college if he started playing the game; he wasn't that brilliant to begin with. But he didn't want to lose this girl, not yet. "How often do you play?" he asked.

"We haven't started yet this year," Daniel said. "We've been looking for another player. We only play a couple of times a week. Really. It won't hurt your grades if that's what you're thinking about."

"I sort of was."

"Well, that's good," Kate said. "Because we don't want a fanatic."

"We do want someone who'll stay with it though," Daniel said. "Why don't you give it a try and see how it works out? Nobody's demanding a contract."

"I know."

"Try it," Kate said, and smiled at him. "What the hell?"

He smiled back and nodded yes.

CHAPTER FIVE

The four of them were sitting in Daniel's room after supper, beginning to play the new game he had spent the summer contriving. They had already chosen their characters: Kate was Glacia, the Fighter, again, Jay Jay was still Freelik the Frenetic of Glossamir, a Sprite, and Robbie was Pardieu, a Holy Man. They sat in a circle on the floor, pencils and graph paper ready to chart their dangerous and difficult course, and Daniel had put up the small screen the Maze Controller used to hide the pages of the scenario he had invented to take them on their imagined trip.

Beginning players used rule books, and as their skills grew more advanced they progressed to ever more complicated and imaginative books of adventures, departing from them when they wished. Daniel used a combination of advanced books and things he had invented. He had to, because Jay Jay with his photographic memory had memorized nearly every book that could be bought. Daniel didn't even want to think how much money Jay Jay had spent. But Jay Jay was rich, and those things didn't mean much to him.

Holding the dice in his hand, Daniel began to talk. The other three looked at him with rapt attention.

He knew they were visualizing everything he told them, and he was aware how real it was, for he had been a player once himself.

"A half day's walk from a small town there is a wasteland of gnarled hills, covered with withered trees and dried grass. Beneath these hills is the entrance to the forbidden caves of the Jinnorak. As long as anyone can remember, no one has entered these caves, and it is rumored that within them lives a mutated people, once human, now changed from generations in the foul depths to creatures unrecognizable and vicious. But perhaps that is just a rumor, and perhaps the last of them have died. Still, there are other dangers, but it is also known that there are wondrous things within, for those brave and clever enough to take them. Shall you enter?"

"Yes," Kate said, and the other two nodded.

"The entrance is only five feet high," Daniel went on. "As you enter, you find you are in a small room, pitch-dark, with the sound of running water."

"Give the dimensions of the room," Jay Jay said, writing.

"Six paces wide, twelve feet long. On the right there are two doors."

"Whose pace?" Jay Jay demanded.

"A human's."

"Okay, eight feet. I can see in the dark. I see the doors."

"Is there writing on them?" Kate asked.

"Yes," Daniel said. "But it is in an unknown tongue." He threw the dice. An eight. "Pardieu can understand the message, but it will be garbled."

"It says Ladies' Room and Men's Room," Jay Jay said, and rolled on the floor laughing.

"Come on, Jay Jay," Daniel said sternly. "Stop fooling around."

"Sorry."

"What do I see?" asked Robbie.

"Journey here forever, unless . . . and the rest is unknown to you."

"I think we should feel the doors," Kate said. "If the running water is behind one of them it might be magic water and we don't want to let it out." She threw the dice. A twelve. "What can I do?"

"You can open one of them," Daniel said.

She felt herself entering the landscape of the game now, and her heart began to pound. She had brought some armor, a short sword, food, a lantern, and a few coins in case there was anyone to be bribed. Pardieu had his magic spells, and Freelik had his own powers as well as the ability to deceive. It was dangerous to light her lantern in case there was a monster in the room who would then be able to see them and attack them. But darkness frightened her more. Darkness was one of the most terrible things she knew, with the sound of breathing; the thing that had happened that night . . . but she wouldn't think about it now. Now there was only the game, where she would take revenge on creeping, soft breathing things, where she would flash her sword and kill, and conquer. She lit her lantern. The small room was empty. She could see the writing on the doors and she couldn't read it at all. It was in the ancient Jinnorak tongue.

Jay Jay knew why he had been fooling around. The game always frightened him a little at the beginning—having to make that commitment. It was, he

knew, something deep and invasive once he got involved in it. It was a fantasy he ate, slept, and
dreamed. More than the excitement of the perils, he
liked the satisfaction of winning. Freelik really didn't
need the treasure; Sprites could always do for themselves; but treasure was pretty and satisfying to own,
and you could give parties with it, have feasts, sing,
and tell stories and dance all through the enchanted
nights in the moonlight under the trees. It was for
this later pleasure he would go into the terrible
mazes. And besides, in a way, he liked tempting the
unexpected. The human world seemed far away now,
pathetic and boring.

Robbie, safe in the cloak of Pardieu the Holy Man,
walked with sure steps over the damp crumbling floor
of the maze. Glacia's lantern swayed in her hand and
cast its glow into the dark shadows ahead. A terrible
shriek rent the air. Six gigantic Gorvils leaped up
from a hidden pit, snarling their rage at having their
terrain invaded. Dimly in the distance he could hear
the reassuring clack of the dice. His small dagger
firmly in his hand, he sprang at the nearest Gorvil,
striking it in its center eye. It screamed shrilly and
ran away, waving its little webbed arms. Glacia was
whacking everywhere, the strongest of the strong. "I
will enchant one!" Freelik cried. "It will tell me
where the treasure is!"
How happy Pardieu was to be here on his sacred
search, warm in the company of his trusted friends,
guiltless and good. It was a fine thing to have a mission.

Daniel smiled. They were in it now, they *really*

liked his game. Kate's shoulders were tense, her eyes
squinted as if she could actually see into the unknown. Jay Jay was giving forth little squeaks of excitement, telling everyone what to do, as usual. If
they had really been in the maze the Sprite would be
hopping around. And best of all, Robbie was working
out well, taking it all very seriously, planning his
moves. He played intelligently and thoughtfully, but
not without daring. Daniel didn't like a safe game. It
was hard to be the Maze Controller: you had to be
sure the game wasn't too easy, but you couldn't let everyone get killed either. He watched carefully as Jay
Jay mapped out the maze to scale on his graph paper,
making notes, remembering everything. Jay Jay was
by far the smartest of any of them, himself included,
and it pleased Daniel the most when he could get Jay
Jay totally baffled, which unfortunately was never for
long. This world he had created, here in his room,
with his close friends participating so eagerly, was the
best of all possible worlds. It was worth all the trouble he had gone to this summer to create the new adventure. Michelangelo couldn't have felt any better
when he finished painting the Sistine Chapel. A work
of art was a work of art, no matter on what level.

CHAPTER SIX

They had worked out a routine now where they played the game two or three nights a week and both afternoons on weekends. That left weekend nights free for going out, and the other weeknights for studying. Kate was taking two easy English literature courses, a poetry-writing course, and psychology. She had already read most of the required novels before she'd come to college, and the poetry class was a joke because she could dash off a poem in an hour.

Eng Lit I was held in a huge amphitheater with rows of seats rising so high that the professor looked like a tiny doll standing in front of his lectern, speaking through a microphone. "I am sure many of you have read *Huckleberry Finn* before," he said. "I have read it twenty-two times." The class groaned, a wave of sound. "Every time I read it I see something different," he went on. "As we grow and mature we understand new meanings in a great novel."

Bor-ring, Kate wrote in her notebook, and passed it to Robbie, who was sitting next to her. It had turned out they were both in the same gut course, so now they sat together all the time and saved seats for each other. It was one of the most popular courses in the school, mostly because it was not hard.

Zzzzzz, Robbie wrote, and passed her notebook back. They tried to keep from laughing. There was something about being with Robbie that made Kate feel very silly and relaxed and young. It wasn't because he was a Freshman and she was a Sophomore, because they were the same age—and she wouldn't have cared if she were older. Those things didn't matter to her. It was more that Robbie was terribly sweet and totally unthreatening. They had fun together. He was also very handsome. She loved his gentle face and perfectly proportioned swimmer's body. She found herself looking at him more lately than she had intended to. She knew she was starting to care about him in a way that was more than just a good pal, and she didn't like that at all.

She'd been in love. Everyone at Grant said that if a love affair lasted more than five months you were living on borrowed time. They all knew they were growing, changing, finding different goals, and you couldn't expect to be the same person you were several months ago—so how could you stay in love, or the other person stay in love with you? Love was dangerous because unless you were very lucky one of you was bound to get hurt. At least, you got hurt the first time. After that you learned. "They break your pretty balloon just once," her last year's roommate had said.

Dawn, the beautiful American Indian girl who Kate had thought would be such a confidante. "I'd never tell you my problems," Dawn had told her. "It would hurt me too much to see you get upset."

How could you answer that? No, I won't get upset, I won't care about you? Please upset me, that's what I'm here for? Kate wondered if Dawn was just saying that so she wouldn't have to listen to *her* complain. If so, Kate couldn't blame her for that; who wanted to listen to a lot of troubles? You fell in love alone because you were supposed to be grown-up, and if it didn't work out then you got over it alone.

So last year Kate had been in love, and it had lasted six months, and everyone knew it would eventually end, except her. She had really believed in that romance. Steve . . . funny, charming, a good writer, a shit. He just got bored with her. He was on to other things. She was expected to understand. He didn't want to get married, neither did she; he didn't want to live with anybody, neither did she; he wanted to go to Nepal. Then he would do something else, he'd see. She could come to Nepal if she wanted, but she'd just be dead weight. It was over. Besides, she didn't have the slightest desire to go to Nepal.

So she nursed her broken heart and kept silent, and tried to think about the bad parts of the relationship so she could get over it faster. Remember how there was never enough room in the narrow dorm bed for the two of them to fall asleep properly. How he hogged it all anyway. How he threw his underwear on the floor, the slob. How he never made plans, so they always got to the last show at the movies after the opening credits. How he kissed her so sweetly and left little love notes in her clothes and made her feel beautiful and special. . . .

People were gathering their books and papers and standing up; the class was over. She had dreamed her way through it. That was another thing love did; it ruined your concentration. She hoped Robbie had taken enough notes for both of them.

"Do you want to buy some food and go have a

picnic?" Robbie said. "There won't be many more terrific days like this one."

"No . . . I don't know."

He looked hurt. "Are you all right?"

"Sure. I have to study this afternoon."

"Okay. I'll see you at dinner then."

She went off toward the library and then when she
knew he was gone she walked back and sat on the
ground under a tree. Students were sitting in pairs
and groups on the strips of lawn between the large
red-brick class buildings, enjoying the last good
weather of fall. She had been mean to Robbie, but
she couldn't help it. She didn't want to have a picnic
with him on a beautiful fall day, storing up
memories, feeling open and mellow and vulnerable—
not yet, anyway.

And she didn't know how she would feel about
having sex ever again, after the long-buried but never
forgotten Incident in the Laundry Room. No one
had been allowed to touch her since then, and if anyone did she didn't know if she would be able to stand
it.

It had been the night she knew it was all over with
Steve. For a while she had pretended, but finally she
knew he didn't even want her for a friend. She didn't
want to brood, she wanted to keep busy. There was
laundry piling up that needed to be done. It was Saturday night, when almost nobody used the laundry
room. She wouldn't have to wait for a machine. Everybody else was having a good time with the person
they were in love with. She went down to the laundry
room and found herself alone.

She separated the whites from the colors, dumped
the clothes, sheets, and towels into two machines,

poured in the detergent, and was fishing in her handbag for quarters when the lights went out. Suddenly the room was plunged into pitch darkness. It was weird because there was not one machine on, not even a dryer. It was absolutely still. She wondered if a fuse had blown. She turned around, but it was so dark after the previous fluorescent brightness that she couldn't even see where the door was. Then she heard the tiny click of a cigarette lighter.

She saw the flame, and saw it glint off the sharp, shiny point of a switchblade knife. That was all—just the blade, held high—and then she heard the sound of breathing.

Soft, soft, quick excited breathing. She couldn't even hear footsteps, so silent was his tread, but the knife blade, shining gold and silver, came nearer, and so did the breathing. She knew without any doubt that it was a man, and that he was going to rape her.

The most terrifying thing in the world was a knife. A gun had a certain unreality to it; it could even be a toy. But you could not pretend a knife was a toy. And this one was long and sharp. The hand that held it was not trembling at all. Only the breathing was ragged: soft, excited, almost like sighs of ecstasy. She realized then that he probably would kill her, either before or after he raped her, and that her blood and pain would be part of his pleasure. She could feel her heart pounding so violently it seemed to fill the dark room. She crouched and ran, silently, away from that glittering blade, toward the tall dryers. He followed her, still in that wordless grim silence that was even more frightening than any words could have been.

Hide . . . hide. She was small and slim, she could slip into narrow spaces. But the bank of dryers stood there locked together, flush against the wall. Kate ran her hands across them, feeling for a space, wondering if she could crawl into an open dryer, knowing she would be more trapped inside than she was now.

There was a small air space behind the bank of dryers, between them and the wall, for the heat to escape. She slid into it, hearing his breath coming closer. Her eyes were becoming accustomed to the dark and she could make out shapes. Then she realized that at the end of this little passage there was a wall, and if he were small enough to follow her she would be trapped and he would slash her to death.

Carefully, silently, she turned around and crept out again, then ran, too close . . . feeling her heart turn over as he took a swipe at her. She felt wetness trickling down her arm. She began to sob, in silence, choking back the tears and her tiny, terrified animal sounds so he could not hear her and find her. She hit one of the ironing boards and fell, too frightened to feel any pain, and then jumped up again and ran, trying to get to the exit door before he did. Then he snapped off his cigarette lighter so there was no light at all. Now he and his knife could be anywhere.

Running swiftly down the line of ironing boards, Kate knocked them all over, leaving them on their sides or backs with their metal legs held high. Let him trip over one, make him fall, please God. . . . Where could she run now? If she ran into him he would grab her, slit her throat. . . .

She knew she was going to die and that there was no point to it, no purpose, only the unfairness and cruelty of it. She felt everything inside her seem to empty out: the hope, the love, the feeling. She was a shell, an object. She was nothing.

Then the door to the laundry room burst open and there were voices, perplexed, annoyed, and the silhouettes of three other women illuminated by the light in the hall.

"What the hell? Why are the lights out?"

One of the women switched on the overhead fluorescent light. It was blinding. Kate blinked. And when she opened her eyes again, in that instant before he fled, she saw the face of her would-be rapist-murderer clearly. He was in his early thirties, lean and feral: a drifter or someone who worked in the town. He was no one she knew.

Afterward she never really could figure out why he hadn't killed all four of them, herself and the three other women who had come to do their wash. She'd read about incidents like that in the newspapers, one maniac holding a whole dormitory of women in his power. But he had chosen to run away instead, and she was alive.

She and the three other women put a notice on the dorm bulletin board. BE CAREFUL—THERE IS A RAPIST WITH A KNIFE AROUND THE CAMPUS. HE WAS LAST SEEN IN THE LAUNDRY ROOM OF HOLLIS EAST. DO NOT GO ANYWHERE ALONE WHERE YOU COULD GET TRAPPED.

The cut took six stitches. She told the doctor she had been mugged. There was nothing else she wanted to tell. She was sure she wouldn't be able to identify him if she saw him again; she'd been too frightened. She told Dawn to watch out, but never expressed any of the conflicting emotions that were tearing her apart. She did not tell her mother, because she didn't want to upset her. She signed up for a karate course, which she continued all summer when she went home to San Francisco. Her instructor, who was a woman teaching all-woman classes how to defend themselves from men, told Kate she had the fastest reflexes she'd ever seen in a student.

During the weeks and months after The Incident in the Laundry Room, as Kate began to think of it, it began to seem as if part of the nightmare had been her fault. She shouldn't have been so stupid and careless as to go down there alone when she knew it would be deserted. It was also Steve's fault. If he hadn't left her they would have been together that night and she wouldn't have been alone and available to be murdered. Her father had left her too, abandoned her . . . every man she'd ever cared about had turned out to be untrustworthy and selfish. You hoped happiness would last, you loved and believed in them, and then they said good-bye. You couldn't trust anyone but yourself. Maybe that was the lesson life was meant to teach you.

It was then she began to realize everything she had ever written was childish and superficial. The Mazes and Monsters game, which she had played innocently and pleasantly with her friends, began to become more important. It became her release and her social life. She had no dates—treating the men in her dorm and classes casually, keeping them as friends and discouraging anything more. Friends didn't desert you. She trusted Jay Jay and Daniel; they were like brothers to her, even though Daniel was so sexy and attractive to other women.

After a while the pain of the remembered night became dulled, lying at the back of her mind, pushed aside for other things. She tried to live her life day to day. Nobody ever suspected she was upset at all.

Kate got up from where she had been sitting under the tree, and began to walk slowly to the dorm. Still time to grab some lunch and then get part of this week's required reading out of the way. She thought of Robbie's sweetness, his growing dependence on her, and wondered what she wanted to do. Maybe he would be the one, at last, who would love her and not go away. Then she could let out all the feelings she'd been saving up; her love and warmth and giving sexuality. But first she would have to test him, and she didn't know how to do that. Maybe it would be better just to withdraw for a while so she wouldn't have to deal with any of it.

CHAPTER SEVEN

Robbie couldn't figure out why Kate had suddenly become so distant. He felt hurt and confused. He'd thought she really liked him as much as he liked her; they'd had fun together and were always able to make each other laugh. From the first minute he saw her, at Jay Jay's party, his feelings for her had grown. He'd been trying to get up the courage to move their relationship to the next level—love and sex and maybe even sharing a room together—but now she had cut it all off without a word of explanation.

When he tried to talk to her about it she was always busy. It seemed as if lately he was always chasing after her and she was rushing away somewhere. He didn't want to make a fool of himself, but he didn't know what to do, and he couldn't stand the thought of losing her without ever understanding why.

They continued to play the game, but there they were in another world, not Kate and Robbie, so it was different; and whenever they had finished playing for the night she would run to her room. One night Robbie waited until he was alone with Daniel and then asked him.

"Daniel, is Kate mad at me?"

"Not that I know of."

"She's acting different. I feel like that guy in the commercial: you tell me to change my toothpaste and then she'll like me again."

"Was something going on that I missed?" Daniel asked.

"I don't know," Robbie said, feeling miserable. "Maybe I imagined it."

"Kate had a hard time last year," Daniel said. "She broke up with the guy she was going with and it left her kind of defensive."

"Is she still in love with him?"

"Oh, no." Daniel gave him an appraising look. "You're really interested in her, aren't you."

Robbie shrugged.

"You are," Daniel said. He smiled. "Well, if it works out, the two of you can share a room and then we'll have the extra room to play the game the way we planned last year."

"Very funny. If *you* wanted some girl it would work out that way. Not with me and Kate."

"Maybe it's just as well," Daniel said calmly. "If the two of you did get involved and it didn't work out, it would fuck up our game."

"Don't you ever stop being so logical?"

"Nope."

It was hopeless. Robbie thought of putting a note under Kate's door, but that seemed childish. He tried to think of something funny to do, the sort of nutty thing Jay Jay would think of, but he didn't have that sort of imagination. He thought how ordinary he was, and he decided Kate was right not to care about him. He had probably bored her.

Then one day she came into his room, looking contrite and timid. "I'm sorry," she said.

His heart leaped. Kate . . . "Why have you been keeping me out?" he asked. "What did I do?"

"It wasn't you. Can we start again?"

"*Yes!* You want to go to the movies tonight?"

"I'd love to." She smiled. "There's a lot of stuff I haven't seen. Let's drive into town and get the paper."

They went to see a double feature of *Halloween* and *When a Stranger Calls,* because they both liked scary movies, and afterward they went to Fat City, the only halfway decent cheap restaurant in town, where most of the college students hung out. The walls were dark wood, with old movie posters hanging on them, and the lights were dim. There were booths as well as tables, so you could sit and talk in privacy. Because it was late and a weeknight the place was quite empty. The jukebox was playing for free.

Robbie and Kate sat across from each other at a booth in the corner. All evening she had been the same old Kate again, laughing and comfortable to be with. He ordered a hamburger and beer, she ordered white wine and her usual health food salad.

"I've got to get you off that stuff," she said, gesturing at his hamburger. She picked a French fry off his plate and popped it into her mouth. "Don't you know that when they slaughter an animal it gets scared and its system gets filled up with fight-or-flight hormones, and they get into *your* system?"

"Nobody killed whatever went into this hamburger," Robbie said. "It died of natural causes."

"In this place I can believe it."

Robbie reached across the table and took her hand. "Kate . . . I'm not the kind of person who hurts other people. I might do something stupid by accident, but I would never lie to you."

"I don't think you would."

"You don't act like that's a very big plus."

She was playing with his fingers. "People seem to think telling the truth is such a big deal," she said. "Like you should get a medal for it. There are a lot of things people would never want to hear, *never,* but other people don't think about that because it's so worthy to be *honest.*"

"I know."

"I was going with someone last year," she said. "He told me he wanted to move on. He was being honest. I didn't like hearing it."

"I guess that hurt." He wanted to give her something, tell her something bad that had happened to him too, as a way of sharing and making her feel less alone. "I'll tell you the worst thing that ever happened to me," he said. "I have this older brother, Hall junior, my only brother actually. He's three years older than I am, and he's terrific. But he used to fight a lot with my parents. They never got along at all. He ran away when he was fifteen, and my dad sent the cops after him. The police brought him back. He was going to be sixteen then, it was his sixteenth birthday, April Fools' Day. My parents had a big party for him, a combination welcome home and birthday party. And in the middle of it, when nobody was paying attention, he ran away again and never came back."

She was looking at him with such softness and understanding in her eyes that he almost told her the rest of it . . . but he couldn't, not even to her. "Never?" she said.

"Never. We never even got a letter or a postcard or

a phone call. It was like he disappeared off the earth. It's been such a long time, and I keep wondering what happened to him."

"That must be so terrible," Kate said.

"Not knowing is the worst part," Robbie said.

"I'm so sorry . . ."

She got up and led him into the shadows by the jukebox, and they danced slowly and closely together, her head on his chest, their arms wrapped around each other, both of them being very gentle. They looked at each other then and kissed.

"I love you," Robbie said.

They left Fat City and drove back to the dorm, and went up to her room. She drew him inside and locked the door. Since he had last been in her room she had painted rainbows on her walls. She turned on the music, very softly, and they stood there in that rainbow room and began to touch each other with wonder, as if this had never happened before for either of them. He was so filled with love for her he thought he would die of happiness. She led him to her narrow bed, and they made love perfectly and easily. For one moment, only one, she seemed to be frightened and drew back, and her body stiffened; but then she smiled at him and relaxed again. He felt as if he were dreaming, because he had dreamed of this moment so often in the past weeks that now it seemed as if the fantasy and the reality blended into something that he was only wishing would be.

"I love you too," she said.

Afterward, lying in the darkness, holding her, he was unexpectedly plunged into the deepest depression he had ever known. He felt that he had betrayed her, had lied already, and betrayed Hall, because it was

Hall's story that had touched her enough to make her love him. A small part of him had been glad when Hall left—some evil, deeply hidden part—and he had always felt guilty for it. But, Robbie tried to tell himself rationally, Kate had already decided she wanted him when she came back. His story hadn't won her; it had only been a further way of sharing, to become closer to her. He tried to fight off the depression, holding her tightly, trying to synchronize his breathing with hers.

He remembered that April night with such clarity it seemed to be happening all over again . . . the party guests making noise downstairs, music playing, moonlight shining through the branches of the big tree outside his bedroom window and making patterns on the floor. He had gone upstairs to be alone for a while. He was thirteen, and the people downstairs were older, none of them his friends, and he was bored. He was lying on his bed in the dark, still dressed because he might want to go back downstairs to the party, and wondering if everyone would be so glad to see *him* if he had run away. His parents were pretending that nothing bad had happened, and they were celebrating, trying to make it all up to Hall for whatever had made him miserable enough to leave.

Then the door opened and his brother came in. "Robbie?"

"Hi."

Hall junior, tall, handsome, blond, the older brother Robbie had always worshiped and been jealous of, sat down on the edge of his bed and put his hand on Robbie's shoulder. "Do you have any money?"

"Money?"

"Yeah. I know you hoard it."

"What do you want money for?"

His brother's voice was hoarse, strained. "I need it."

"Okay. I'll lend you some. How much do you need?"

"It's not a loan," Hall said.

Robbie stared at him then in the moonlight, the perfect, classic features, the dark shadows underneath his eyes like those of a sick person, and he felt his throat close. He understood. "Don't . . ." he said helplessly.

"I have to. This time I'm never coming back."

"Why?"

Hall's fingers closed tightly on his wrist. "You won't tell? You promise me you won't tell? They'll kill you if they find out you helped me."

"Don't go. . . ." And he was getting up, taking the money he had saved from its hiding place in his desk drawer: one hundred and sixty-two dollars, allowance and money he had earned doing odd jobs, and he was handing it to Hall.

"Thank you." His brother looked at him and smiled a thin little smile, and then the money disappeared into his jeans. "I'll keep in touch."

But Hall never had. He did in Robbie's dreams, walking into the room just as vividly as if it had been real, and he said he had been unhappy but it would be all right now. Then Robbie would wake up and remember it was not all right at all.

He didn't tell his parents about the money, nor that he had even spoken to his brother before the second and last disappearance. Hall was gone before anyone realized he had left. Robbie remembered his mother screaming, that long, shrill scream of the bereaved, as if she had just been informed of her son's death. He knew he wouldn't forget that sound as long as he lived. Then she started drunkenly smashing all his father's expensive watches, as if to tell him that all the things he'd worked so hard to get were meaningless and vain.

Robbie was doubly guilty. Guilty for helping Hall to run away, and for being a little bit glad. Later, when Hall didn't write or call and Robbie realized what "never coming back" really meant, he began to feel the sorrow and the pain. What had seemed, at the time, to be part of an exciting adventure, now had turned into the most terrible thing that had ever happened to him in his life.

CHAPTER EIGHT

Daniel was seeing twins, on different nights of course. Their names were Cindy and Lyndy, and they were so spectacularly beautiful that one of them would have been enough; two seemed like wretched excess. And they were bright. He had met Cindy in his math class. She wanted to be a doctor. When he had seen Lyndy in his American History class, naturally he'd thought she was Cindy, and he'd sat down next to her and started talking to her, until he realized she was laughing.

"Oh, no," she groaned. "I'm the *other* one."

"There are two of you?"

"There aren't two of you, are there?" she asked hopefully.

Since there was one of him, they shared. Lyndy wanted to be a lawyer. They were both interested in their future careers, planned to stay single until they were well established in their professions, and then get married and have one child each. Or twins. They saw other men besides Daniel, and while Jay Jay seemed jealous and Robbie admiring, Daniel sometimes had the disquieting feeling that his sex life was only comedy relief for most of the people in the dorm. If only they hadn't been *identical* twins. . . . It was like a joke. Still, it was unusual, and he had to admit he liked the idea. Kate teased him about it, good-naturedly, and asked him whether he planned to take the two of them out together on their birthday.

"They have the same birthday, you know," she said.

"Then they can go out with someone else."

"What a rat! You can't screw them and then not take them out on their birthday. And you have to buy them a present." She giggled. "Give them the same thing in different colors."

Robbie had practically moved into Kate's room now, and they were inseparable. Daniel decided to wait and see if their romance survived the term, and if it did, then he would suggest they all use Robbie's room to play the game. He didn't like having to use his own room for everything: studying, sleeping, entertaining the twins—who roomed together in a different dorm—and playing the game too. What he liked least about college life was the lack of privacy. At night everyone played their stereos, all full-blast, and people thundered up and down the halls and talked in loud voices. If you wanted to study you needed to almost hypnotize yourself, or buy earplugs, or go to the library, which was a nuisance. The library was just a ten-minute run from the dorms, but it closed at eleven, and now that the weather had turned sharply colder and it rained often, a chill, unpleasant rain, people liked to stay put.

Daniel had always been a loner. That was why he liked to run. For his mandatory gym class he chose track, although he disliked having to compete in something he only wanted to do for pleasure. Robbie was still on the swimming team, Jay Jay was taking fencing—mainly because he liked the paraphernalia, particularly the mask—and Kate was continuing her karate. None of them planned to go home for the brief Thanksgiving holiday. Kate said it would be too expensive to fly to California and she didn't want to spend her whole vacation driving to get there and back. Jay Jay and Robbie didn't want to go home to see their families. And Daniel thought it would be nice for the four of them to stay in the nearly empty dorm and play the game every day. The others agreed happily.

They all told their parents they were going camping, so as not to hurt their feelings.

On Thanksgiving day they ate turkey sandwiches washed down with beer, played the game for nine straight hours, and then went out to take a walk in the cold night air to clear their heads. They walked past the huge, dark dorms, where only a few lights showed in windows, past the empty class buildings of the Grant campus, and along the narrow sidewalks that led into the town. Small houses were set side by side on the outskirts of Pequod, each with its car in the driveway, and inside these houses families were finishing their Thanksgiving dinners. Daniel could see them through some of the windows: sitting around dining tables or watching television. In one house he saw a father and son playing cards under the light of a lamp in front of a picture window, and he suddenly felt very lonely. He was sorry he hadn't gone home for the holiday. There wouldn't be many more family times—then he'd be an adult and out in the world alone. In the eyes of the world he was an adult already.

Ahead of him Kate and Robbie were walking with

their arms around each other. Daniel wondered how long it would last. He liked Robbie, you couldn't not like Robbie—but he just wasn't *enough* for Kate; she was special. This was just fun and games. Not that there was anything wrong with that. . . . And there was Jay Jay, all alone, in his fat down coat and Mickey Mouse Club hat, looking like a kid; Jay Jay who had never been a kid. Daniel felt a wave of sad affection for Jay Jay. Really, when you thought about it, Jay Jay had nobody to love but his mynah bird.

And what about me? Daniel thought. When he'd been very young he had been a devotee of the TV show *Star Trek,* and he'd always identified with Mr. Spock, the logical, objective, half-alien with no human feelings. Now, at nineteen, he wondered if he was turning into that sort of creature. He'd never been in love, never felt really insecure, never been hurt. Whenever he was disappointed he could always reason it out with common sense. Maybe it was better to be someone like Kate, willing to care enough about someone that she could take the risk of having her world come smashing down. Better to be Robbie, walking around with that goony look on his face, carried away with his dream of romance even if he knew it wouldn't last. Maybe even better to be Jay Jay, always living on the edge, looking for excitement, never satisfied. It was better than being Mr. Spock.

But Daniel had never found anyone who seemed the right one to fall in love with. There was always something wrong with her—she was too silly, too demanding, too unfeeling, always too something. Sex was easy for him, but love seemed impossible.

On special occasions his mother always said: "Next time . . ." and made a wish. "Next time we'll celebrate for *you*." She would pick out one person whose turn it seemed to be to have something nice happen and she would say her little charm to him.

Next time . . . Daniel said to himself, and wondered.

CHAPTER NINE

The weather turned just after Thanksgiving, as if winter could not hold off any longer. Chill winds blew, and it snowed. All dressed alike, in their down coats or jackets, jeans, boots, scarves wrapped around their faces, the students trudging from class to class seemed like the inhabitants of some totalitarian country; asexual, dogged, unfrivolous. Underneath their colorless uniforms, however, they seethed with life. People fell in love and out of love, they had food fights in the cafeteria, they gave impromptu parties where they drank and smoked whatever they could get their hands on and shared without reservation, they surrounded themselves with the music that spoke to them of their own inarticulate dreams—and they always studied, in a constant state of terror. It was important to get good marks, because after you graduated you would have to make a living. Most of them tried to make plans. The world seemed both open to them and closed. Open because anything was possible, but closed because it was so hard to get a job. They wanted success, fame, riches; and if that was not to be then at least they wanted security. The world was so insecure, there was little to believe in, but they would have money. People didn't protest very much this year at Grant, although there was one student who stood outside the library every morning, her face raw with cold, and shouted: "Save the whales!" At Grant there was room for everyone.

Jay Jay felt he was losing his mooring. Everyone he cared about had someone to hold on to, but he was alone. He sat in his warm room and talked to Merlin, his best friend. "Poor Jay Jay," Jay Jay said. "Poor Jay Jay."

"Poor Jay Jay," Merlin said, finally.

"Speak to me," Jay Jay said.

"Birds can't talk," Merlin said sternly.

"Where's Jay Jay?"

"Poor Jay Jay."

"Good," Jay Jay said, and filled Merlin's little bowl.

He was so sad. No one had time for him anymore. Kate was always off somewhere with Robbie, and Daniel had his merry sex life. Only poor Jay Jay, doomed to be a mascot, a child . . .

And he was so bored. He put on his old record of Steely Dan doing "Deacon Blues," a song he played more and more often lately. *Drink Scotch whiskey all night long, and die behind the wheel.* . . . He could get on his motorbike and ram it into a wall. No, that was too ordinary. If he died, he wanted attention, he wanted to become a legend. Then they would all be sorry they had neglected him. He would be remembered forever, like those two students who had disappeared into the caverns long before he was born. If they had lived, they probably wouldn't be anything at all.

He wasn't really certain he wanted to kill himself; maybe he just wanted to play a trick and scare his friends. Still, the thought of doing away with himself gave him a little shiver of anticipation. Nobody had ever committed suicide at Grant.

He wrote a note to Kate. *Please feed Merlin every day, and remember me.* He put on his down coat and leather aviator's helmet, took his flashlight, looked sadly at Merlin for what might be the last time, and went down the hall. He slipped the key to his room and the note under Kate's door, and went out into the cold.

He knew where the forbidden caverns were; he had ridden past them the first week he arrived at school, just to see. The snow the night before had been light and the ground was frosty, but still he left tire tracks. Good . . . it wouldn't do for them to be unable to find him. The caverns looked the same as they had before. The same green sign with its warning, the same chain across the entrance. The hills looked rocky and dismal under their light dusting of snow, and the afternoon sky was the color of iron. He shivered with the cold and anticipation. Parking his motorbike in the shelter of some rocks, Jay Jay slipped under the chain and entered the caverns.

He swung his flashlight around to see what was there. He was in a smallish room, like a kind of entrance hall, and on either side there were tunnels high enough to walk in, leading off into the depths. He surmised the underground chambers were laid out somewhat like the branches of a tree . . . or a maze. His eyes widened with wonder. This *was* a maze—it was just like the game! The walls were made of some kind of damp stone, and far away, softly, there was the sound of dripping water. Great pale stalactites and stalagmites gave the caverns an eerie look, showing how ancient this place was. It was almost beautiful.

Carefully, slowly, Jay Jay stepped forward, moving the beam of his light. His quick mind memorized where he had been. There, in the right-hand chamber, was a large black pool, with water dripping into it from the vault above. Oh, it was so wonderful, so glorious, so Tolkien! Gollum could live there in that cold, black, bottomless pool. Jay Jay could almost see him now, rising, hissing, turning his serpentine head this way and that in search of the delicate little morsel in the down coat. Suddenly the most exciting plan he had ever had in his life began to form in Jay Jay's mind.

These caverns *were* the game. If a clever Maze Controller, himself of course, were to chart them, and then use real props . . . A cloak, for instance, with a bottle in the pocket containing a potion that could be either magic giving all knowledge or poison . . . real lanterns, real swords, real costumes, and a real treasure . . . They could all chip in for the treasure. That would give them more of an incentive to find it. The little charms, amulets, statues, writing on the wall, hidden scrolls, he would purchase himself and hide all around. The monsters, of course, would have to be imaginary, but there would always be the real danger of getting lost, or slipping and getting hurt, or even drowning. He shivered, partly with fear, partly with delight. He was a genius!

The caverns weren't so cold and terrible. They were actually rather cool and pleasant, and he imagined they retained the same temperature all year round. They would be perfect to play in on warm days, and not too bad if they began the new game in

winter. Of course, he'd have to wait until they finished playing Daniel's game. Daniel had worked so
hard on it they couldn't just abandon it, even though
now it seemed very dull and colorless to Jay Jay compared to what he had just concocted. First, he would
have to talk the others into his plan. He was sure he
could do it. Nothing scared Kate, Robbie was a fol-
lower, and Daniel liked difficult problems to solve. After he had convinced them, Jay Jay planned to let his
character get killed in Daniel's game. That would
make the game much less interesting for the others. It
would be a kind of sacrificial suicide. He laughed
aloud, very pleased with himself. The sound rang off
the walls, echoing in a pleasantly diabolical way.
How funny that he had come here planning to kill
himself and had ended up with a greater desire to
live than he'd ever had before.

He picked his way carefully out of the caverns into
the mundane world. The early winter dusk had
fallen. He got back on his motorbike and rode into
town, where he bought some sandwiches and sodas,
and a dozen boxes of Pepperidge Farm croutons to
drop as bread crumbs so he wouldn't get lost. He also
bought extra batteries for his flashlight. Tomorrow,
when the hardware store was open, he would buy a
real lantern. This would do for now.

Back to the caverns, his own adventureland of
endless possibility. Jay Jay hummed happily as he began to investigate the first three chambers, dropping
his croutons, arranging little piles of stones to give
himself added clues to direction. He was aware how
dangerous these mazes were, and he had no intention
of ending his life. He felt a little frightened, which
pleased him, and also very elated. At nine o'clock,

ravenously hungry, he sat down with his back against a large rock and ate his sandwiches and drank his sodas, which were still cool. White paint, he thought, would be good for a secret message, or perhaps even luminous silver paint if he could find it. He knew there wasn't anything he couldn't find if he wanted to. He would invent ancient runes—aha!

Feeling very tired and cozy after his supper and his athletic and intellectual efforts, he lay down, pulling the hood of his coat over his head to act as a sort of pillow. It wouldn't do to go back to the dorm tonight, then nobody would worry about him. He would go back tomorrow. And meanwhile, somehow it seemed as if sleeping here gave him proprietorship, making the caverns his own. He slept, and dreamed of the game, dreamed that they all loved him. A whole tribe of Sprites was sitting on little stone mushrooms, all applauding for him. *You are the cleverest of all, O Freelik the Frenetic of Glossamir!* they cried admiringly in their tiny voices. They were wearing silken robes in pale, iridescent colors, and every one of them looked just like him.

The next morning was cold and clear. Jay Jay rode back to the dorm in triumph, his motorbike a charger; feeling that he had indeed discovered a treasure. He was gratified to see that the others were very upset over his disappearance, particularly Kate.

"Where did you go?" she demanded. "I was scared to death."

"I'll tell you when I'm ready," he said smugly.

"I fed Merlin and put the cover on his cage," she said reproachfully. "That was a terrible note to leave. I didn't know what you were going to do. If that was another one of your stupid jokes it wasn't funny."

"I'll tell you tonight if you're free," he said.

"We're playing the game tonight," she said. "Aren't we?"

"I'll tell you before the game," Jay Jay said. "When we're all together."

Sitting in Daniel's room, in their circle, Jay Jay told them his plan. They looked at him and then at each other, confused, each waiting for someone else to tell them what to do. He could tell that they were both horrified and intrigued.

"It's awfully dangerous," Daniel said.

"That's the point," said Jay Jay.

"You spent the night there?" Kate said. "All by yourself?"

"Yup."

"Did you see bones?"

Jay Jay smiled. "Wouldn't you like to know?" Bones . . . of course, he would have to get some bones too. "However, if you're too afraid to try my idea . . ."

"There's a difference between being brave and being reckless," Kate said.

"We're still playing *this* game," Daniel said. He sounded hurt.

"Jay Jay shrugged. "Think about it. We have plenty of time."

Robbie hadn't said a word. "What do you think, Robbie?" Kate asked.

"I'll do whatever everybody else decides," Robbie said.

"Don't you have your own opinion?" Jay Jay asked acidly. It annoyed him the way Robbie always deferred to Kate. Just like a henpecked husband.

"I think it would be kind of exciting," Robbie said.

"You see?" Jay Jay said. "He's the only one with imagination."

"Let's just play my game till we finish it," Daniel said. "I worked like hell on this game."

Jay Jay smiled his guileless little smile. "There's plenty of time," he said. "I'll bring this up again."

Kate glanced at Daniel as if to say, *He'll forget it. It's just another of his crazy ideas.*

But Jay Jay knew he would never forget it, and he wouldn't give up. He had never been so excited by anything in his whole life.

CHAPTER TEN

Robbie was not allowed to sleep in Kate's room every night; she said the bed was too small and he disturbed her. He understood. It was difficult to pay attention in classes, do homework, and keep alert in the game when you hadn't had a decent night's sleep. For him it was even more difficult than for her, because he had to keep up his stamina in swimming practice. Her practicality was mature and sensible, and he agreed with her plan that they only sleep together overnight on weekends, but still he couldn't help feeling a little rejected. If she really loved him she would find a way . . . He drove into town and went to the thrift shop and bought a double mattress which looked quite clean, and dragged it up the dormitory stairs and into his room. He bought a set of sheets and a blanket in the shopping mall, made their bed, and brought Kate into his room triumphantly to show her his surprise.

"Now we can live together," he told her.

A flicker of fear came into her eyes and her face was grave. "It's too soon," she said.

"What's too soon?" Her rejection hit him like a physical pain. He could actually feel it, a tightening in his chest. "We're together all the time anyway."

"Robbie, I never lived with anybody before. I'm not ready. I love you, but sometimes I like to be all alone."

"Why would anybody want to be all alone?"

"It's too soon," she said again, sadly. "I've got all these pressures of school . . . us being together is the best thing in my life, but please don't try to change it yet."

"I'm never going to leave you," he said, "if that's what you're worried about." Over her shoulder he could look out the window at his ugly view of the parking lot. He wondered if she thought his room wasn't good enough, not romantic enough. "We can put the bed in your room if you'd rather."

"It's not whose room we live in," she said.

"I don't understand."

"Robbie, it's really sweet that you bought the bed. We can use it weekends. It'll be a lot more comfortable." She took his hand and smiled at him. "Trust me."

He locked the door quickly and drew her down on their new bed, to use it and thus make it real. She didn't protest. But he could feel something in her drawing away from him, and it maddened him and made him feel afraid. For the first time his lovemaking was wild, possessive; not tender, not sweet. She had always been the strong one, she made the decisions, she was the leader, but not this time, not now. He became so frenzied that he didn't even care whether she liked it or not. He tried to make up for all the times he'd never been able to understand her as well as he wanted to, to obliterate that stubborn core that resisted all the love and need he wanted to lavish on it. He wanted—for once, at last—to win.

It was the best sex he'd ever had, and as soon as he

was finished he felt guilty, because he'd *liked* not caring what *she* wanted. He looked at her nervously, wondering if she knew what he was thinking.

"Wow," she said. Her tone was totally noncommittal. He didn't know if he'd won or lost, and he certainly didn't dare ask her.

It occurred to him, in the days that followed, that he had expected love to make his life complete, and had never expected that a relationship might be two difficult people trying to become one. He couldn't imagine how he could have been so stupid not to have known it after the example he had right under his nose at home with his battling parents. But they were from another era, nearly dinosaurs, and he had planned to be different. He had planned for everything to be perfect. He'd thought he really had everything figured out, but now he looked at his life and realized he'd been asleep. His schoolwork was piling up on him. It seemed as if there were never enough hours in the day, and he wondered if he could get a leave of absence from the swimming team, tell the coach he was worried about exams. Other people did that, or else they got thrown off the team for not keeping up. He knew he'd been wasting a lot of time having fun, going to movies with Kate, just being with her, playing the game with his friends, daydreaming. It was as if there were certain gaps in his memory: time vanished.

But he did nothing about it. He kept on with swimming practice, he kept spending evenings with Kate when he knew he needed to study more than she because she was so quick, and he kept playing the game. The game was a great emotional release for him because it kept him from worrying about everything else, for a while anyway.

At night he began to dream again about his brother. Sometimes Hall was sixteen, looking the way he had when he ran away five years ago, and sometimes he was an adult Robbie hardly knew. If Hall was alive he would be taller, filled out, perhaps he'd have a mustache or even a beard. He'd be different. Maybe he was a junkie; skinny, sick. Or maybe he'd been dead for years and these were only wishes that would never come true.

The dreams were more complicated now. No longer did Hall come to sit on his bed in the moonlight and talk to him. Now Robbie found himself in a maze, with walls and floor of graph paper, filled with a strange bluish light, and he was running down these frustrating corridors after his brother. It was so neat, like a hospital, or a sketch made by a player. Maybe the dream symbolized that Hall was in a hospital somewhere, perhaps with amnesia. Robbie was always running, out of breath, trying to call out and finding that he had no voice. He could never run fast enough; his legs would ache and he would sink to the floor, drawn inexorably down like someone with a wasting disease. How his legs cramped and pained him. How futilely he tried to shout to tell Hall he was here, to stop and wait for him . . . He would wake up drenched with sweat, crying. His tears felt scaldingly hot, the tears of frustration. They almost burned his cheeks. He would lie in bed for at least twenty minutes, trying to collect himself, to get out of the dream into the real world again. It was just as well he didn't spend every night with Kate. He never wanted her to see him like this.

But then, inevitably, she did. She held him tenderly, rocking him like a baby. "It's your brother, isn't it," she said.

He nodded. "I couldn't get to him."

"Was he in trouble?"

"I don't know."

"It's not your fault," Kate said. "It's not your fault."

But of course it was.

Now the brother who had never been close to him—who had, in the two years preceding his disappearance, undergone a personality change, becoming inaccessible—became kind and close to Robbie in his dreams. This was the Hall he remembered when he was very young, the brother who had patiently played catch with him in the backyard, who had told Robbie grown-up jokes he was not to repeat to his parents but could to his friends, even though Robbie only pretended to understand them. Robbie waited for his dreams with fear and anticipation. Fear, because of that paralyzing feeling of frustration; anticipation, because each time he felt he was coming a little closer to finding out how he could help Hall. He was sure that no one could dream so vividly, and so often, unless the dreams were trying to say something to him.

And then one night in a dream the most extraordinary thing happened. He was following Hall, and suddenly he was not Robbie at all—he was Pardieu the Holy Man. Looking down he saw his brown robes, the sandals on his feet, and around his waist the rope holding the little leather bag of potions and miracles. *Wait!* Pardieu cried, running. *I am Pardieu! I will help you!* But Hall was gone.

Pardieu looked in his bag of magic spells. There was the coin of wishes, to undo what had been done. There was the incandescent liquid, which gave the ability to see into the mind of any being who was possessed of intelligence. His fingers closed around the last, most prized spell of all: The graven jade Eye of Timor. It was a mystery how it had gotten into his pouch, for he had never before been clever or worthy enough to win it. The Eye of Timor could be used by only the highest level of Holy Men, for it gave the user the greatest power of all—the power to raise the dead.

When he awoke from that dream in the morning, for the first time Robbie did not cry. He lay in his bed thinking, feeling at peace. It was as if he were surrounded by soft feathers. He did not understand why, but for the first time instead of dread and frustration he felt a gentle, blissful hope.

CHAPTER ELEVEN

Christmas vacation was coming soon, and people were already planning their escape. Kate, Jay Jay, Daniel, and Robbie had decided to have a last great game session before they departed for home, the game to be preceded by a private party with an exchange of gifts. The life of the dorm and the people in it swirled around them as lightly and unheeded as winter snowflakes. Some students had put up a tree downstairs in the common room, and decorated it, and decorations and wishes for Happy Holidays appeared on the bulletin board, along with an address where you could send Christmas cards to the hostages in Iran. A serious editorial in *The Grant Gazette* warned that potential accidents to our nuclear power plants might make this one the last Christmas ever. The immediate concern in Hollis East, however, was finding a free ride home to save train or plane fare.

Although Jay Jay had no shortage of money, Robbie was going to take him and Merlin, since he could drive through New York on his way to Greenwich; Daniel planned to take the train to Cambridge; and Kate's mother had sent her a round-trip plane ticket to San Francisco.

"Are you going to miss me?" Robbie asked Kate.

"Of course. Are you going to miss me?"

"Like crazy."

Kate went with Jay Jay to buy food for their party, which they decided would be held in his room. Parties were always held in Jay Jay's room. They went to the gourmet section of the supermarket in the shopping mall, and in five minutes Jay Jay had already exceeded their budget. He even insisted on buying champagne.

"You and I should do stuff like this more often," he said.

"I know. We should."

"It's not my fault."

"It's mine," Kate said. "Next time Robbie and I go to the movies, you come too."

"Okay."

They were filled with warm Christmas spirit, and sang carols all the way home to the dorm in her car, the backseat piled high with bags of extravagant delicacies: huge, out of season pears and grapes, imported cheeses, pâté, English biscuits, a fruitcake that Jay Jay planned to soak in brandy.

They began the party at five o'clock, toasting each other with champagne. Jay Jay had arranged the food very nicely on top of his desk, and had taught Merlin to sing the first line of "Jingle Bells," which they all cheered wildly. They had locked the door so no one would crash their party. Then they handed out the presents. Kate and Robbie exchanged thin gold chains to wear around their necks, and she gave Daniel a pair of very sexy-looking sunglasses she knew he'd been thinking of buying for himself, and Jay Jay a real find from the thrift shop: a top hat just like the ones in the old Fred Astaire movies. He put it on immediately. She gave Merlin a swing for his cage, with red and green ribbons on it. She and Jay Jay were the only ones who remembered to give Merlin anything. Daniel gave everybody records, and Robbie, who had conferred with Daniel on this decision, did the same for him and Jay Jay. Jay Jay gave each of them a beautifully lacquered little box, in which he had placed four perfectly rolled joints.

Then they tore into the food as if they were ravenous. It was not really because they were so hungry, but because they wanted to get to the best part of the evening: the game.

They were only dimly aware of how much the game had taken over their lives already. All they knew was that nothing else, not even this special party with its atmosphere of affection and luxury and celebration, was as real to them as the game. And each of them felt, in some secret, guilty way, that they wanted to get the party over with so they could go into Daniel's room and enter their world.

"You have found the talking sword of Lothia," Daniel said. He held the dice in his hand and looked at the three eager faces of Glacia, Freelik, and Pardieu. The dice he held were both chance and power. As he surveyed the underground perils he had laid out so carefully, he wondered whether all of these adventurers would still be alive at the end of this night. He didn't want them to die. He was as excited as they were as they fought their way deeper and deeper into the maze, winning battles with strength and wits, amassing plunder. He knew he had to be objective in order to be an effective M.C., but he wanted them to find the treasure. It didn't belong to him—it belonged to the evil King of the Jinnorak, who was very much alive; horrible, smoke-breathing, covered with scales, feasting off human flesh when he could find it, and the flesh of his part-human slaves when he couldn't. If Glacia, Freelik, and Pardieu could survive until they came to the throne room of the King, and could kill him, it would be as if they had conquered all the evil in the world.

Glacia grasped the talking sword of Lothia and gazed into its polished surface. The light of her lantern glanced off it, gold and silver, and her heart turned over with fear. But this was *her* sword, no one else's, and it would obey her commands. It would kill her enemies and it would speak to her of secrets none of them yet knew. "What lies beyond that door?" she demanded.

"I can only answer yes or no," the sword answered.

"Is it treasure?" Glacia said.

Soft click of the dice. "No."

"Is it danger, then?"

"No."

"Then it's neutral?"

"Yes."

"Good," Glacia said. She turned to the others. "Shall we advance or go the other way?"

"Wait," Pardieu said. "Talking swords have been known to tell lies. How do we know this is a truthful sword? We must test it."

He was right, of course. Glacia was disappointed; first because she had been so pleased to have the aid of the sword, and second because she had never thought to test its loyalty. She of all people should have known better. Nothing was to be trusted at first sight.

"Do you cut stone?" she asked the sword.

"No."

"Can you kill people?"

"Yes."

"Do you always tell the truth?"

"No," the sword said.

She looked at Pardieu and Freelik in angry exasperation. "What do we do?"

"Wait," Freelik said. "Sword, can you talk?"

"Yes," the sword said.

"Do you always tell the truth?"

"Yes."

"Did you tell the truth just now?"

"No."

"It tells the truth every third time!" Freelik squeaked triumphantly. "Now we can control it."

Glacia smiled. She raised the sword high, filled with the sense of her own power. The third answer had been that the unknown room was neutral. "Let us advance," she said to the others.

They passed through the neutral room in safety, moving ever nearer to their goal. Up a narrow, winding staircase they went, steps that kept moving down every time they climbed higher, forcing them to run just to stay in the same place, until finally—after considering the consequences of not having it later—Pardieu threw his one-use-only spell of paralyzation and made the stairs stand still. It would be a long time before he could earn another such spell, and he would most probably need it for a randomly encountered monster, but if he hadn't used it for the stairs they might have been trapped there forever. He thought that a Holy Man had more responsibilities than anyone else. He had to make more complicated choices, and he could heal as well as hurt. That was good, for Pardieu did not like to cause destruction, even of evil beings. He could slash with his sword as well as any but Glacia, but it made him feel guilty to kill, even though he did it only in self-defense. If he could use his magic spells to charm wicked spirits into being good, it was better.

Once in every generation there was a Holy Man, who learned all his secrets from the Holy Man who had come before him. Pardieu's mentor had been a legendary Holy Man who had vanished many years ago, but who some said would never die and had merely chosen to spend his last days in peaceful retirement. Pardieu was not so sure. Sometimes, as he made his way through this treacherous maze, he felt that his mentor had been there before, perhaps was there still, waiting for him. The great one had gone away alone. He had enough power to do that, without a band of companions. But even the most experienced of Holy Men sometimes found themselves in unanticipated trouble.

Pardieu's hand tightened around the little pouch of spells and potions he wore attached to his belt. He had given away a very strong one, but he had kept the most important one. Let others sing their songs and tell their legends of the olden days. He was the one who by his heroism would rescue and bring back the greatest Holy Man of all—The Great Hall.

None of the others knew it, but tonight he was not Freelik—he was Jay Jay. He had already gotten bored with the game. Compared to the way he wanted to play it, in the real mazes of the caverns, this was child's play. He went through the moves, pretending for the others, but he was waiting for his chance to die. Now that he intended to die, it wasn't so easy. He couldn't make an obvious blunder; the others were too smart for that, especially Daniel, who felt responsible for the flow of the game.

Now Daniel had called up a bunch of the undead, and there was a fierce battle. This was going to go on all night, Jay Jay just knew it, and he felt dismayed. Getting rid of the undead took ages if they were the ones who weren't afraid of light, which these obviously were not. He prayed for an unlucky throw of the dice. If everybody got tired they would quit after they routed the undead, and then he'd never be able to convince them to start his new game in the caverns. What a rotten way to spend Christmas vacation—still in suspense!

Kate was rolling great numbers tonight; he wished they were in Las Vegas. She was sending the undead back where they came from at a fast rate. Come on, Daniel, undead are boring, kid stuff. Let's get on with it. . . . Hurray, the last of the undead had fled, leaving their black rags behind them. Now their brave troupe was advancing into a room where there was a pit, and deep inside the pit was glitter. It could be precious gems, or perhaps it was a trap. Daniel wouldn't let them have such a big treasure so soon, would he? Maybe it was just a thin layer of diamonds, and under it were lethal spikes. Jay Jay remembered the pit with spikes from an old game, and it didn't take much imagination to add the camouflage. Jay

Jay knew Daniel's mind pretty well by now. He wondered if Daniel knew his.

A smart Sprite would use his sonar to test the pit before jumping into it to gather up the treasure. Tonight Jay Jay did not intend to be a smart Sprite.

"Freelik jumps into the pit!" he cried, feigning excitement. "He has his hands out to gather the jewels. How much can he take?"

Clack, went the dice. "The pit is filled with sharp spikes," Daniel said sadly. "The precious gems were a trap. The Sprite is impaled and dies."

"No!" Kate cried. "Pardieu, save him! Use your spell to raise the dead."

"Pardieu does not have enough points yet to raise the dead," the Maze Controller said. "Freelik is dead."

"Oh, shit," Jay Jay said, pretending to be very disappointed. He moved back out of their circle, out of the game.

"It just won't be the same without him," Kate said.

You bet it won't, Jay Jay thought, and waited.

At three in the morning they were rehashing the game. Lying on the floor of Daniel's room, tired and bleary-eyed, finishing up the last of their party food which Jay Jay had brought in after he got killed, they went over what had gone wrong. They all agreed Freelik should have used his sonar; that was a fatal blunder. Now Jay Jay would start again as a beginner, with a new character, and they would complete the game until they won or everyone got killed. None of them was particularly enthusiastic about this.

"If Jay Jay has to start with no powers he's not going to be any help," Kate said. "Besides, it's more fun when we're all equal."

"Well, *I* didn't kill him," Daniel said.

"You did so," Jay Jay said.

"You weren't paying attention," Daniel said.

"Let's not argue about it," Robbie said peaceably.

"What do you want to do, Jay Jay?" Kate asked.

"Well . . ."

Seductively, Jay Jay laid out the pros and cons of stopping the game right here. Then he went on with his suggestion about playing in the caverns. As the Maze Controller, and having already thought about how to bring the game up to this higher, more vivid level, he would arrange everything. They would love it, he promised them. It would be something no one else had ever done. It wouldn't be just a fantasy—it would truly *be* the game.

They were sleepy, disappointed by the loss of Freelik, and vulnerable. Jay Jay promised them wonders. He watched them begin to weaken, to come around to his side. Kate was afraid of the dark, so she would hate the dark caverns, and therefore, being Kate, she would force herself to go into them. Jay Jay knew he had won her. Robbie was always so agreeable that Jay Jay knew he would say yes as soon as Kate did. Robbie certainly couldn't admit to being afraid of something that didn't scare Kate. As for Daniel, his intellectual curiosity was greater than either his pride in his old game or his fear of danger. He needed a new frontier as much as any of them. Daniel smiled and nodded, and even looked excited now. Jay Jay felt a great glow of triumph.

"Then we'll play in the caverns after Christmas vacation," Jay Jay said. "All in favor say aye."

"Aye!" they chorused.

Then they all looked around at each other excitedly and smiled with anticipation. "And the game has to be our secret," Daniel said. "If the Dean finds out we're using the caverns we'll be expelled."

The nodded conspiratorially.

They thought they were beginning an adventure.

PART TWO:

RANDOMLY ENCOUNTERED MONSTERS

CHAPTER ONE

Kate found it hard to throw off the spell of the game at first when she went home to San Francisco. Here at home she was a different person: a daughter, a sister, an old school friend. Robbie called her every day, and they agreed not to discuss the game on the phone in case anyone picked up the receiver. But after a few days back with her family she took up her life just where she had left it.

She loved the big old airy house with the bare wood floors, the old rag rugs her mother collected, the antique quilts she'd bought before they became fashionable and so expensive, the silly painted antique toys. Her mother believed in plants instead of curtains, so from her bedroom window Kate could see the faraway hills and bay sparkling through a forest of green leaves. There was always a cat or the dog underfoot, or jumping into a lap to be loved. How could her father have left all this?

There had been some changes since she'd been away at college. Her mother, who was both frightened and exhilarated by law school, had lost weight and started wearing jeans. Her younger sister Belinda had grown three inches and had her braces removed; she was taller than Kate. Belinda had gone completely boy-crazy. There was always a group of noisy, giggling little girls in her room, talking about boys, and those same sex objects—gangly, shy, pimpled—came ringing the doorbell at all hours as if their families didn't own a phone. But there were also plenty of boys who did use the phone, and Kate had to fight to get a chance to use it to speak to her own friends.

Her best friends Liz and Janny came over and they made tofu in the kitchen, a long drawn out process. Liz had decided to try becoming a vegetarian. She was at Harvard, and Janny was at Berkeley: the three of them had known each other since first grade. Kate had never told them about the Incident in the Laundry Room—it had been too painful and now it was too late.

"How's the food at Grant?" Liz asked.

"Vile. Beyond vile."

"How's your love life?"

Kate smiled. "Great! I'm in love, and he loves me. His name is Robbie, and he's really gorgeous. Blond hair, *green* eyes, and he swims. And he's smart."

"Do you live together?"

"No. He wants to, but I don't."

"You're right," Liz said. "When you live with a man you have to get along with his roommates too. You really have to like them because you're all on top of each other."

"He doesn't have any roommates," Kate said. "I just like to be independent."

"How come all these soybeans make so little of this gunk?" Janny asked.

"That's the way it is," Liz said.

"Are you sure it's a lot cheaper to make it? It's a lot of trouble."

"It's good—you'll love it."

"I have had three tragic romances since September," Janny said.

"Tragic for who?" Liz asked.

"That's a good question."

"We're thinking of going to Europe this summer," Liz said to Kate. "Do you want to go?"

"This summer?" It wasn't even Christmas yet and they were making plans for next summer. Kate could hardly imagine summer, it was so far away. "Is it expensive?"

"Not the way we're going to do it."

"Let me think about it."

"Okay." Liz busied herself efficiently with stirring and straining.

Neither of them had said: *Bring Robbie.* Kate realized they didn't think her romance would last that long. She herself had kept from thinking about it. She thought how much she would really like to go to Europe with her two lifelong friends, the places they would see, the adventures they would share. She couldn't bring Robbie if they didn't each bring a man because she'd always have to be with Robbie and it wouldn't be the same. She thought guiltily how being in love made you so *committed;* you couldn't go off with other people for a long period of time because you missed the person you loved, and knowing he missed you made you feel like a rat. Maybe she could go to Europe with Robbie next summer, just the two of them. They could meet Liz and Janny somewhere for a week or so. She'd see how things went.

The first part of Christmas vacation passed very pleasantly for Kate—there were parties almost every

night, and sometimes just a few friends got together
for dinner or to go roller-skating or dancing. Even
though her mother had a lot of studying to do, she
had managed to decorate the house as she always did
with fragrant pine branches and wreaths, and there
was a big tree Kate and Belinda and their mother
decorated together with all the old ornaments they'd
had ever since they could remember, which her
mother saved carefully every year for the next Christmas. Kate's favorite was the tiny winged horse her father had bought her when she was little. He'd told
her its name was Pegasus, and it was legendary. Each
Christmas after he'd left, the little winged-horse deco-
ration had made her feel sad, but now she felt nothing but a resigned nostalgia. She knew that somewhere
deep below there was real hurt, but she refused to
allow herself to feel it anymore.

She had spoken to her father on the telephone, and
he had insisted that she come to stay with him and
Norine for a few days. Norine, his twenty-three-year-
old wife, whom Kate called Chlorine behind her
back, who embarrassed Kate because she was too
young and sexy in a trite-looking way to be married
to her father.

"I could just come for the day, Dad."

"Don't just come for the day. Come for the weekend. What are fathers for?"

I'll tell you what they're for, Kate thought.

"Besides," he went on, "you have to try our new
hot tub."

"The attack of the giant mold," Kate said. The
game jumped into her mind.

"It's not moldy, silly girl, it's clean."

"I'm not taking my clothes off," Kate said.

"We won't. Bring a bikini. And your running shoes. We'll run and you'll feel terrific."

"Okay," she said, trying not to sound ungracious. She wanted to see him, she missed him, but she couldn't stand to see him with Chlorine. But she'd just have to get used to it, the way she'd gotten used to everything else.

"I have a blind date this weekend," her mother told her. "Actually I met him once—I was introduced to him at Marie's party last month. I know it's going to be a disaster, but Marie says he's the best bachelor in California."

"I.e.: breathing," Kate said. Her mother laughed. "You're going to wear makeup, I hope."

"Of course. I always wear lipstick."

"Lipstick isn't makeup. You have to do your eyes too, and wear blusher. I'll teach you."

"All right," her mother said, surprisingly compliant. Kate realized she was beginning to notice there was a whole new life out there waiting for her to take a piece of it. She wanted her mother to have a good time and be popular. She shouldn't have to be alone.

As she put eye makeup on her mother in front of the mirror, demonstrating what she should and shouldn't do, Kate felt as if she were the sophisticated grown-up and her mother the child. It was a nice feeling and made her feel even closer than usual.

"I haven't told you much about Robbie," Kate said.

"Tell me."

"Well, he's really a very sweet person. I don't think he could ever do anything to hurt anybody. He's gentle and considerate . . . kind of quiet . . .

very sensitive. He loves me a lot. And he's so good-looking you can't believe it."

"He sounds too good to be true," her mother said. "How old is he?"

"Same as I am."

"Maybe I should go out with eighteen-year-olds."

"You could. Some of them like older women. Dad never had any trouble going out with young girls."

"Some of them like older men," her mother said gently. She peered at herself in the mirror. "I don't look too bad with this stuff on."

"You look terrific! And Mom . . . have a little haircut. Just get that old permanent trimmed off. Your hair will look a lot shinier."

Her mother laughed. "Okay, okay. When you come back from your father's you can give me a report about the best *ex*-bachelor in California, and I'll tell you about my adventure."

"How come that guy you're going to go out with is still a bachelor?" Kate asked suspiciously.

"He's divorced."

"Well, just be careful."

"Yes, dear."

She left her mother still laughing and went to her room to pack. What was so funny about a little daughterly concern? Her mother had led a pretty sheltered life.

Her father's house was in commuting distance of her mother's, but it seemed to be in a different world. He had two acres of land, trees, a hot tub, a Jacuzzi, and privacy. On the upper floor he had a sun deck where in summer you could sunbathe nude. He greeted her in his running clothes, his hair damp with fashionable sweat, his tanned skin as brown as a coconut. She was sure he used a sunlamp in the winter.

"Kate! You brought the sun!" He hugged her. He did not smell of fashionable sweat; he smelled of men's cologne. "Norine! Kate's here!"

"You look good, Dad," Kate said.

"I'm up to five miles a day," he said proudly. "Every day, even in the rain." He patted his stomach. "Coming down. Fifty sit-ups every morning."

"Wow."

Chlorine came walking languidly out of the house, wearing a string bikini and a cowboy hat. Her long, sun-streaked blond hair hung down to her large breasts, a thick hank of hair on each side as if she had carefully separated it in the middle. She had a pretty, starlet kind of face, black-dyed eyelashes, and the body of a *Playboy* centerfold. She gave Kate a sisterly sort of hug. Kate preferred not to think of it as a stepmotherly hug.

"Hurry up and put your bathing suit on," Chlorine said.

The guest room was cool and dim, the shutters closed against the sun. There was the splash of bright flowered cotton fabric against white wicker, and a blooming poinsettia plant on the dresser. A pile of the new magazines lay neatly on the night table next to the bed. There was a poinsettia plant in the bathroom too, and a brand-new cake of expensive-looking soap. The room was immaculate; so had the house seemed as Kate walked through it. He's found someone else to take care of him, she thought; just like the one he traded in, only younger.

She put on her bikini and went outside, where they were waiting. They sat in the hot tub and drank iced

tea with fresh mint in it. They sat in the Jacuzzi and
drank cold white wine. Her father asked her about
college and Kate told him what he wanted to hear:
that he had absolutely nothing to worry about. She
did not mention the game, although she knew he
would have found it fascinating. He always wanted to
do whatever he thought young people were doing.
But for her it was not just a game, it was an emotional thing about all the most private fears and fantasies of her life, and she couldn't share it, even with
her parents. Besides, he wouldn't understand and he
would think it was crazy. Chlorine read *L'Officiel*,
quietly letting father and daughter have their little
talk.

After a while they had lunch under a tree: chicken
salad with walnuts in it, the way Kate's mother used
to make it. It was Kate's favorite salad, but she could
only swallow a few bites. She thought she would
throw up. He's even got the same recipes, she
thought.

"I thought you ate chicken," her father said.

"I do. Just that I'm full . . . all that tea and
stuff."

"We don't eat meat anymore either," her father
said.

Kate helped Chlorine take the dishes back to the
kitchen. Her father, as in the olden days, didn't move
a muscle to help. He's found himself another love
slave, Kate thought in wonder. How does he do it?

"Still thinking of getting a job, Norine?" Kate
asked by way of conversation.

"No, I don't think so. Maybe later."

"Don't you get bored just cleaning and cooking?"

Chlorine shrugged. "I go to the gym every day. I

have to take care of my wardrobe. I get a manicure and pedicure and bikini wax. It takes me a whole day just to wash my hair. I do my gardening—those plants all over the house, I grow them myself. I'm busy all the time."

After lunch Chlorine went to her room to take a nap, leaving Kate and her father alone together.

"Want to take a run?" he asked eagerly.

"I'm kind of tired."

"Okay. We'll just sit here and talk." He opened another bottle of cold white wine. "You're not too full for a little more wine, are you?"

She shook her head. Might as well get smashed. She wished she had a joint. He probably had one, but she didn't want to ask him.

They sipped their wine in silence. "Kate," he said finally, "I want to tell you why men get divorced."

She didn't say anything. She wasn't sure she wanted to know, after wondering all this time, because she was afraid of what he might say. Whatever he said would be about him and her mother, and there were places in their lives where she did not want to walk.

"A man and a girl are dating," he went on, "and she's very seductive, very unattainable. She's sexy. He falls in love with that girl. Then they get married, they have children, and suddenly she's living the marriage script her parents taught her. She thinks a home has to be a safe, boring place where the children can grow up. She *wants* it to be boring. She's not sexy anymore. She can't help it; it's the way she was brought up. The home has to be a haven for the children. The man wants more. He leaves."

"Chlorine is boring!" Kate burst out.

"Norine? What makes you think she's boring?"

"She's a dumb cow," Kate said. "You think she's sexy because she has big tits and she's young."

"No," he said. "I think she's sexy because she thinks *I'm* sexy."

Kate felt embarrassed. She didn't want to know about her father's sex life. She wondered if part of what he said was right. At least *he* thought it was right, and he knew his side of it.

"I just hope you two don't have any kids," she said. "I'd hate to see them spoil your lives."

"Kate . . . it wasn't you and Belinda. Don't you understand? It was the way women of a certain generation were brought up."

"It's your generation too. You were just afraid to get middle-aged."

"I thought you were sophisticated enough to understand," he said.

"I'm trying."

"It's going to be different this time, with Norine and me." He smiled. "She's pregnant. You see, I don't have anything against a family."

"You two are going to have a *baby*?"

"In June. A little Gemini."

Her hand was shaking as she filled her glass with wine. She drank it down. "Well," she said, trying to sound pleasant because he looked so proud and pleased. "I guess I'll have a little sister or brother."

She knew now he was gone for good.

CHAPTER TWO

Long before she was Kate's mother, Meg Porter had grown up as a perfect child of the Fifties. She fervently believed every movie she'd ever seen, and when life did not turn out like the movies she never questioned the movies; she thought something was wrong with life. She was a cheerleader in college, leaping around with pom-poms, and she was also an honors student. She was a mischief-maker who never did anything really bad, so she didn't get in trouble. People thought she was cute. When she was at college her friends used to say: "I have to get married before all the good ones are taken." Surrounded by the "good ones," popular and secure, Meg waited for her own special Mr. Right. She knew when he came along she'd know it immediately, just like in the movies.

Mr. Right was Alan Finch. She found his name romantic and English. He was a veteran, a former lieutenant. They were always lieutenants in the movies. He even looked like an actor; the nice one who got the girl at the end. He was four years older than she was and seemed experienced and sophisticated. She met him on a blind date in Senior year, and after that first date neither of them went out with anyone else.

They were married right after she graduated, and moved to San Francisco because Alan had always wanted to live there. It didn't frighten her to leave her family and friends. It made her feel grown-up. Alan would be her family and friends now—her very best friend, and they would live happily ever after.

They got a little apartment in Berkeley, which they painted themselves, and after they had Kate and Belinda they moved across the bay and bought their house. Meg learned how to be a gourmet cook and how to take care of plants; she tended the children and the cats and dog; they bought furniture, books, records, quilts, rugs, antique toys, a car. Every time she and Alan acquired something together she felt it was another brick in the good wall that was going to keep them safe and secure forever. The thing that made their little world complete was the children. Kate and Belinda were bright and beautiful and fun. Meg worked hard to make their home a haven for Alan to return to every evening after a dangerous day out in the market, gambling with other people's money, making his conquests. She was happy to live through him. His glories were hers too. She pictured the two of them growing old together.

When he told her they had already grown old together she was shocked. What did he want her to be that she wasn't? She begged him to tell her what he wanted, and he answered that he had been cheating. She was willing to forgive him. They had been married fifteen years and had a whole life they'd built together; cheating wasn't enough to tear that down. He said he was bored, sad, disappointed. He acted as if it were her fault. She didn't understand. She had never been bored. How could he be sad and disappointed when he had everything they'd dreamed about when they were engaged and planning their future?

He tossed her and the children away as if they were biodegradable.

After a while Meg got over her anger and bitterness. She decided Alan was crazy. She had her two wonderful daughters, and they were her best friends. She loved them fiercely. They made her laugh. They were so vulnerable under their coolness that she wanted to stand like a Valkyrie and protect them, but she knew she couldn't. The best thing she could do for them and for herself was to have a new life of her own.

She went out on blind dates. They were the former "good ones," now on their second or third go-round, but they didn't look so good anymore. She wondered why they didn't treat her the way men had in college.

When Kate went to spend the weekend before Christmas at her father's, Meg Finch had her last date. She had met him briefly at a party the month before, where her hostess recommended him as "the best bachelor in California."

The first thing he said to her was that he was dismayed she had cut her hair. He said he had preferred it curly; it was sexy, like pubic hair. She thought of jumping out of his car, but he was driving fast, down a residential street that was far away from any transportation, and it was raining. He took her to a bar called Fantasy: wall-to-wall mirrors, blue, red, and green lights reflecting off them, a young man in a full-length mink coat leaning languidly against a white piano. Her date asked her about her life. At least that was familiar.

Meg told him about law school, how frightened she had been at first because she thought everyone else would be so young, and how happy she was to find quite a few women her age in her class. She told him how she admired those other women for starting all over again, for fulfilling old dreams or daring to reach for a new one.

He said he bet none of them had ever had an orgasm.

She felt like crying, running away, or screaming at him. But she did none of those things: she blushed. She was back in the time tunnel to the girl she had been when she was dating at college—passive, agreeable. Then the colored lights in the bar swirled around and a floor show started. It was an S&M show. Whips and chains. Meg walked out and took a taxi home.

After the weekend Meg told Kate about her date. They both laughed over the telling of the story, now safely in the past, but underneath Meg was angry. She announced that had been her last date, and she meant it. From now on she would go out only with friends. If a man wanted to see her it would have to be on her own turf, at dinner in her own home with her daughters. She wanted normalcy, not sparring and humiliation.

Meg was planning to cook a big Christmas dinner—that was comforting. She had invited friends and told the girls to ask their friends too. Not everybody had a family that made a big fuss over holidays. Kate had brought Christmas presents for herself and Belinda from their father, and the girls insisted on opening them right away. The presents looked as though Norine had picked them. Kate had received sexy lingerie: a satin teddy and a nightgown and peignoir. Belinda had been given a plaid flannel bathrobe. They were both disappointed. But since each of them loved the other's gift, they traded happily. Their father never gave them the right thing; it was as if he didn't know them at all.

And then Kate broke the news. Alan was about to become a father again. Meg knew Kate and Belinda were only pretending they didn't care; as for herself, she was numb. The man who had walked out on her six years before was a stranger now. They would always be tied together by their children, but he no longer had the power to break her heart. Men remarried and started new families; he wasn't the first. She wasn't even really surprised. She only wished that instead of just telling Kate he had picked up the phone to tell her too, like a friend.

But that was another of her romantic fantasies that one by one were being replaced by reality. Long ago she had dreamed that she and Alan would be best friends. Now she knew they would never be friends at all.

She decided she wouldn't let it matter. She was still a romantic. The world was askew, but she would always have dreams. She would have her own life now, on her own terms, and she would make it work.

CHAPTER THREE

Jay Jay looked at the outside of the Park Avenue apartment building where he and his mother lived, collecting himself now for the stress family confrontations always seemed to bring. Other people liked going home; he went home because there was nowhere else to go.

"Good-bye!" Robbie yelled behind him, putting his little car into gear. "Merry Christmas!"

"Good-bye," Jay Jay called back. "See you soon."

The car drove away and he was alone; Merlin in his cage in one hand, his suitcase in the other, his cowboy hat on his head to remind him that he was the great Jay Jay, the one of mysterious glamour. The doorman, in his dark green winter uniform, came out to the sidewalk.

"Mr. Brockway."

"Good afternoon, Paul."

He had graduated from being Jay Jay to being Mr. Brockway when he went to college. It was Paul's way of being nice; it was ridiculous, but he rather liked it. All those lonely years at high school where the other kids were so much older they looked on him as a rather amusing mascot, but never a friend, the humiliation of graduating at fourteen when everyone else

was eighteen, and tall, and having a sex life and social life that didn't include him—all of that was somehow shut off into the past when he became a College
Man. Mr. Brockway. There wasn't one soul from high
school he even spoke to now, not that he'd spoken to
them very much then either.

"Help you with your bag, Mr. Brockway?"

"Thank you."

The doorman took his bag to the elevator and Jay
Jay gave him a dollar.

The marble floors of the lobby were as polished as
ever, the mirrors gleamed, not a bulb was out in the
crystal chandelier. The enormous Christmas tree
loomed in the corner, decorated with colored balls
and lit. There were Hanukkah candles on the mantel.
No tenant was to be ignored in this season of goodwill and holiday tips.

Jay Jay let himself into the apartment with his key.
His mother, Julia Brockway, was a rather famous dec-
orator, with some very well-known, rich clients, and
her large, high-ceilinged apartment was a showplace
for her new ideas as well as a home. He noticed that
she'd moved the furniture around in the living room
again, and this year's tree was decorated with nothing
but hundreds of tiny perfectly tied red-and-white
checked bows. She always kept things around that
smelled: sachets, pomander balls; incense, perfumed
candles, sticks of vanilla. She even put special per-
fume on the light bulbs so they scented the room
when they were lit. This Christmas the theme seemed
to be cloves and cinnamon.

"I'm here, Mom," he called.

She came floating out of someplace in the back
vastness of the apartment, looking chic and slim and

beautiful. He looked like her; the same pointed face and mass of golden curls, the small-boned quickness, but it was more suitable on her. She was wearing a white silk bathrobe and had all her makeup on, so he knew she was getting ready to go out.

"Darling," she said, in her light voice that was like water. She could be Queen of the Sprites. She put her hands on his shoulders and kissed the air near his cheek so as not to mess up her makeup. Then she looked him over. "I think you grew a little. Did you? I hope so."

"I'm not growing anymore," Jay Jay said. "Where are you going?"

"To a cocktail party at the French Embassy. Then dinner at a new place in SoHo that got a good review in *Vogue*. Everything nonfattening. Even the champagne, apparently—it has less sugar content." She clapped her hands. "Let me show you your Christmas present!"

"Now?"

"Of course now. You'd see it anyway."

She led the way to his room. His heart sank. He knew already what it would be, and he felt the anger roaring through him, choking him. She always killed his identity, she made him disappear into her own fantasies—please don't, Mom, say you didn't do it again . . .

"*Voilà!*" She flung open the door. She had redecorated his room completely; he couldn't even recognize it.

"Oh, shit," Jay Jay said.

When he had left for Grant in September he had left a cozy, warm, masculine room with antique furniture and tan-and-white-striped fabric on the walls.

He'd just gotten used to it. When she had changed the last room he'd gotten to like he had thought the new one was too staid and stuffy, but after a while he had grown to like it too. And now all the warmth had been stripped away to the stark white bareness of High Tech. It looked like a goddamn hospital. Everything was built-in and hidden, the bed was a four-poster made of steel things that looked like girders, a mover's pad was the hideous cover, and the brightness of those shiny unadorned walls was blinding.

"Where's my stuff?" he screamed.

"It's in the cabinets," she said. "Don't you scream at me. I worked my tail off to get this ready for you in time for the holidays."

"I liked it the other way. Where's my furniture?"

"Don't you *like* your new room?" she asked. She looked hurt.

"Don't I like it? I just told you I hate it. Why do you always act like you're deaf when I talk to you?"

"Maybe because you *scream* when you talk to me," she snapped. "Do you know how many clients would give their eyeteeth to have a room like this, done by Julia Brockway?"

"Your clients remove their eyeteeth by hand every night and put them in a glass of water," Jay Jay said.

"You're a fresh little kid."

"My room is my turf," Jay Jay said. "It's my nest. My cave. I don't want you changing it around when I go away. And Merlin hates it too." Merlin was blinking his eyes. "Tell her, Merlin."

"Birds can't talk," Merlin said.

"Coward," Jay Jay said to him. "Mom, when you change my environment without my permission you

obliterate *me*. You're going to make me schizophrenic."

"I doubt that," she said. She pouted now, and
crossed her arms over her breasts like the statue of a
saint. "You know I'd never do anything to hurt you,
Jay Jay. I just thought it would be interesting."

For you or for me? he thought, but he didn't say it.
His poor mother; she would never understand him.
Right now his beloved antique furniture was probably sitting in some client's bedroom. His mother
treated all the furniture in their apartment with the
same cavalier attitude as she did Jay Jay's, except for
a few pieces that were irreplaceable and to which she
was devoted. Even those, he suspected, she loved for
their investment value. He wondered if there was
anything—or anyone—in the world that had his
mother's purely emotional affection.

He and his mother made up finally, in a way.
Their fights never lasted long. She was an orderly person, and as she was always in a hurry to go somewhere, she didn't like to leave an untidy unfinished
argument behind. He apologized for being too surprised to realize her goodwill; she apologized for
shocking him without warning. She did not promise
not to do it again. Redecorating his room was the
only thing she knew how to do for him.

As soon as she had left for her cocktail party Jay
Jay took all his old movie and movie star posters out
of the closet, got a hammer and some picture hooks,
and banged the nails into her newly enameled, very
expensive walls. The posters made the room look a
lot better. He hung Merlin's cage from the top of the
frame of the four-poster bed. "Poor Merlin," he said.

"Poor Jay Jay."

At least she'd had the decency to leave him his television set. He found it tucked away in one of the built-in cabinets, bolted down to a pullout, swiveling shelf. Jay Jay went to the kitchen, where the cook had left some cold chicken and endive salad in the refrigerator for him. There were also two bottles of his mother's best white wine chilling there; he supposed in case she brought some friends home with her after dinner. He appropriated one for himself. The cook had also baked his favorite brownies.

He took the food and wine into his room, locked the door, fed Merlin, lit a joint, and settled down in front of the TV to watch a rerun of *The Maltese Falcon,* one of his favorite films. He'd seen it about twenty times.

"Don't get paranoid, Merlin," he said. "Nobody's going to stuff *you.*"

The wine and the pot made him feel mellow. He would be busy this Christmas vacation; there were a lot of movies he had to see which hadn't opened yet in Pequod, he would have to start planning the details of the game, and he had to buy his family presents. His mother's, his father's and stepmother's and stepsister's . . .

"What did you think of that bitch, huh, Merlin?" he said. "She didn't even ask me about college."

Every Christmas Jay Jay's father gave two parties: his Christmas Eve party, which was famous, to which he invited his most illustrious or notorious authors, many of whom were well known in other fields; and celebrities he'd gotten to know through the years— and his Christmas Day party, which was smaller, not so exciting, and for family. No one ever turned down an invitation to one of Justin Brockway's parties.

Since his marriage to the ballerina Orinda Wells, Justy had added the greatest stars of the ballet world to his party list. With the sudden rush of movie star autobiographies he had also added many actors and actresses, who particularly liked coming because Justy never allowed the press to come. His guests could behave as badly as they wanted, with complete lack of publicity—but no one ever behaved badly at one of Justin Brockway's parties. They wanted to be invited again.

Jay Jay was always invited to the family party, the one on Christmas Day. That wasn't the one he wanted to go to. The guests were aunts and uncles and cousins he saw once a year, and underlings from Justy's office who had no place to go, and the food was leftovers from the party the night before. He wanted to go to the exciting party on Christmas Eve. This year he intended to.

The Christmas Eve party was black tie, but of course he couldn't wear his tuxedo because then the fecalite would know he had planned to crash. It had to look like an accident. He decided to wear his white suit, with a black silk shirt and a white tie; an antique pocket watch hooked to his lapel and draped in his pocket. After agonizing minutes of decision he decided to forgo wearing one of his hats. They would never understand. He had bought the presents at Tiffany's. He was set.

Justin Brockway owned a beautiful town house in the East Sixties, on a tree-lined street with a private patrol. It had four stories, a bowed window in front, and a beautiful garden in back. As Jay Jay got out of his taxi he saw with excitement a line of chauffeur-driven cars dropping people off in front of the house.

He ducked into the phone booth on the corner and waited until he saw the street was clear, then he sprinted to the house and walked innocently to the front door and rang the bell.

The door was opened by a uniformed maid hired for the occasion. She smiled pleasantly and took his coat. He retained the packages—his badge of legitimacy—and walked into the living room. His heart was pounding. The room was filled with everyone in New York he wanted to know, the babble of their happy voices rising tantalizingly, their elusive eyes glancing around for people *they* wanted to know. The tall room was wood-paneled, its back wall of windows overlooking the wonderful garden. Justy and Orinda had put tiny white lights in all the trees outside, and in the hedge. It was like a fairyland. A butler carrying a silver tray offered Jay Jay a glass of champagne. He declined, for now. He looked for his father and finally saw him, talking to a small, baldish political expert and a large, loud movie actress in a caftan. Now Jay Jay would show her a little acting.

"Dad!" he said. "Wasn't it *tonight?*"

"Excuse me," his father said quickly to the other two. He put his arm around Jay Jay's shoulders and led him to the corner. "Well, Jay Jay, how nice to see you," he said politely. His eyes were a little startled, but he was smiling with aplomb.

"I thought it was tonight," Jay Jay said. He thrust the presents at his father.

"Your mother . . ." Justy said, with an air of weary patience. "It's tomorrow. But now that you're here, of course you must stay. How are you? Is school all right?"

"Oh, yes, I'm fine, school's fine."

"Good. How were the marks at midterm?"

"All A's."

"Of course they were. Go put your packages under the tree and say hello to Orinda." His father was already scanning the room for Orinda, raising a finger to catch her attention, steering Jay Jay in her direction. "There she is. I'll catch you later."

Orinda Wells Brockway, the white swan, embraced Jay Jay in her delicate wings. She seemed so fragile he thought he could probably lift her, but he knew how strong she was. "Jay Jay!"

"I thought it was tonight," he said.

"You're coming tomorrow too, I hope."

"Well . . . I guess so," he said, as if such a prospect had not been necessary to think about before.

"Good, then we'll have more time to talk. This is a madhouse. Jay Jay, why didn't you call me for ballet tickets? I'm dancing twice next week; don't you want to go?"

"I'd love to," he said.

"Good, we'll arrange it tomorrow. Now you must see Sarah—she's gotten so big and beautiful you won't recognize her." She was looking for the baby now, leading him to the child and her nurse. He felt as if he were the baton in a relay race.

His half sister, Sarah Brockway, was two years old, a robust, happy child with dark curls. She was wearing a ruffled white dress and was held in the arms of a sensual-looking young blond woman of about twenty, the au pair girl Inger. Sarah recognized him and rewarded him with a big smile. Inger, whom he had been lusting after ever since he first saw her, rewarded him with indifference. He would have preferred it to be the other way around. Orinda had already disappeared into the crowd of her guests.

"Merry Christmas," Jay Jay said to Sarah and Inger, and went directly to the bar.

He had a glass of champagne, lit one of his thin brown cigarettes, and stood looking around with the air of a fascinating sophisticate. Inside he was quaking. Here were legendary people he'd seen on television being interviewed, and on the screen, and whose books he had read. He had known for years that they were his father's friends, but he had never met them. He drank another glass of champagne and accepted a canapé. Through the double doors to the dining room he could see a sumptuous buffet supper waiting; inviolable perfect food displayed until the secret signal that it was the right time.

"And who are you?" a musical, accented voice asked.

His heart turned over. Petrova, the greatest Russian ballerina, bone-thin, radiating nervous energy; great violet eyes, hair wrapped in a white turban, dressed in white, a perfectly behaved white Afghan hound standing beside her, white leash wrapped around her tiny hand.

"Jay Jay Brockway," he said.

"I am Svetlana Petrova," she said gravely. She knew he knew, but it was part of the game of being just a normal person. She took a long black Russian cigarette out of her evening bag and he lit it for her. She gestured at the one he was smoking. "That is a cigarette I don't know," she said.

"It's not as interesting as yours," Jay Jay said. He held out his pack and offered her one.

"Please," she said, and offered him one of hers in

return. "We will have—what is that funny thing?—a taste test."

He planned to save hers forever. He was so awed by her he couldn't think of a thing to say. He thought of patting her dog.

"My little harlequin," she said.

"Why am I a harlequin?"

"The face . . . it's wonderful. Nobody ever told you that before?"

"Only Picasso," Jay Jay said.

She laughed. "You know Federov?" she asked, turning and linking her arm in the arm of the man who had just come up behind Jay Jay. Federov! The greatest male ballet dancer with the golden hair and famous love life. Jay Jay could hardly believe he was standing here with both of them at once. "This is Justy's son," Petrova said.

She *knew*! The fecalite must have actually *mentioned* him some time to these people! *He,* Jay Jay, spoken about in his absence, to *them*!

Suddenly it was easy: people talked to him, introduced him to other people, laughed at his jokes, made a fuss over him. He even had people to sit next to when dinner was finally begun. Joe Henry, the Pulitzer Prize-winning novelist who often got drunk at parties and punched someone (but never at Justin Brockway's parties), talked to him about the possibility of life in outer space. Well, not really to him alone—to four other people too.

I fit in, Jay Jay thought. I really do.

Then why wasn't he having a better time? He had just as good a time at the parties he gave at college. As he finished the strawberry trifle and chocolate mousse he had figured it out. These people here in this room had a shared history of fame and achievement; his was only in the future. He was still an outsider.

He pictured his ideal party. It would be several years from now, and everyone would be just as illustrious as the people here, but they would all be *his* friends: the ones who had climbed to the top together. Kate would be there, and she would be the Pulitzer Prize-winning novelist. Perhaps she would also write scripts; only for him of course. He would be the Academy Award-winning actor. Merlin often appeared with him on interview shows. Daniel would be the great computer genius who had made millions from the games he had invented, and who had a villa in the South of France—where they were all invited every summer. Jay Jay's friend Perry, who had been in pre-med at Grant, would have discovered the cure for cancer, and was up for the Nobel Prize. Everyone knew he would get it. Robbie . . . what about Robbie? He had started too late to be an Olympic swimmer. Poor Robbie, too average to keep up with the rest of them, his affair with Kate long over, had disappeared from their lives. Jay Jay's father, of course, would not be invited, unless he wished to crash. But his sister Sarah, who would be just about the age Jay Jay was now, would be devastatingly beautiful, and she would be there with the son of one of the people who was here now. She would be a little diffident, because she knew she had only been invited through Jay Jay's generosity.

Jay Jay closed his eyes and smiled. His party would be so chic that even his mother would be there.

CHAPTER FOUR

When Julia Brockway was a little girl, she once over-heard one of her teachers tell another that she was "a cold fish." She was Julie Burns then, an enchantingly pretty little blond girl who was tidy and punctual, and she thought for a few days about what a cold fish might be, and if it would keep her from being popular, give her bad marks, or in any other way upset the balance of her life. She decided it wouldn't, and put it out of her mind.

By the time she was in college, and boys were falling all over themselves to make a good impression on her, she realized there was something about her that was different from the other girls, and that it was valuable. Other girls seemed to suffer from an excess of emotion; they wept when boys they loved didn't call, they claimed to have broken hearts. Boys always called Julie Burns. Her inaccessibility made her seem like a mirror; they saw themselves reflected and were happy. The first and only man she fell in love with was Justy Brockway, and he immediately suggested they live together. He was a genuine eccentric, a genius, a charmer, and she was sure living with him would be more fun than anything she had yet experienced, so she agreed. They took an apartment together, off campus. Each told the college authorities they were taking the apartment with a relative, for financial reasons. Living in sin, in 1962, could still get you expelled.

When Julie discovered she was pregnant, she and Justy discussed whether she should have an abortion or they should get married and have the child. They decided on marriage. He couldn't imagine that having a baby would interfere with his life in any way, and she thought it would make her an adult. Actually, having Jay Jay interfered with their life together very little. Their small apartment was always filled with friends, any of whom could be called upon to serve as an impromptu baby-sitter. Jay Jay's first summer they left him with her parents while they went backpacking in Europe. The following summer they went in grander style, and Jay Jay stayed with his paternal grandparents. By then Julie and Justy knew people they had met in Europe, as well as people from college, and their European student friends often came to stay with them for extended periods, thus providing the Brockways with even better baby-sitters because their guests had to do something to pay them back for the free lodging.

Julie couldn't understand why her few married friends gushed on about their babies. It was her opinion that a child had to accommodate its parents, not the other way around, no matter what the baby books said. Justy felt that if they treated Jay Jay as an adult he would become precocious, which was what he wanted. He couldn't have stood it if his son hadn't been bright. Since Jay Jay was obviously brilliant, and quite quickly gave a reasonably good imitation of a small adult, Justy was pleased.

As soon as Julie and Justy graduated, they moved to New York, where he got a job in publishing. At first they had a rather wretched little apartment, because they had very little money, but Julie began to realize that she had a talent for decorating, and that she liked it. She did some interesting things with their apartment, and then she took a few courses, and began to read all the decorating magazines. When Jay Jay entered First Grade at four, able to read but unable to tie his shoes, Julie got a job as a receptionist at a decorating firm. She was well liked, eager to learn, and no fool, and soon worked her way up to an assistant. Justy was an editor now. They moved to a better apartment. Julie decorated it, and Justy began giving parties for specially chosen people, instead of just free-for-alls. In return, they began to be invited to parties where they met people who would be helpful in their careers. They both discovered they were fascinated by success.

If they hadn't been so busy doing interesting things they would have noticed earlier that they had fallen out of love, if indeed they had ever been in love, and that they no longer interested each other. One afternoon, Justy decided to bring home a young woman he'd just shared an excellent lunch with—he was feeling so mellow he decided he deserved to take the afternoon off and go to bed with her. Besides, she was an author he was trying to steal from another publisher, and she had been trying to get him into bed for months. On that same afternoon, Julie brought home the handsome married president of a large corporation, who had been trying to get his hands on her for months. She, however, had no intention of giving in. She intended to show him her apartment, which she had decorated so cleverly, impress him, and tell him she couldn't possibly do anything with him because her son would be home from school and her husband home from the office.

They all met at the same time. The four of them were very civilized and had a drink together. Afterward Justy and Julie discussed it, the way they had discussed whether or not to have their baby. This time they discussed whether or not to get a divorce.

Julie wondered why she wasn't more upset. Other women took the breakup of a marriage as a trauma, the way the girls at school had taken the end of a romance. She and Justy were very rational and pleasant about it, and they decided it would be more interesting to live apart. After all, neither of them had really had a chance to have love affairs; they'd been married so young. They were twenty-six already, and soon they would be too old. They decided she would keep the apartment and Jay Jay, and Justy would pay whatever their lawyers decided was fair.

For one moment Julie thought perhaps she was making a mistake. Justy was probably the only person she had ever met, or ever would meet, who was as cool and rational as she was. Perhaps they could continue in a marriage of convenience, as friends . . . But no, that would be embarrassing and hard to explain. Men would think she was fair game. Better to strike out on a life of her own.

The divorce was amicable. The married corporation president, fascinated that Julie was still elusive, and impressed by her talent, introduced her to a few of his important friends. One of them, a rich woman who prided herself on discovering new artists, let Julie decorate her New York pied-à-terre.

The apartment was photographed for *Architectural Digest* and *Vogue*. Julie began calling herself Julia— after all, she was a grown-up now at last—and quickly acquired as many clients as she could handle. She bought the Park Avenue co-op. She was happy.

She took a few lovers and discovered a disturbing truth about herself. She really wasn't at all interested in sex. She loved parties, meeting intriguing people, getting dressed up, having stimulating ideas on how to improve her environment, but she didn't care if she never went to bed with a man again. Women didn't interest her either. She began to go out mainly with homosexual men, who were easy to be with and didn't expect or want her to go to bed with them; and clients who were too afraid of her to make a pass.

She had read enough magazine articles to know she had a low sex drive. She did not, for one moment, delude herself into thinking she was saving her body for a meaningful relationship. She asked her gynecologist to give her a hormone test, just to be sure she was all right. She was fine. After that her lack of libido didn't bother Julia at all. As long as it didn't make her breasts sag, it didn't matter.

When Justy remarried, Julia sent him and Orinda a lovely crystal bird from Steuben. Things from Steuben went with any decor. When Jay Jay graduated from high school, Justy bought him a Fiat Spider convertible. Kids loved cars. Julia couldn't understand why Jay Jay sold it. She and Justy always gave people perfect presents.

She also couldn't understand why Jay Jay got so upset whenever she redecorated his room. He was like a fussy little old man, set in his ways already. She was appalled when she saw the craters he had dug in her expensive lacquered walls with those nails from the picture hooks. Five layers of white lacquer—for that! She couldn't bear imperfection. Even though the posters were hanging over the holes, she knew they were there.

She thought perhaps this coming spring, when Jay Jay was at school, she would put natural sisal on his bedroom walls, to hide them, get lots of potted palms, and do a bed with white mosquito netting all around it, and an old-fashioned ceiling fan like something from a Sydney Greenstreet movie. Jay Jay was so crazy about those old films, maybe he would like that sort of room. The mynah bird would fit perfectly into the setting. The more she thought about it, the more excited she got.

Of course, it would be a surprise.

CHAPTER FIVE

In the room in the Brookline house where he had
spent his childhood, Daniel stood on his toes, raised
his hand as high as he could, and touched the ceiling.
He remembered what an honor it had seemed to have
this attic room, all alone up here on the top floor: his
private domain. The room had seemed enormous.
Now it was small, and he had to stoop to shave in
front of the bathroom mirror because his mother had
installed it low when he was a child and nobody ever
remembered to have it changed. This room, this
house, enfolded him in memories, and for a moment
he looked at his college self and wondered how he
could have been crazy enough to agree to play the
game in the caverns. He must have crossed over into
some kind of madness. It was too dangerous. He'd
have to back out.

But then he started to think of reasons why it
wasn't too dangerous after all. They could try it and
if it didn't work they could stop. If he was the one to
break it up now, the others would think he was just
jealous because he wasn't M.C. anymore.

Why should he care what they thought? He cared
what Kate thought, because he admired her intelligence and courage. She had integrity: he never

wanted her to think he didn't. The girls he went out with, the ones who made everything so easy for him, seemed vapid compared to Kate. He'd been only half kidding that first day back at Grant when he said he was thinking of giving up sex. It was only that it was always the wrong time to stop. Maybe he'd give it up this Christmas vacation and see if he survived. Perhaps he'd reach a higher level of consciousness, the way people did when they fasted.

He laughed and went downstairs to join his family for dinner.

There was his mother: small, trim, a brown rinse covering the gray in her hair now, her blue eyes always inquisitive. She looked at you intently when you spoke to her and nodded often. She liked to refer to herself as "a creative listener." She was also a creative talker. And there was his father: the perfect tweedy professor. His brother Andy and Andy's girl friend Beth had come for dinner too. Andy and Daniel had a strong family resemblance, but Andy was taller and his hair was sandy instead of dark. Beth was tall too, and willowy, with blond hair and skin that seemed as smooth as glass. They made a striking couple; people sometimes turned around to look at them when they went jogging or bicycling together.

There was a fire in the fireplace, and outside stars glittered in the black sky. The Hanukkah candles were nearly all lit. This year their parents had decided to give Daniel and Andy money instead of presents, because that was what they really needed most. His father had opened a bottle of California zinfandel, and poured a glass for Daniel.

"I've decided to learn about wine," his mother said. "Everybody I know is into gourmet cooking, but I don't have time, and it doesn't relax me. So I've decided: wine. Tell me how that tastes."

"Fine," Andy said.

Daniel tasted it. "It's okay."

"Just okay, or good?"

"Good. Listen, I'm not an authority. We drink Ripple at school, unless Jay Jay picks it."

They all settled comfortably on the floor in front of the fire. A Chopin concerto was playing softly. "You know," his father said, "a time comes when you think of moving ahead in life. A very interesting thing happened to me recently. The Vice-President was at Harvard giving a speech, and it seems he'd read my book, and he asked that I be invited to the party afterward."

"Your father's book," his mother repeated proudly, her eyes shining.

Ten years ago, when Daniel was a little kid, his father had written a book called *The Crisis in Regulation: The Public Interest and Vested Interests*. It had received a limited but appreciative response, mainly among his academic colleagues. When he was old enough to read it, Daniel had tried. It was not his field, and he had been bored, but he was impressed that his father had done it.

"So I went, of course," his father continued. "And he was very cordial, but more important—interested in my ideas." He paused, looking at each of them to be sure they were taking it all in. "He said: 'Goldsmith, you might be on our team.'"

"Washington?" Andy said.

"That seemed to be the idea," his father said. "He didn't actually make a commitment, but he implied that I might be called to Washington. I don't know what else 'on our team' means."

"I thought you were happy at Harvard," Daniel said. He couldn't imagine his father in Washington.

"Frankly," his father said, "I think I've done as much as I can here. Look . . . if it was party talk, I'll survive. But I feel something is going to happen, and if it does, I'll be glad to go."

"That's fantastic, Doctor Goldsmith," Beth said. She raised her glass. They all drank a toast to his future.

"I had a small triumph myself," his mother said. She was trying to act casual, but Daniel could see how excited she was. "You remember Kevin, the little black boy in my class who was almost autistic? The one with the alcoholic mother, the father who disappeared? Doctor Francke kept telling me: 'Autism is chemical, Ellie; you're not going to get through to that child.' But I wouldn't give up. I said: 'Look at that traumatic home life! Some children are more fragile than others. Kevin is one of the fragile ones.' " She took a sip of wine and smiled. "Well, this morning, he was smearing away with his finger paints, and just as I handed him the cobalt blue, he *spoke!*"

"What did he say?" Daniel asked, fascinated.

" 'April is the cruelest month,' " his father said wryly.

"Don't be silly, Harold. He said: 'No.' "

"Well, that's good," Andy said.

"You're darn right it's good," his mother said. "He could have pushed the blue paint away, or just used it passively, but he had a preference and he made a choice. And he verbalized it! I know he can talk—he has an entire vocabulary just waiting to explode out of him, but it takes time. And I'll give him that time."

"How do you feel about going to Washington, Mrs. Goldsmith?" Beth asked.

"Whatever Harold wants is all right with me," she said.

"What about your work?"

"Beth, don't start that stuff with my mother," Andy said. "You'll get her all upset."

"I'm not upset," his mother said. "I can pursue my career in Washington. Besides, if it happens, it won't be for a long time, and I can make great progress with Kevin in the meantime."

"Your mother will be valuable wherever she goes," his father said.

Daniel felt the little currents moving through the room: ambition, fear, hope, control, compromise. All through the long years of their marriage his parents had ridden those dangerous currents; two people paddling in tandem in a light canoe, keeping their balance, moving ahead. No matter what her own triumphs, she always put them aside for his father's. It was true that someone else could continue with her work, but someone else could go to Washington instead of his father, and what would it really matter to anyone but Harold Goldsmith? And, of course, his wife. Maybe she cared as much about having her husband move up in the world as he did.

Beth sat in front of the fire with her face edged in gold. Her skirt was spread out like a nest, and Andy kept cracking walnuts with his strong hands and dropping the nutmeats into it. "I heard the most awful story today," Beth said. "A man had a Dacron tube grafted into one of those arteries leading to the heart; you know, that operation they've been doing for ages. He died a few years later of an apparent heart attack, and when they did an autopsy they found he'd grown a rare kind of cancerous tumor around the Dacron graft."

"Poor guy," Andy said.

"Do you know what that means?" Beth said. "It means that it's possible that synthetics cause cancer."

"Something else to worry about," his mother said. "Half the country will have to go nudist."

"Remember that thing they did on TV?" Daniel said. "On *Fernwood Tonight* when Martin Mull had those mice in little polyester leisure suits to show that leisure suits cause cancer?" He laughed, remembering. He had liked that show, it was funny.

"Nothing is safe anymore," his mother said angrily. "They do a satire on television and a couple of years later it comes true. There isn't anything too far-fetched or horrible to imagine. We're destroying the planet."

"With leisure suits?" Andy said. He laughed and popped a handful of shelled walnuts into his mouth.

"Go laugh," his mother said. "You're going to have to live in that world. Somebody's going to have to do something about it."

"Daniel will do something about it," his father said calmly. He smiled at Daniel. "The future of mankind is in computers. We'll have energy conservation systems, new transportation systems, community participation systems . . . we'll get rid of poverty, waste—"

"Wait a minute!" Daniel said. "I can't do all that."

"I didn't say you'd be the only one. But you'll help."

Why wasn't he happier about saving the world, when everybody else seemed to want to?

"What about people who just want to tend their own garden?" Daniel said.

"No room anymore," his father said. His mother nodded. "No room for nonparticipation. Be thankful you're bright and have something to contribute."

"I wish it would snow for Christmas," Daniel said, to change the subject. "Remember the great big snows we used to have every winter? Now it doesn't seem to snow till February."

"The weather is changing," his father said. "We're tampering with the environment. You want snow? Good, that's something you care about. Figure out a more efficient . . ."

Oh, shit, Daniel thought, closing out the sound of his father's voice. He wanted a simple snowball fight and his parents wanted him to win the Nobel Prize. Could you have both? He wanted to please them, but he had only one life, and he didn't want to end up old and bitter.

"Dinner is ready," his mother said.

They sat in their accustomed places, passing around the platters of food. Since Daniel's visit from college made him a sort of guest, they had all his favorite things to eat: little squab chickens, a bowl of stuffing on the side, peas, sweet potato casserole with marshmallows on top. They were his favorite foods because he was used to them; they reminded him of every special dinner since he was a child. For dessert his mother had bought a huge, gooey cake.

Beth nodded at Andy. He disappeared into the kitchen and came back with a bottle of cold champagne and a tray of glasses.

"What's that for?" his father said.

Andy grinned like the Cheshire Cat and popped the cork. "Beth and I have an announcement," he said. He looked at her.

"We're getting married," they said in unison.

A shriek of joy and hugs and kisses from his mother, happy handshaking and a kiss for Beth from his father, a goofy smile from Daniel. Daniel felt so strange. He'd always thought of Andy and Beth as sort of married anyway, but now that they were making it official he was a little bit rocked. They would be on their own now, drawing away from the others, making a family of their own. They were lucky, he thought, to be able to make a commitment. So lucky . . . it was what he wanted to be able to do.

"When?" his mother asked.

"June," Beth said. "We want a traditional wedding, I'm going to get a white dress, have bridesmaids, everything. We're going to Mexico for our honeymoon."

"Mexico is very interesting," his father said.

"And affordable," Andy said.

"I suppose now you'll want to look for a nicer apartment," his mother said.

The two of them looked at her in surprise. "What for?" Beth asked.

"Well . . . that place you're in looks so . . . temporary. People get married, they get dishes, silver, furniture . . ."

"We have that stuff," Andy said.

"Maybe you're right," his mother said. "After you have your first child you'll have to move anyhow."

"We're not having children," Beth said. "Certainly not for a long time, anyway, and then only one."

His mother looked horrified for a moment, then carefully composed her face. It was her habit not to argue with her children; she wanted to be their friend. But there were bright blotches of pink on her cheeks.

"The world can't be that bad," she said, "not to want children."

"It's not the world," Beth said calmly. "I'm not sure I want to be a social worker forever. I'm applying to law school, and after that I might go into politics."

"You can go into politics and have children," his mother said.

"We have time to decide," Andy said. "Beth's only twenty-four."

"At twenty-four I had you already."

"It's a different world, Mom."

"I *know* that," his mother said sharply. She busied herself with pouring more coffee, cutting more cake, forcing it on them, insisting, even though they were full. It was as if by starting to serve dessert all over again she could erase time, make what he and Beth had just said disappear. "I guess then," she said finally, "it's up to Daniel."

"To do what?" Daniel asked. "Talk them into it?"

"No," his mother said. "To have children. You can't both let me down." Her tone was light, but forced. She wanted them to think she was just joking, and yet she wasn't, and she wanted them to know that too.

He couldn't make her any promises, but a part of him wanted a lot of kids, a houseful of them, all happy and noisy and having fun—and him teaching them games and playing with them.

After dinner Daniel and Andy went outside to shoot baskets in the hoop in the garage door, the way they had done since they were little boys. It was a joke now, because Andy was a professional and Daniel just fooled around, but they liked to keep up the tradition. The air was cold and crisp, with a bite to it, but not the sort that forecast snow.

"You know," Andy said, "I always envied you. Everything was so easy for you. It was always so hard for me. But now I don't feel that way anymore. I think it's hard for you too."

"It is," Daniel said. "I always envied *you*."

"Me?"

"Yep."

"I never knew that." Andy tucked the old basketball under his arm and put his other arm around Daniel's shoulders, walking with him as if he were explaining a court maneuver to a student. "You can do anything you want, Daniel," he said. "You can be anything you want. They don't mean to hassle you. Whatever you decide to do with your life, they might make a fuss at first, but they'll go along."

"I guess," Daniel said. "But I have to live my own life anyway."

"All they want is for us to be happy," Andy said. "Their idea of what's supposed to make us happy isn't always ours, but they mean well."

"I know. I love computers . . . do *you* think it's selfish to want to make up games for them? Somebody has to make up the games in the world."

"You couldn't have said it better."

"It didn't impress them much," Daniel said. "Hey, I'm really glad that you and Beth are getting married."

Andy grinned. "We're all excited about it."

They walked together back into the warm house that smelled of pine cones which Beth had gathered and tossed into the fire. Daniel and his father sat down at the small table in front of the window, the way they always did at night, and played chess. The chessmen waited for him, in their same positions, while he was away at college, and he wondered what his father would do when he was gone for good.

But he wasn't going to think about that now. He had to concentrate to beat his father, so Daniel gave the moves his full attention. It was very important to him to win at games. He didn't care about winning at sports, or in life, but games were different. A game was the only thing that was exactly what you wanted it to be.

CHAPTER SIX

Back in high school, before Ellie Kaufman had ever met Harold Goldsmith, the girls were fond of making lists of the qualities they wanted in a future husband. "Good personality" and "Sense of humor" were high on the list. "Good character" and "Intelligent" were added dutifully so one would not seem to frivolous. "Attractive" was at the bottom of the list, mainly because it was such a given—who would dream of marrying an *un*attractive man?—that it was added as an afterthought. Ellie had no list. There was only one thing she wanted in her future husband: He would have to be better than she was in everything.

It was not that she had a low opinion of herself; quite the contrary. She knew she was attractive, bright, had a good character, and boys seemed to like her personality. But she knew she couldn't stand to live with a man who wasn't better than she was—not just as good, but better. How else could she respect him? How else could she defer to him? How else could he take care of her? If she was going to settle for a man who was the same as she was, then she might as well take care of herself.

She met Harold at college. She knew right away he was better than she was, but he never acted as if he knew it, which was fine with her. "Conceited" was definitely not on her list of attributes. They were married right after she graduated, and they had Andy while Harold was in graduate school. They were of that group of people who met at college, stayed at college, and simply never went home again. If she hadn't met and married Harold she would have gone to graduate school; as it was, she never stopped taking courses.

It was the early 1950s, and so Ellie always had an excuse for taking the courses so she wouldn't seem to be thinking of deserting her husband and baby for a career. Harold was a professor so her courses were free. She'd have to be a fool to waste that opportunity. She took art appreciation, painting, sculpture, pottery, and psychology. When Harold got appointed to Harvard she certainly couldn't give up a chance to study there, so she began working for a Master's. Andy and Daniel were both in school so she had enough free time. Her friends worried about the effect on her children's mental health, as if she had deserted them.

"I'm not going to *work*," Ellie told her friends. "It just seems a shame to waste all those credits."

When she had her degree in Art Therapy it seemed not only silly but a sin to waste her education, so she got a job working with emotionally disturbed children. The children were a mix of rich and poor, so in a way she could claim she was really doing social work even though she was being paid. She loved all the children, even the ones who bit her.

When Andy got his degree in Recreational Therapy and his own apartment, and Daniel went away to Grant, Ellie was ready to tell her friends that she had entered a career as a way of letting go of her sons less painfully. But by then her friends had been through the women's movement, and they told her they admired her for knowing what she wanted all along. She stopped making excuses.

Here she was, married twenty-seven years, a very different person from the unformed creature who had married Harold Goldsmith because he was better than she was—and now she knew he was better than she was only because she loved him and chose to think so. They had never had a fight that was bad enough for them to think of a divorce, she had never cheated and was sure he hadn't, and they still had a good time together. The fact that she and Harold had been responsible for creating two adults who would live after them and do good things in the world made her feel immortal, a part of eternity.

The discovery that one of those adults—Andy the *meshugge*—had chosen to betray her immortality by refusing to have a child of his own filled her with horror. It wasn't that she wanted to play Grandma. She had enough little children to worry about at the hospital. It was that Andy was ending the greatest thing in life she had been able to do.

How could she explain that to him? How could she tell him what a family really was? Even if your children and grandchildren went to the four corners of the earth and you never saw them again, a part of you was walking somewhere on that earth and that mattered. Otherwise you disappeared. Did *Daniel* know? Could *he* understand? She didn't have to worry about Daniel finding a nice girl; the phone never stopped ringing when he was home. The girls called the boys today, not like when she was young. Harold joked and said he wished he were nineteen years old now instead of back then. But she worried about what was going on in Daniel's head. The sensitive, tender, loving little boy who had told her everything, shown the most amazingly mature perceptions, had grown up and away from her.

All the psychology courses she'd taken didn't help her when she tried to understand her own child. You couldn't, after all, read someone's mind. Maybe Daniel was just going through the natural searching and separating that teen-agers had to do. You couldn't even call them "teen-agers" anymore—they had to be "young adults."

Then that made her a middle-aged adult. The time had gone by so fast she couldn't stand it: a blink of the eye and it was over.

CHAPTER SEVEN

The mixed feelings Robbie always had when he walked into his parents' house in Greenwich were intensified when he came home for Christmas vacation. Holidays, particularly Christmas, were supposed to be joyful times, but the home in which these holidays were celebrated was tumultuous and filled with anger. Home, as he had always believed other people's were, was a refuge of warmth and love. In his he felt torn apart, his loyalties going first to one parent and then the other, and sometimes even—as if it were a selfish and unworthy thing—to himself. To protect himself he had adopted a surface calmness. It went with his all-American good looks, his good manners, his gentle ways; so he almost seemed to have erased himself. There was no one who did not like the Robbie Wheeling he had created. His parents' friends said he made up for the tragedy of the older son.

There were pictures of Hall junior on the piano in the living room, just as there were pictures of Robbie: the happy babies smiling in the sun, the proud young boys with their huge baseball bats, and finally the teen-agers. Robbie's photos were always the same; he only got older. Hall's changed a great deal. In his last photograph he seemed almost paranoid, startled by the camera, ready to spring. Cat and Hall senior, his parents, had not seen how extraordinary this photograph was or they would not have put it on display for people to see—but how could they have noticed, when the real Hall junior had looked exactly the same way and they saw him all the time? Robbie himself had only noticed it later, when Hall was gone and he was trying to understand.

Hall's room was waiting for him exactly as he had left it. The cleaning woman dusted it, and there were fresh sheets on the bed. It was a way of saying he might come back. And what if he did come back and discovered his room had been turned into something else: a den or a guest room for instance? He might become angry and leave again.

Whenever Robbie walked past his brother's room, which was next to his along the upstairs corridor, he could hardly bear to glance inside, and yet something drew him to look. The past always came back when he saw that plaid bedspread, the maple dresser, even the pile of old magazines, their pages yellow now. They had been old magazines when Hall left; he just hadn't bothered to throw them away. Merry Christmas.

The house had been quite nice once, done in traditional style with a great deal of flowered chintz. The fabric was faded now and worn down to the stuffing on the arms of the chairs, but his mother never got around to doing anything about it. They did not entertain anymore anyway, except for a few very close friends. His father took people to the country club. He went to the city early and came back late, by which time his wife, who had been drinking alone and storing up the grievances of over twenty years, would fight with him. There was no need to redecorate their environment; the feelings would be the same.

During the holiday Robbie saw his friends from high school, went to parties, called Kate every day, and swam. He wanted to keep in practice, and since the high school was closed for vacation (he knew the coach would have let him in for old times' sake) he went early every morning to the YMCA. The large, damp, echoing tiled room that smelled of chlorine was empty during the time he chose to go. The diehards who had to get in their laps before the commuter train were gone, and it was too early for the lunch-hour fitness freaks. Robbie warmed up, sprinted, cooled down, and then just did leisurely laps, reluctant to leave. He found swimming hypnotic. Back and forth, turning, moving with careful, endless strokes through that walled, tiled maze that looked like the little squares on graph paper. He was in the maze, and in his dream of the maze; Robbie, Pardieu . . .

When he had to go home eventually, after his swim, he always felt more relaxed. Still, he was counting the days until he could get back to college, to Kate and his friends, and to the game.

His mother was cooking Christmas dinner for him and his father and her father, who was eighty years old and widowed. Cat, his mother, was the youngest child. There were no aunts, uncles, and cousins this year: some were on holiday in warm places, lying in the sun, others were far away in other states with their own families. The four of them seemed a pathetic little group somehow. His father was in the living room watching football on television, on the new set he'd bought, with a screen that looked like a movie screen. He was drinking martinis. Dinner was not for several hours, and Robbie knew there would be trouble by then. His mother was in the kitchen drinking vodka with her father. She no longer bothered with martinis. Robbie could smell the turkey in the oven. It smelled good, and she had made his father's favorite chestnut and oyster stuffing. Everybody hoped she wouldn't burn the dinner as usual, and she knew what they were thinking, so she was sitting in the kitchen even though there was a long time to go and she had set the timer.

"Tell your mother to put out some cheese," his father told Robbie. "Didn't we get a wheel of that nice black-rind cheddar from the Pattersons? Sure we did. What's she doing, waiting for it to spoil?"

Robbie looked at his father. Even at his leisure he was well dressed, like a country gentleman: navy blue blazer, open-neck shirt, black velvet slippers with his initials on them in gold, on his wrist one of the seven watches he had replaced with identical ones. Lean, tall, slightly tanned, a fifty-dollar haircut. His mother hated those black velvet slippers. She called them "his royalty shoes," and laughed when he wore them.

"Dad wants cheese," Robbie said, entering the kitchen.

"I am getting it ready for him," she said. There were so many things going on in her tone that Robbie couldn't begin to think about it. If her words were glass and shattered on the floor in a hundred pieces each one would be an emotion.

She sliced a wedge of the black-rind cheddar and put it on a cheese board with some crackers and a small knife. She was wearing a dark red party dress.

She was still so beautiful, his mother; tall and slim and blond with aristocratic bones. Liquor had not made her puffy or smudged her features. It made her face melt, but only when she was very drunk, and right now she was only partly drunk. She looked like her father. At eighty he looked much younger, and he drank a lot too. He smiled at Robbie.

"Have a steady girl?"

"Yes, sir."

"Living together, I bet. Young people today . . ." His voice was pleasant, conversational. He took a sip of his vodka. "The old people are getting like the young people. New morality. The old widows at the club, always chasing me. Come over to say hello, how are you. I suppose they want me to take them out, go to bed with them. Not that I can't still do it, you understand. But I don't want to get involved. You go to bed with a woman, next thing she wants you to move in, marry her. Am I right, Cat?"

"I don't know," Robbie's mother said. She gestured wearily at Robbie to take the cheese to his father.

"Is she drunk?" his father asked.

"Not very."

His father looked at his watch and grunted.

"Grandpa's talking about sex," Robbie said. "He's funny."

"Jesus," his father said.

He sat down and watched the game with his father for a while, and then he went back to the kitchen. His mother's mood had changed. Now she was getting angry. He knew the phases so well he could anticipate them. The level of vodka in the bottle had gone down considerably.

"I wouldn't do it now," she said. "I wouldn't marry

the first man I fell in love with. Or the second, either. I'd go out and live first. Find out who I was. Did you ever try to live with a man who doesn't talk?"

"You ought to have a cook," his grandfather said.

"I don't mind."

"You should have people waiting on you. He's successful. I don't like to see you dragging heavy bags of groceries from the market."

"What do you think I've been doing my whole life?"

"It isn't right," he said.

"I'd rather he talked to me," she said.

"You talk to each other a lot," Robbie said.

"Fighting isn't the same as talking," she said. "Maybe it is. But just once I'd like to have a conversation where I didn't end up hoarse."

"Can I help with anything?" Robbie asked.

"We should have eaten at the club," she said.

Dinner was late. His mother put Christmas carols on the stereo and lit candles on the dining room table. She had covered the table with the white linen cloth she used for parties, and was using the dishes with Christmas trees painted on them.

"Turn that down, Cat," his father said, annoyed. "How can I hear this?"

"It's Christmas and we're going to have music and conversation," she said. She was very drunk now. "Turn that thing off. We're going to act like a goddamn family."

"You're drunk," he said.

"I have plenty of reasons."

"When the hell are you going to have dinner ready?" He was none too sober himself. "Everybody's starving except you."

"It's ready now," she snapped, and turned off his beloved new TV.

The turkey was overcooked. Robbie could tell the moment he saw the dark, leathery skin. His father was carving it angrily. "I need an ax for this damn thing," he said. "You get drunk and you burn the Christmas dinner, as usual. I should have eaten at the club."

"Oh, *you* should?" she said. "Alone with all the families?"

"I wouldn't take you in that condition."

"This is my home and I can be in any condition I like," she said, her cheeks flushed with rage. "I am a talented, well-educated woman, and I could have been someone, I could have had a life. You made me drink. I drink so I can get through the day. All my life, it was always duty. What you wanted. What everybody else wanted. Not what I wanted. Nobody ever asked me that."

"I hate when you drink," he said. "You act like a hostile bitch."

"And I hate oyster stuffing," she said. "Those disgusting little fishy gray things."

Robbie closed his mind to their fight and ate quietly. He knew they were not fighting about dry turkey or oyster stuffing, or about how much liquor had been consumed that day, or even a wasted life ending in a lonely house with no guests and no laughter—they were fighting about something so deep they could not speak of it. He knew what it was, and it frightened him, because there would never be any end unless Hall came back. Even now, drunk as she was, she did not say: *You called the police.* And he did not say: *He would have left anyway.* Your fault, they were both shouting; your fault, yours . . . Robbie wondered if he would ever be old enough so these arguments did not make him cringe and want to leave.

His grandfather sat quietly, chewing his food, used to this chaos. Like Robbie, he had no other choice. But unlike Robbie, he had no guilt to share either . . .

After dinner Robbie drove his grandfather home. As he came back to his parents' house he could see the lighted tree through the living room window, the fire in the fireplace burning merrily, and his mother in her dark red party dress sitting in front of the flames drinking, all alone. A party should never end with someone all alone, and yet they all were: his grandfather with his dreams of old widows, his father in bed, his mother by the fire, and himself. He wondered if each of them felt as lonely as he did.

At least his sentence was not indeterminate. He would be going back to school soon.

CHAPTER EIGHT

No one remembered who had first nicknamed Catherine Forsythe "Cat." Her father said it was he because she was so agile and quick. Her mother claimed it was she, because Catherine was so quiet, sneaking up on you, watching with round green eyes. Nobody ever thought to call her "Mouse." She was much too big.

She was one of the tallest girls in her class at school, but slender and graceful; athletic, aesthetic, and bright, and always with that cool aristocratic beauty that made boys write poems to her. Hers was an old eastern family, and she was brought up to be what her father called "a gentlewoman." A gentlewoman, she thought, had more character than a lady—a lady languished in a hammock, but a gentlewoman could handle anything. She went to boarding school, and then she went to Vassar, because her mother and grandmother had gone there. Her great love was music—she dreamed of becoming a professional pianist—but her parents would not hear of sending her to Juilliard. It was necessary for a gentlewoman to have a well-rounded college education, preferably at the school that had smoothed the edges of her forebears. Cat's music was an excellent choice: she could play the piano at home while taking care of her husband and children. It would bring pleasure to her family and herself. Her becoming a professional was only discussed once, and dismissed immediately. Professional musicians had to practice eight hours a day, and then they had to travel. They could not have a normal life.

Cat met Hall Wheeling at a party. She was a Senior in college. He was different from the other men who wanted her; his ambition burned so brighly it was like sexuality. He radiated sparks. When he spoke to her of what he would become, the great things he would do, she felt her throat close as if she were go- ing to cry—his life would be a wonder. He was work- ing in New York, so they had weekend dates. She married him gratefully a week after she graduated. She was a virgin. Eleven months later she was a mother.

Marriage to an ambitious, successful man was not what she had expected. All of that energy he had was for other things, other people. When she went to par- ties with him she saw the Hall Wheeling she had fallen in love with; but now he was enchanting people from his business world. At home he was tired, quiet, busy with work he had brought home from the office. He wanted "to unwind." She realized that without either of them ever knowing it he had won her the way he would win a contract. She had been the challenge, the project. Now she and their baby, Hall junior, were like a building he had designed: completed, strong, perfect, built to last for- ever, and he was off to the next assignment. She looked at the other wives, busy in their own little worlds of home and children, and she realized this was what marriage was. She was doing just what a woman was supposed to do. But she felt betrayed.

They had Robbie. She hardly ever played the piano anymore. The only free time she had was when the babies were napping, and then she couldn't make noise. The rest of the time she was doing all the things you had to do for a helpless infant, or chasing after an active toddler, and it was so far from her dreams of the aesthetic gentlewoman's life that she could not believe she had ever been so naive. She had never known what having children entailed. No one had ever told her. Perhaps she was selfish . . . She was afraid to tell anyone how she felt, for fear they would tell her there was something wrong with her.

She needed her music: she felt it and heard it in her head, straining along the tendons of her arms and fingers like electricity. When she did have a chance to play the piano she realized she had lost valuable time she might never get back. She wasn't as good as she had been. And now, at five o'clock each evening, she had begun to drink, "to relax," and the drinking had become as seductive as the music. She tried to teach the boys to play the piano but they were not interested. They had no talent at all. She began to think that she had deluded herself; that she had no talent either. She loved and needed her music, she missed it, and finding it out of reach she began to will it further away. She would go back to it when the boys were grown. That was what other mothers did. Now she could drink, and forget.

But the truth was she drank to remember. On the outside she had never changed from the quiet, sweet, cool girl who inspired poetry. Inside she was furious. The woman who tried to please everyone, to run a lovely home, to make her husband praise her; the woman whose generosity of spirit saw only good in everyone; that woman was burning inside, seething with anger. All the time she was growing up people had lied to her about life. Her parents had lied, her teachers had lied, her friends had lied, the world had lied; and even her husband, the one who was supposed to love her more than anyone else, had lied. When she got drunk she dared to say what she thought, and then it made other people angry. She had to make an impossible choice: turn her rage against herself and suffer, or vent it on the world and lose everyone. Not knowing which to do she did both.

When Hall was fourteen she found out he was taking drugs. How could his school allow people to sell pills and marijuana to a little boy? How could this happen? She and her husband had moved to the suburbs so their children would be safe. Where were the police? Where was safety, sanity? Hall wouldn't tell her where he'd gotten the stuff. When she searched his room he screamed at her. When she cut off his allowance he sold drugs to other children so he could get some for himself. Then she found out he'd been going in to New York.

She couldn't control him. He was almost as tall as she was, and he had become a stranger. He had an addiction, but so did she, and how could she do anything but argue with him and pray for him and cry? When he was fifteen years old he ran away.

His father called the police. He told her that young boys who ran away became male prostitutes, got kidnapped, raped, beaten, killed. The police found Hall and brought him back like a prisoner—the prisoner of his parents. He was desperate and devious and he fooled them both. They thought he had learned how dangerous the world was out there and would stay home and be their son again. They gave him a birthday party to celebrate the fresh, new start they would all have together, all forgiven in love and hope for the future.

He ran away and never came back.

The pain of her failure would stay with her as long as she lived. There was not a morning she woke up without the sense that something hideous had happened, and then there was always that moment when she remembered what it was. She could tell herself that society had betrayed her son, or that he had done it to himself, but she could never really believe it wasn't her fault, and his father's, for things they had neglected to do. No one had told her what to do. Life had lied to her again. She wondered what she had done right with Robbie that she had done wrong with Hall, but she would never know.

CHAPTER NINE

It was New Year's Eve, 1980—the start of a new decade. That made it even more exciting, and although all of them pretended New Year's Eve was silly, it meant a lot to them. Kate was going to her friend Janny's New Year's Eve party. The three of them had planned it together; she and Janny and Liz, but it was at Janny's house. When they made the guest list they discovered they had seven men for every woman, which was awful, so they told people to bring dates. Then they worried that only the women would bring dates.

"The guys will get mad and leave," Janny said.

"No they won't," Liz said. "They get free food and liquor and a nice warm place to hang around in—they'll stay."

They had recruited three friends to act as disc jockeys. At midnight they planned to set off firecrackers in the backyard. They wished they could have been able to afford real fireworks, but this would have to do. If people didn't crash, and if nobody got too drunk or stoned, and if the neighbors didn't complain about the noise, it would be a terrific party. Kate was only sorry that Robbie couldn't be there. It was sad to be by yourself on a sentimental night like this, especially when there was a man you cared about.

Cared about . . . why hadn't she thought: *a man you loved?* She really did care about Robbie a lot; she wanted to protect him and cuddle with him and be with him, but was that real love? Love should be your heart turning over when you saw him, a melting feeling when you had sex, being willing to die for him if you had to. Being away from Robbie this Christmas vacation hadn't been a lonely terrible time. She was happy with her old friends, and she felt warm and comforted every day when he called, but she hadn't been counting the days until she could be with him again. She knew she'd be with him. Was this why romances at Grant broke up so fast: being too sure of somebody, wondering why there wasn't more excitement? It made her feel guilty. She knew she hadn't closed herself off from love this time, because she trusted Robbie completely. Yet, there was something missing in him, spaces she couldn't figure out. Maybe he didn't even know what they were.

She didn't have anybody to talk to about it. Her mother was more naive about love than she was. Liz and Janny didn't know him, and they didn't expect anything to last anyway. They would roll their eyes and laugh and chorus, "Next!"

Poor Robbie . . . But at midnight on New Year's Eve, when he called as he had promised to, she started to cry. She cried because he was so good and faithful and kind and she didn't deserve him, and she also cried because the firecrackers were going off in the backyard and she was missing them, and it made her feel like a perfidious rat to care.

When Robbie heard Kate cry on the phone he was

so moved he almost started to cry himself. He was at his friend Nick's party, and there was so much noise he had to hold his hand over the other ear. It was a total free-for-all because they knew it was the last real party before they had to go back to school. Everyone had gotten very dressed up, and they had bought champagne to serve at midnight. The television set in the living room was on, and they had watched it, counting in unison, all excited, as the ball fell down the tower in Times Square. Then they blew horns and yelled, "Happy New Year!" and kissed each other. When it was midnight in California the long-distance circuits were still busy, and Robbie had been panicked that he wouldn't be able to get the call through to Kate at exactly twelve o'clock her time, and then it wouldn't count. He liked the ritual of it; it made him feel secure. If he could be the first person to speak to her on the first minute of the first day of her new decade, it would bring them both luck.

"Don't cry," he told her gently. "I'll be with you soon. Just ten more days."

"I know," she said tearfully.

"I send you a kiss," he said. "This is a real kiss, okay? I mean, I'm kissing *you*, it's coming right through the telephone wires to land on your face." He kissed into the phone. "Got it?"

"I got it." She sent one back to him. "That was yours."

"It felt great," he said.

"I have to go now," she said.

"I love you."

"I love you too," she said. "Talk to you tomorrow?"

"Of course."

After they hung up he stayed there for a while by the phone, feeling peaceful, until a girl he hardly knew came over and gave him a kiss. Robbie wished she hadn't done that. He didn't want to kiss anybody but Kate; it was necessary to be undefiled.

At midnight on New Year's Eve Daniel was in bed with a girl named Sharon whom he'd seen a couple of times during the holidays. She was an economics major at B.U., a Junior, and she had her own apartment, which she shared with two other women who were away. She was enthusiastic and outgoing and very sexy, and she liked to be with him alone more than she liked to be with him at a party, so she had dragged him home from the party at ten o'clock. After nearly two hours in bed they were both quite tired, and they were sipping champagne and eating cookies.

She ran her hand through his thick hair. "Happy New Year," she said.

"Happy New Year."

"You're the only man I know who's prettier than I am."

"I'm not pretty, Sharon, come on!" Daniel said, annoyed. She always made him feel like an object.

She grinned. "You're gorgeous, how's that?"

"Okay."

"And bright. And a nice guy. And a terrific lover."

"Thank you."

"These cookies are stale," she said. She got up and went into the bathroom. She had a beautiful body, very firm and smooth and curvy. He poured a little more champagne and turned on the small black and white television set she had on the floor next to the bed. The reception was terrible; he couldn't tell if it was snowing in Times Square or the snow was on the screen, or even if it *was* Times Square. He supposed she hardly ever had time to watch TV anyway.

He felt depressed. The sex had been great, and she was a nice person, but he didn't care about her and he knew she didn't really care about him either. He never knew what she was thinking, and when he tried to ask, it always turned out that what she was thinking had very little to do with him. That was just as well—it would be unfair if she had more feelings for him than he did for her. This was just right the way it was. He should be pleased.

But New Year's Eve was a special time, and he wished he were in bed with a girl he loved, not here with someone who was almost a stranger.

The stranger, with whom he had just engaged in all sorts of erotic, pleasant, and intimate acts, came back and got into bed.

"Can you stay all night?" she asked.

"Sure."

"Good. Where do your parents think you are?"

"All-night party. That's where I *was*."

She laughed. "I got my own apartment so I could stop lying to my parents. They do control the money, after all. They're sending me to school, so I like them to be happy. Commuting was the pits. I lived in the dorm for a year, but when I had to go home for holidays my parents acted as if I was still their little girl. This way they can tell themselves what they want to hear."

"True."

"My roommates and I are going to London this

summer," she said. "If you want to sublet this apartment, you can."

"What's the rent?"

"Four hundred a month, but it has two bedrooms, so you can share."

"Thank you," he said. "I'll think about it."

"You get it all furnished, of course," she said. "It's a steal."

He thought how his friends at school would probably think he had spent a sophisticated, romantic, sexy New Year's Eve—a typical Daniel's New Year's Eve—practically attacked by this luscious creature, now in bed sipping champagne together.

A typical Daniel's New Year's Eve, he thought sadly, was lying here casually discussing a real estate deal.

Jay Jay spent the same New Year's Eve he had spent for as long as he could remember: alone while the rest of the world was at a party. His mother had gone out in a long white evening gown, trailing a cloud of Opium and *two* dates, both of them gay. Jay Jay had prepared a little supper of champagne, Scotch salmon, Brie, and grapes, and was lying on his bed watching television. Merlin was his date. For a special holiday treat Merlin got some grapes too. When all the midnight nonsense was over, Jay Jay switched channels until he found an old movie. He had called Kate, Daniel, and Robbie earlier, but they were all out at parties, like normal people. He'd spoken to Kate's mother, who seemed very nice and was entertaining a few friends; there was no one at all home at Daniel's house; and Robbie's mother was completely drunk but friendly. Jay Jay had the feeling she was lonely and glad to have someone to talk to, even if it was just a kid who was a school friend of her son's. She talked to him for fifteen minutes. He didn't mind; in fact he liked it.

So the old year was over and good riddance. The new one was going to be much better. He turned off the TV so he could concentrate and got out the pile of new Mazes and Monsters Challenge Modules he'd bought at the hobby shop. He'd already gone over them several times, checking off perils that could be reenacted with real props in a real setting like the caverns. He pictured the mazes he would invent in the caverns as a sort of deadly and terrifying fun house, with masks and eerie lighting waiting around corners, a coffin, real bones, a sword in a pile of stones, lumpy misshapen creatures made of rags and stuffing, coins, fake jewels, the robe with the mysterious potion in its pocket, and a pile of the Perilous Sand. But best of all would be the real bottomless pools, the pitch-dark uncharted labyrinth; the shivery feeling that no magic scroll could ever help you if you got lost. He, of course, would have a compass and a map.

He would need all the time he could get to prepare the game he had in mind. While the others were studying for stupid Winter Finals he could be working out the game, because he never needed to study. But it was really going to be complicated to get all that stuff, like a kind of scavenger hunt. The more Jay Jay thought about his plans for his new game the more excited he got. He knew that tonight he wouldn't be able to sleep at all. It was pointless to hang around New York anymore now that the important holidays were over. He could split tomorrow, go back to school early. His mother wouldn't care.

That would give him ten days, all by himself, to get started.

PART THREE:

RAISING THE DEAD

CHAPTER ONE

Back in the dismal winter landscape of the deserted university, Jay Jay made it vibrant with the colorful creatures of his imagination. The school authorities had turned down the heat to save energy, but Merlin's heater kept their room nice and warm. Once, he ran into the security guard, who asked for identification—not because Jay Jay looked like a local vandal, but because he seemed too young to be there at all—and for some reason, after he had ascertained that Jay Jay was in the dorm legally, the security guard seemed sorry for him. Jay Jay couldn't understand why, since he was having the time of his life.

He went methodically down his list of necessary props, checking off each one as he found or bought it. He hadn't yet decided what the treasure should be, but there was plenty of time for that. Smaller treasures, to keep the adventurers going, were easier. But he had the feeling that the monsters in the caverns would be the real treasure.

By the time the rest of the students had come back to the dorm, Jay Jay had everything he needed, neatly hidden away in one of the rooms of his caverns. He had now begun to think of them as *his* caverns, not *the* caverns, just as this production now was

his game. Good-bye to Freelik the Frenetic of Glossamir, who had only been a player. Now he was the
Maze Controller: the director, the scriptwriter, the set
decorater, even the producer. He had begun to map
his maze from the labyrinth of his caverns, and he
kept the map hidden in his room where no one could
find it. This was the most creative project he had ever
done in his life, and it fulfilled him almost completely. The only thing he still needed were his actors, and they were sequestered with their noses in
their books, cramming for Winter Finals.

He also needed human bones; his special scary
present for Kate. For these he went to his friend
Perry, who was in pre-med.

Perry was a simian-looking person with a gnome-
like mind. "What do you need human bones for?"

"I just need them," Jay Jay said. "I'll trade you the
use of my motorbike for two weeks in return for two
days' use of the bones."

"*If* I let you have them, it would have to be on a
weekend. I'd have to steal them out of the anatomy
lab and that's the only time no one will know."

"A weekend is just when I want them. Friday night
till late Sunday night."

Perry squinted his eyes like the mad scientist. "I
have to know why you need them, though."

"You don't have to know," Jay Jay said. "You want
to know."

"Same thing. I can get them and you can't."

"Okay, but don't tell anybody. I don't want anybody else to get the idea of invading my territory. I
thought of it first and it's *my* thing. Okay?"

"Okay."

"A couple of us are going to play Mazes and Monsters in the caverns," Jay Jay whispered triumphantly.

"Oh, boy, you are really nuts!" Perry said.

"Do I get the bones?"

"Why don't you use animal bones? All you have to do is boil the carcass—"

"You're going to make me throw up," Jay Jay said.

"You really going to play in the caverns?" Perry said. Like most of the people at Grant, he had heard of the game and knew that it was popular on the campus, even though he didn't play it himself. "You know, you could get lost in there and die."

"We know," Jay Jay said.

"You're not going to lose my bones?"

"If we get lost and die in the caverns with your bones, they'll come to look for us, and then you'll get even more bones. That ought to make you happy."

"And I get free gas for the motorbike," Perry said.

They shook hands on their deal. Jay Jay said he'd let him know the date. He knew Perry would probably tell a few people, but it didn't matter. They would never tell the school authorities, and none of Perry's friends played the game. The chance of another group trying to play in the caverns was extremely rare. It was much more likely that they would come to Jay Jay and ask to be included. Even so, Jay Jay didn't want strangers.

"Remember," he said, "secrecy is of the essence."

"Yeah, yeah," Perry said. "It's my ass too, you know."

Oh joy, oh bliss, oh gleeful wonder! Everything was falling into place so well.

Reading Period, when everyone studied for exams, was a time of hushed terror in the dorms. There were no parties. People went to the library. Even the constant blare of music from all the individual stereo sets was muted; background for memorizing. The people who had neglected their work up till now were frantic. There was much trading of notes, and all-night sessions to catch up. Normally pale anyway at this time of year, now most of the students looked sick—with worry, sleeplessness, and the effect of a vast consumption of coffee, junk food, nicotine, and pills to stay awake. Jay Jay looked and felt very chipper. Daniel and Kate, although they studied, seemed normal. Poor Robbie was haggard and drawn. All romances were put on hold during this period of fear. After all, if you flunked out, you'd probably never see the person you were in love with again . . . not to mention never getting a decent job; suffering the wrath of your parents, the disdain of the world, and the loss of your own self-respect.

One night around eleven thirty, when he had returned from his secret nightly trip to the caverns, Jay Jay came tapping on Kate's door, carrying a Thermos of hot coffee.

"Coffee break, madam."

She looked pleased to see him, and put her book down immediately. "How sweet. Thank you."

He sat down on her bed and poured coffee for both of them. "How's it going?"

"Oh, it's okay. I just sometimes wonder how the professors *know* what the authors had in mind. We have to spit back whatever they tell us in class. And I think: If I'm a famous writer some day, will people make up what they think I meant and then make other people agree with them?"

"Probably," Jay Jay said. "Unless you write the textbook yourself."

"It doesn't matter," Kate said, suddenly looking depressed. "I'm never going to be a famous writer—or any kind at all."

"How can you say that? We're all going to be famous. That's the plan."

"Whose plan?"

"Mine," Jay Jay said.

"Then you'll have to get rid of my writer's block. I can't be a writer if I don't write anything."

"You'll think of things. Right now you're at school; there's too much input from other sources."

"Maybe." She sipped her coffee. "How are your plans for the new game going?"

"Fantastic. Just wait."

"I worry about you at night, Jay Jay. I know you're in the caverns all alone."

He was touched. She, his love, his friend, worried about him! He wished he had brought her something better than coffee, but it was what he'd had left from his evening in the caverns and it had been a spur-of-the-moment idea to share it with her. "You don't have to worry," he said. "I'm careful, and I know my way around pretty well by now."

"You couldn't. They're too big."

"The Pyramids were not built in a day."

"May I quote you?" They laughed. It was a matter of pride with both of them never to say anything banal unless it was on purpose. "You know what I was thinking, Jay Jay? You're almost halfway through college and you want to be an actor, but you've never taken an acting class."

"I know," he said calmly.

"But why not?"

He thought about it. It wasn't to spite his father, because his father didn't care. It wasn't because he was afraid of competition. He knew he was good. Why, then? "I guess," Jay Jay said finally, "it's because I have the game. I don't need anything else."

"It's not the same," Kate said.

"Yes it is." He told her then about his feelings in the caverns; how he was the producer, scriptwriter, set designer, and everyone else. "Most of us actors end up wanting to do everything else too," he said. "We like the power."

"Maybe then you won't be an actor after all—maybe you'll be a director or a producer," she said. She sounded rather pleased. "You really have the soul of an entrepreneur."

"I could star in my own movies," he said. "I'd write in a part for myself. Maybe just a cameo, but effective. Or a lead. It would depend on how I felt."

"Sometimes I dread life after college," Kate said. "I absolutely refuse to settle for a boring job. Don't let me, Jay Jay. If you see me copping out, you remind me how when we were at Grant we knew we could do anything."

"Okay," he said. "But you have to do the same for me."

"I have to study now," she said. "Not everybody's a genius like you." She smiled at him. "Thanks for the coffee break."

"Anytime." He went back to his room humming a little tune. She wanted him to be her friend after college; it wasn't just a part of his fantasy of all of them doing great things together. It was real. Neither of them would ever let the other one betray their potential.

Life after college seemed so far away he almost couldn't imagine it. Kate telling him he was halfway through college was like telling someone he was middle-aged. He was entering the second half of his Sophomore year; he wasn't "halfway through college." Exams were coming soon, and of course he would get his usual A's, and then they would start the game—his game. That was the only thing that seemed real at all.

CHAPTER TWO

It was the first night of the new game in the caverns. The four of them went there in Kate's car. Since people were always rushing in and out of the dorms, no one paid any attention to them and their duffel bags of equipment, which they put into the trunk. They had thrown the dice in Jay Jay's room to see what they could take with them, and whatever they needed Jay Jay seemed to have ready. They each had a real sword—which was actually a hunting knife in a sheath—and they had lanterns, coins, amulets, food, and costumes. Kate, as Glacia, had her chain-mail armor, to be put on when they got to the deserted area near the caverns. Robbie, as Pardieu, had his rough brown cloak. Daniel, who was to be Nimble the Charlatan, was already dressed in a black turtleneck sweater and slacks; he looked like a cat burglar. It was not in the spirit of a medieval game, but he refused to have anything to do with the black leotard Jay Jay had bought for him. Jay Jay told him he'd change his mind as soon as he found out how the rough, damp passages they might have to crawl through would mess up his clothes, and took the leotard along.

They hid the red Rabbit in a small clump of trees

near the entrance to the caverns. Kate and Robbie dressed, and then the four of them tramped together over the hard, bare ground to the chained opening. They paused. "This is the secret kingdom of the evil Voracians," Jay Jay said. "Somewhere within dwells Ak-Oga, the most fiendish monster of them all. He has lived in the depths of this lair for more ages than Humans or Sprites or Dwarfs can know. As great and awesome as is his wickedness, so is the greatness and awesomeness of his treasure. Shall you enter?"

"Yes," they said.

They took a last look at the black sky overhead, filled with bright stars, and then they ducked under the chain, entered the caverns, and lit their kerosene lamps.

Kate's heart turned over. This place was such a blend of all the fantasies she had invented, and reality, that for a moment she almost felt she was losing her grip on what was real and what was not. Except for the lights of their lanterns, the blackness was so vast and absolute that she was not sure she would have the courage to go another step. It was worse than the darkness of the laundry room when that man was trying to kill her, because in the laundry room she had some idea of where things were. But here all was new. The lamplight touched the shiny, black walls with the glitter of gold. Ancient stalactites and stalagmites like stone icicles . . . the faraway drip of unseen water . . . the musty smell of evil . . . but worst of all, that darkness. In that darkness you could lose your sense of direction and wander in circles until you lost consciousness. She was terrified. She drew a deep breath and said nothing.

Now Jay Jay moved lightly to a corner of the small

vaulted room and lit a large battery-powered lantern, the kind used at campsites, which he had put there before they came. It gave the room a reassuring glow, but equally important it made it possible for him to read his Challenge Module, see the throw of the dice, and for all of them to be able to chart the maze with their pencils and graph paper, and mark wherever they were at any given time.

They were looking around in awe. Kate glanced at Daniel and Robbie. She couldn't tell if they were afraid or not. Daniel looked fascinated and Robbie transfixed. She didn't want to be the only one who was scared to death, and if she was, she certainly didn't want them to know it. She tightened her hand on her sword as if it could give her some protection.

There was no need to sit in their customary circle to ask the Maze Controller where they were—*they were there*. "Which way shall we go?" Daniel asked the group.

"Right," Kate said. "To the water." She tried to will herself deeper into the game, to become Glacia, no longer Kate. Glacia wouldn't be afraid. A part of her was thinking that the sound of water perhaps led to a hidden pool, and that Jay Jay would want them to see this, and so he would have put inducements in that other chamber; perhaps some charm or treasure. The other part was trying to block out Jay Jay, and to make this game, which *was* real, as real as the imaginary one they had played in the dorm. She felt that separating the real from the fantasy was a way of keeping her sanity, but if she didn't let herself get into the game it wouldn't be any fun.

Glacia . . . I am Glacia . . . why do I always hold back? I'm always afraid, pretending I'm not, do-

ing things to test myself. I am Glacia, and I have
sworn to seek out the evil monster Ak-Oga, and seize
the treasure. Glacia turned right with the others and
walked with very gingerly steps toward the sound of
the dripping water. They went through a narrow tunnel and then came out upon a large room with a
black pool at one end. It was breathtaking. There
was something eternal about this place. She felt she
had dreamed that bottomless black pool a thousand
times. She felt the danger singing through her blood,
and the mystery, the fantasy, the sheer beauty of
something that was at the same time so menacing.
She shone her lantern around the corners of the
room, and screamed.

A human skeleton lay propped against the wall, lying in an attitude of exhausted despair. It wasn't the
remains of one of the students who had vanished so
long ago; those bones had been found. It was someone else. Oh, God . . . it could be them!

Glacia the Fighter never screamed in fear.

"Alas," Pardieu said sadly. "Who can that be? Some
wanderer, perhaps, on a mission such as ours."

"Be careful," Nimble the Charlatan warned. "It
could be a trick. Sometimes these skeletons have powers."

Just as he spoke the empty eye sockets of the skull
glittered with a mad light, all greenish and skittering.
The dice clicked softly on the stones. "What do you
choose to do?" the Maze Controller asked, his voice
coming disembodied from the shadows of the black
room.

"Is it evil?" Nimble asked.

"No."

"Is it helpful, then?" Pardieu asked.

"Perhaps."

Glacia remembered another adventure from a long time ago. "We will have to touch it," she said, trying to keep her voice steady and calm. "The glittering eyes may show us a clue if we turn the head."

"I am afraid to disturb the bones of those who rest in peace," Pardieu said in his kind, reverent tones. "It is a sacrilege."

"I am not afraid," Glacia said. She strode to the skeleton and touched the head with the tips of her fingers. Her stomach churned. Slowly, slowly, she moved the skull to either side, hoping there might be some magic to open a trap door or show up invisible writing. Nothing.

Then suddenly, as if it were on wires, the entire skeleton rose swiftly in the air and flew away into the dark above her. "Ahhh . . ." The sound came from her own throat and from her companions: awe, terror, fascination, a gasp sharpening into a shriek.

Behind where the skeleton had been lying there were tiny luminous letters written on the wall.

"Who among us can read these?" Pardieu asked.

Nimble the Charlatan walked closer and looked at the letters. Then he turned, his eyes shining with triumph. "I can," he said. "They are the ancient runes of my people. I learned them as a child, and I still remember some of them. It says: 'Eat of the bitter herb.' "

"It it a trick?" Glacia asked. "Where is the herb? Will it give us wisdom, or kill us?"

"First we must find it," Nimble said. "Let us search this room and then go on."

Glacia, proud and strong as she was, was glad Nimble had become the new member of their band.

He was so calm and sure. She felt a great confidence by his side. Irresistibly drawn to the black waters of the pool, she knelt and dropped a small stone into its depths. The stone sank away and disappeared instantly. "But be careful of the water," she said. "I think it has a hypnotic lure."

"If you feel it calling to you," Nimble said, "take my hand."

That little bastard Jay Jay is a genius, Daniel thought, admiring and jealous. He was annoyed too, because Jay Jay's fun-house tricks were so simple and yet they worked on everybody's mind, even his own. He knew how Jay Jay had lit up the bulbs in the skull's eye sockets, he had immediately figured out the wires and pulleys that made the skeleton fly away, and having the "ancient runes" in Hebrew was both ingenious and irritating—irritating because he had never thought of doing it. All Jay Jay had needed to get his hands on was a Passover Haggadah for kids; the one with the translation on the opposite page, and he obviously had. Bitter herbs! Here he was, hoping to make up games for a living after he graduated, and Jay Jay as a vacation sideline had created a minor Disneyland.

Everything was perfectly thought out, even the way Jay Jay kept in the shadows whenever he consulted his rules, in order not to disturb the reality of what was happening to them. All the time they had been moving about, awestruck, Jay Jay had been scattering rice to make a trail so they wouldn't lose their sense of direction and get lost. He also had a map and a compass. Daniel took his pad of graph paper and a pencil from his knapsack and began to chart the maze. He put a little mark where they were now, with some symbols denoting the pool and the skeleton and the Hebrew writing, so he would be able to look at the map later and know just which room was which. He wished he had been the one to think of this game.

"There is nothing to eat in this room," Kate said. She picked up a few grains of the rice Jay Jay had dropped and looked questioningly at him.

"No," Jay Jay said. "That's so you won't get lost. Leave it there."

"Let's move on," Daniel said.

They went back through the narrow tunnel into the first room, and then they turned left, Daniel leading the way. Kate followed, and then Robbie. Their lanterns made wavering shadows and glistening light on the walls, where something sparkled in the blackness. Mica, I bet, Daniel thought. Jay Jay brought up the rear, dragging along his battery-powered lamp, but he had turned it off to make the journey more frightening.

What a strange and wonderful place this is, Daniel thought. All this time it was right here and I never went in to investigate it.

"A wandering monster!" Jay Jay cried. "Over there!" He switched on his lamp and tossed the dice. "A Gorvil . . . followed by three others!"

Gorvils were stupid, soulless, and attacked anything even when they weren't hungry. They were covered with scales, had short webbed arms, huge fangs, and a large eye in the center of their lizardlike foreheads. They were over seven feet tall, and vicious. Daniel took out his knife . . . no, his sword. He wanted to get into the game and stop analyzing everything. This was an imaginary Gorvil, part of the game he knew; not Jay Jay's manufactured, theatrical prop. There was no point in being jealous; it was self-destructive. Now he could go into the fantasy on his own terms, not someone else's, and enter the adventure of his own imagination.

"Kill them!" Glacia cried, waving her sword.

"Kill them!" Pardieu cried, rushing forward, his sword drawn too.

"Kill them!" Nimble growled fiercely, and stabbed the nearest Gorvil again and again, while it bucked and lunged to kill him with its fangs and its black blood poured in torrents over the floor of the maze.

"They are all dead," the Maze Controller said.

"Be careful," Glacia warned. "There may be more."

"Indeed," Pardieu said. "They will surely come to seek revenge. The noise they made as they died was frightful."

Gentle Pardieu felt sickened with guilt and remorse as he surveyed the mutilated bodies of the dead monsters. A Holy Man should resort to violence only when he could not overcome evil with reason or spells. He still had his charms safely tucked in the little leather pouch he wore attached to his belt, and he had not used them. No, he had flung himself into the fray with reckless abandon, as if he were a Fighter, which he was not. Holy Men had been given their magic spells to compensate for their lack of warlike skills. He could have been killed, and then he would have been of no help to his dear companions. But what really upset him was that he had never known he had this capacity for violence within him.

He had been so proud of his goodness. Pride was a sin. One sin led to another, and thus, he supposed, to his violence. I didn't even think . . . I merely acted, like some instinctive beast . . .

He would have to think on this later, when there was time to rest and meditate. He had to pull the evil out of himself, by the roots; do penance if need be.

"You were brave, Pardieu," Glacia said.

"Perhaps foolhardy," Pardieu answered sadly. "I should have used my spell of paralyzation instead."

"You used that up in the other game," Nimble said.

Game? What game? He felt his pouch, looked inside. Where was The Eye of Timor? He felt icy cold. The Eye of Timor, to raise the dead, had been his; he had felt it, seen it. But that had been in a dream . . . Never mind that the spell of paralyzation was lost, but not this one . . . no! He had to have it. He *needed* it.

The others had stopped to rest, eat, and drink. They had sandwiches of cheese and meat on thick bread, and cold beer. The food stuck in Pardieu's throat. Why did his magic spells appear and disappear? Was this some kind of punishment for his pride and his secret violence? Why had Nimble said he had already used the spell? He had been traveling for such a long time and he was so tired. Yes, he remembered now; he had used the spell of paralyzation to stop the moving stairs, long ago. It had been in a different maze.

The others had eaten now and were refreshed. They rose to go on, tossing their empty beer cans into the corner. He got up too, and followed them. I must

"You are not married," The Great Hall said. "It is a false and sinful marriage."

"No . . ." Pardieu said. He felt as if something of indescribable sweetness had just been ripped from his heart. His eyes filled with tears.

"In order to regain The graven Eye of Timor you must prove yourself worthy," The Great Hall said. "Nothing is free. A Holy Man must be above all the lusts of the flesh."

He knew it was true. He had to sacrifice many things to be holy. He felt sadness rise up in him, and then miraculously, it floated away, leaving only peace. It was good to make sacrifices. Worldly pleasures only weighed you down on your difficult travels through life.

"I am waiting for you," The Great Hall said. "When you are truly worthy, you can come to me."

Pardieu held out his hands. "Please let me," he said. "Would you come back with me? I need you."

"And I need you," The Great Hall said. The blue light faded and was gone.

Robbie woke up feeling cold. He had kicked off the covers and was lying alone. Kate, on her side with her back to him, was curled up fast asleep on the other edge of the bed. He lay there for a few minutes, listening to her even breathing, trying to remember his dream. It was not a sad dream; it was only strange. He felt the possibility of unlimited power, and for the first time he knew that someday he *would* find Hall, that it was possible. It was different from the floating feeling he'd had after other dreams. It was a feeling of reality.

He moved over to Kate and put his arms around her, pressing his body against hers for comfort, and

pulled the covers around his shoulders. He felt cozy
and sleepy now, and safe and strong. He loved her
and would take care of her as long as she wanted him
to—but he knew in his heart she really didn't need
him. He supposed he'd always known that, but for
the first time he could accept the knowledge quite
calmly. He didn't have to try to win anything. He
could just love her, and accept her as she was. They
had so much fun together. A relationship didn't have
to be a struggle; it could be this companionship. He
felt he had reached a new level of understanding, and
drifted into a deep, dreamless sleep.

CHAPTER FOUR

Everybody at Grant was sick and tired of winter. Now that they had passed their exams and there was nothing to frighten them, they tried to find new ways of occupying the long, dark evenings. There was skiing on weekends, and the usual parties in the dorms, and the usual excursions to town to hang around at Fat City or go to a movie, but they were all bored with the sameness of life and wanted more. Someone thought of having a 1950s prom. At last there was something to plan and to do.

Prom fever swept the campus, almost as though it really was the Fifties. Committees were formed. Research was done. It would be a costume party, of course, and the students canvassed local thrift shops, called their parents to see if by chance they had saved any old artifacts, and even went as far as Philadelphia to see what they could rent to wear. The students who formed the band that always played at parties learned old Fifties songs. It would be a formal dance, not a sock hop. They wanted to be sophisticated, glamorous, a little campy; and everyone had to have a date. The prom would be held in the gym.

Jay Jay was terrified that he wouldn't be able to get anyone to go with him. They all came to his parties, but who would want to be with him alone? He zeroed in on the youngest, smallest, most frightened Freshman he could find: a sixteen-year-old scholarship student named Glenna, from a small town in the South; a physics major who was always studying and had had hardly any dates at all since coming to Grant. He hadn't even bothered to invite her to his Brigitte Bardot birthday party.

To his surprise she seemed honored that he had noticed her. To his delight he discovered that she was malleable, and had a hidden sense of fun and style. He bought her harlequin glasses with rhinestones on them, told her how to do her hair, and picked out her dress: candy-pink taffeta with a cinched-in waist, a huge skirt, and a strapless top. He bought white silk pumps and had them dyed the same dreadful color as the dress. He found long white gloves, and because they didn't fit he cut off the tips of the fingers. She was his Cinderella and he was her prince. Together they practiced putting grease on his curly hair to make it stay in a pompadour, and Glenna suggested setting it in rollers and spraying it, which hurt and didn't look right after all their trouble. Then she suggested a crew cut. His Cinderella was turning into the wicked stepsister. Jay Jay decided to stay with the grease.

Before Daniel had a chance to accept any of the invitations he'd gotten, Jay Jay found him the perfect date. He'd noticed her coming out of one of the class buildings on a Monday at noon, and on Wednesday he made Daniel come with him and pointed her out. She was tall and voluptuous, with a wide pretty face that was both tough and vapid, a turned-up nose, large blue eyes, and bleached white-blond hair cut very short so it stood up. She had greased the sides back and was wearing safety pins in her ears instead of earrings, and a ripped black leather jacket with buttons on it for every punk rock group Jay Jay had ever heard of.

"She's right out of *The Rocky Horror Show*," Daniel said, dismayed.

"No, no. Take out those safety pins, put her in a slinky white dress, and she's Kim Novak. Would I lie to you?"

She smiled at Daniel. "She scares me," he hissed. He smiled back.

"Well, you don't scare her," Jay Jay whispered, pleased.

"Did anybody ever tell you you look like Kim Novak?" Daniel asked her.

"Yeah?" she said. "Did anybody ever tell you you look just like John Travolta?"

In five minutes she was Daniel's date for the prom. Her name was Tina, she was a Sophomore, and when Jay Jay had fixed her up she looked exactly like Kim Novak. He was right as usual.

Robbie didn't want to go to the prom at all. Kate had to insist. He had all kinds of weak excuses: it was silly, it was too much trouble, they were too involved with the game to waste time on this.

"I don't know what's the matter with him," she told Jay Jay.

"Just do everything for him—he's lazy," Jay Jay said.

"He was never lazy before."

"Robbie's kind of square," Jay Jay said. "He probably really does think he'll look silly. He'll catch the spirit when we all do it."

"He doesn't mind wearing a costume when we play the game," Kate said. "I guess that's because nobody sees him. It's really funny; lately he doesn't seem to enjoy things the way he used to. He's not depressed—it's more that he's kind of . . . serene all the time. Have you noticed?"

"No," Jay Jay said. "But you see him more than I do."

"Maybe it's my imagination," Kate said.

The night of the prom the six of them went together. Kate was wearing a dark red dress with a strapless top, a waist cincher, and a full skirt propped out with a crinoline. She had her hair up in a French roll, was wearing blood-red lipstick; and she looked perfectly beautiful. Jay Jay thought that Kate could wear anything, no matter how odd, and she would always look better than anyone else. He could see from the appreciative glances she was getting that other people thought so too.

"Maybe you'd better take those glasses off, Glenna," he told his date. "They're a little much."

"It's okay with me," Glenna said, putting them into her pink purse. "I can't see out of the dang things anyhow."

The gym was mobbed with people, all slow-dancing and looking around to check out the clothes. Daniel was wearing a navy blue pin-striped suit, a wide flowered tie, and a hat, and he looked like a sexy gangster. He had decided not to look like a greaser; that wouldn't be worthy of Kim Novak.

"I can't breathe in this dress," Tina complained.

"It's worth it," Daniel said. "You look fabulous."

"Really? Maybe I should change my image."

Kate had brought her camera. "I want pictures!" she cried excitedly. "Everybody has to pose."

She took pictures of them all: Jay Jay in his Fifties tuxedo, pinning a gardenia corsage on Glenna's pink dress, Daniel and Tina glued together dancing cheek to cheek, and then Daniel took a picture of Kate and Robbie smiling and holding hands.

"A perfect prom picture!" Kate said happily. "Wait—I have another one we have to do. I saw it in my mother's yearbook. One of you guys sit on a chair and all the women will sit at his feet looking up adoringly. Come on."

She herded them into the pose, chuckling, making Robbie be the object of their attention. He had finally gotten into the party spirit and seemed to be having a good time. He held his hands out, as if blessing them.

"No, no," Kate said. "You pretend to be telling a story or a joke or something. We're all trying to be popular."

"They didn't do that at a prom," Daniel said.

"No, but they did it in the dorm, so it counts for Fifties."

"Boy, that's wild," Tina said. "They must have been kidding."

A large punch bowl had been set on a table in the corner, filled with something red and sweet. Various people kept putting different kinds of alcoholic beverages into it until it became very potent. The gym was decorated with crepe paper and balloons, and that along with the punch gave the dance the air of a rather decadent children's party. Jay Jay noticed Robbie put down his plastic cup of punch, untasted.

"Robbie's going to drive home," Jay Jay announced. "Since he's the only one not getting drunk."

"It's okay with me," Robbie said.

"Good," Jay Jay said. He took Glenna by the hand and led her outside into the darkness behind the building, where he introduced her to the first pot she'd ever had in her life.

Now that Robbie was here and having fun, he couldn't figure out why he hadn't wanted to come. It had been one of those weird things where he'd had the feeling something bad might happen. He was glad he was going to drive, and he made sure Kate didn't drink too much because he didn't know what was in that punch and he didn't want her to get sick. He'd heard about a party once where someone had put LSD into the punch and everybody had gone crazy. He was sure this was just liquor, but even that wasn't too good for you if you mixed it. Kate looked so beautiful in that red dress; it went with her coloring. Her enthusiasm was catching. You couldn't ever not have a good time with Kate.

Daniel's date looked like a cow, and Jay Jay's looked like a mouse. But they both seemed to be nice people. It was too bad they were just props. Neither of those girls meant anything to Daniel or Jay Jay. Only he, Robbie, was lucky enough to be with the person he loved. He could look at Kate the whole time he was dancing with her because her crinoline was so big they couldn't get very close. He felt he could look at her forever, especially when she was smiling the way she was now, making him feel he was part of what was making her so happy.

When the dance was over they went back to the dorm. Tina, to no one's surprise, had decided to spend the night in Daniel's room. Glenna thanked Jay Jay politely and went off to her own, alone. Jay Jay didn't seem to mind at all. He wasn't interested in a sixteen-year-old Freshman.

"I'll just change and then I'll be in," Kate whispered to Robbie.

He lay on their bed, waiting for her, and his thoughts drifted away to total blankness. He felt peaceful and calm. Not tired, just really good. She slipped into his room like a wraith, wearing her plaid flannel bathrobe that made her look about twelve years old. She had washed off the Fifties makeup and let her hair down. He thought she looked even more beautiful this way. She took off her robe and snuggled next to him, naked and soft.

"Why are you wearing your underpants?" she asked.

He'd forgotten to take them off. He felt her hands at the elastic, helping him. Then they were lying together, skin on skin, her fragrant hair falling across his face. She brushed it back with a graceful movement of her arm and kissed him gently. He kissed her back, sweetly, as one would one's best friend. He felt no desire at all. He stroked her shoulder absently, remembering the way he used to feel—when was it?—a week ago, two weeks? Sometimes he lost time.

He felt her hand on him. He took it away, tenderly so he wouldn't hurt her feelings. He hoped she would understand. It wasn't her fault. It wasn't his fault either; it was as if sex and desire had simply drained out of his life without his even noticing, almost imperceptibly, and now they were gone.

Her eyes were large and dark and sympathetic. "Robbie . . . ?"

"It's all right," he said kindly.

"Of course it is," she said. "This happens sometimes."

It was best to tell her the truth. She would understand. "I can't," he said simply.

"You're just tired. Don't worry about it."

"I can't do it with you anymore," he said.

"What did I do?" she asked. She sounded like a frightened little child now, not the understanding woman she had been pretending to be. He put his arms around her to comfort her. He knew she would not misinterpret the gesture.

"You didn't do anything wrong."

"Are you mad at me?"

"No. You? Never."

"Well, what do you mean you can't do it anymore? You can't, or you don't want to, or what?"

He hadn't even thought about it. "I don't know. Both, I guess. I can't give you an answer."

She drew away from him and sat up, her arms hugging her knees. It reminded him of the first time she had taken him into her room, the night of Jay Jay's party, when she sat on her desk and asked him to tell her about himself. That seemed so long ago, a lifetime.

"I think we should discuss this," she said. "Rationally."

"Please don't be upset," Robbie said. "I do love you."

"I don't understand," she said. "Just because you don't feel like doing it one time doesn't mean you never want to do it again. Does it? I mean, don't be silly. Look, if you don't love me . . . if you met

somebody else, or if you don't want to go with me anymore, don't lie and say you love me."

"I do love you," Robbie said calmly. "Why can't
you understand?"

"I'm trying to."

"Why don't we just go to sleep?" he said.

"I think that's a very good idea."

They lay side by side, on their backs, awake, still as
two corpses. He was hoping he hadn't hurt her, and
that she would finally come to realize that even
though he could never have anything to do with her
again sexually it didn't mean he didn't still love her.
There were different kinds of love. His was pure.

After a while she reached over and took his hand.
"It's all right," she said.

He knew then that she really didn't understand at
all.

CHAPTER FIVE

Kate looked at her body carefully in the mirror in her room. I'm not ugly, she thought. I'm certainly not ugly. It must be my personality. Maybe I'm too strong. She had read that strong women scared men off; there was something called The New Impotence. If there was, Robbie had certainly gotten it. He treated her like a beloved little sister.

He hadn't tried to touch her for a month now, and she knew he never would again. At first she had been devastated. How ironic that she had been so sure of him that her only worry was that the relationship would become dull. Yet he really seemed to want to be her friend, and he was even sweeter to her than ever. Gone was the insistence on being with her all the time, and in its place was an almost instinctive consideration of her need to have time to herself. At least he hadn't disappeared like all the other men in her life. After the night of the Fifties Prom he never asked her to sleep in his room again, nor did he try to sleep in hers, and Kate was too proud to ask him. He had made it clear that the love he talked about was platonic—and that was that.

The four of them played the game together more and more often. As they moved deeper into the caverns and began amassing loot and becoming surer of themselves, the game exerted a stronger pull than ever. Playing the game had become their favorite thing to do. Because of their need for secrecy they played on weekend nights instead of afternoons, and Daniel arranged his sex life around their new schedule. Kate had no sex life now, and she wasn't interested in looking for anyone new. Jay Jay, as usual, had none, and as for Robbie, he hadn't shown the slightest sign of interest in anyone new either. Kate wondered if there was something wrong with him. In some almost imperceptible way he had begun to change. Before, he had been sweet; now he was almost saintly. A guy in the dorm Robbie hardly even knew admired his shirt, and Robbie insisted on giving it to him. Oh, God, Kate thought in horror; maybe he's going to become a Hare Krishna or something! When she and Robbie and Jay Jay went to a movie, or to buy food for the game, Robbie insisted on paying for it all. He said money didn't mean anything. The only thing he wouldn't pay for was their beer, but she supposed that had something to do with his alcoholic mother and his bad memories. He had stopped drinking altogether, not that he ever drank much to start with. He had also stopped eating meat, which as far as she was concerned was a good idea. Apparently having no sex, no meat, and no alcohol was healthful—Robbie seemed to be suffused with a pale glow. Kate knew she should be pleased, but somehow it made her uneasy. It came from his spirit, and she didn't understand it.

But much more disturbing was his physical rejection of her. It was just like being ditched, except Robbie stayed around. She wondered if perhaps she was looking for strange things about him to explain his impotence with her, so she wouldn't have to blame herself. No matter how much she intellectualized it, she *did* blame herself. She had made him go to the prom that night against his will; she had always taken the initiative. But if he hadn't liked it, why hadn't he said something? They were supposed to be best friends. She had to talk to somebody about it, and why not go to the authority? She knocked on Daniel's door.

"Come on in," Daniel said. He was doing a class assignment, but as always he looked pleased to see her. His room was immaculate, and she thought a little guiltily that he would probably think she was a slob if he saw hers.

"Your room is fantastically neat," Kate said. "I bet you've got one of your love slaves cleaning it."

"I clean it," Daniel said pleasantly. "I'll clean yours for five dollars an hour."

"I might take you up on it. Can we talk?"

"Sure. Sit down."

"Would you close the door?"

He went to the door and closed it. Then he sat next to her and looked at her with genuine concern. "What's the matter?"

"I just don't understand men."

He burst out laughing. "*You?*"

"Don't tease me," Kate said. "I don't know so much."

"You're the most perceptive, intelligent woman I know."

She was surprised and pleased. She knew he liked her, but it was the first time he'd ever complimented her. "Do you think I'm a ball breaker?" she asked.

"Who said that?"

"I said it. Am I?"

"Of course not."

"You may have noticed my big romance with Robbie is all over," she said.

He nodded. "Did he say you were a ball breaker?"

"No," Kate said. She sighed. "I think I scared him off."

"Do you want him back?" Daniel asked.

She looked down at her hands; the little hands that could deliver a stunning karate blow. "No," she said. "It was a shock at first, but in a way we're better friends now than we ever were. I still love him, but in a different way. It's not romantic . . . it's more real, I guess."

"Robbie is a genuinely nice person," Daniel said. "Look what happened with you and that shit Steve. He wouldn't even stay around to say hello once in a while. You know love affairs break up every five minutes around here. You're not going through anything that was your fault."

"How can you be so sure?"

"Because I know you would never do anything that could drive any man away. People just leave."

He was being so nice she was touched. She looked at his sexy mouth and for one moment she thought that if she were ever to get involved again she would risk it with Daniel, and then she thought: No.

"You leave people all the time," she said. "Why?"

"They leave me too," he said.

"I bet they don't."

"Who's the authority—you or me?"

"I guess you are," Kate said, and for the first time

felt very cheered up. He was human after all. "Well, when these heartless women leave you, why do they?"

"They get bored. They weren't looking for anything serious in the first place. I don't expect more from strangers than they're willing to give."

"Strangers?" Kate said.

"In a way," he said.

His eyes were so blue. Poor Daniel, she thought. It can't be much fun going to bed with strangers all the time. None of the girls he went to bed with ever seemed jealous of the others, or at least they never showed it, and it occurred to her how insecure that must make him feel. "I bet lots of girls were in love with you," she said.

"Only about a hundred," he said, and grinned to show he was kidding.

"I bet they were and you didn't know it."

"Hey," he said. "Everybody around here thinks I'm Superstud. You know what that does to any woman who's sensitive and caring and smart? She says: Oh, this guy is bad news. He's going to use me for another notch on his belt. So I'll use him for the same thing. Kate, if I really cared about someone, I'd have a hell of a time trying to convince her. My reputation, as they say, has preceded me."

"I never thought about that," Kate said.

"Think about it."

"When I tease you . . . do you mind?"

"No, of course not."

"I bet you had fun getting your reputation, though."

"I can't say I hated it."

"I guess it's like a woman being too pretty," Kate said. "She starts to think men are just after her for her looks. I never thought about that before."

"I have a theory about success," Daniel said. "Success does not turn a person into a big shit. If he's a shit in the first place, becoming a success only enables him to be what he always was, openly and with impunity."

"And if he's nice to start with he stays nice, right?"

"That's my theory. Come on, let's go out and I'll buy you a beer."

"Okay," Kate said. "Let me just get my coat."

They drove to Fat City in her car because Daniel only had a bicycle. Kate realized it was the first time she and Daniel had ever been out together alone. For some reason she was having a little difficulty breathing. This is ridiculous, she thought; he's my old pal. I know him the way no one else does—he's Nimble the Charlatan. He's part of my secret world and I'm part of his.

Fat City was crowded. Noisy groups were eating and drinking at nearly all the tables. They had to look for an empty table, and while they were working their way there people they knew said hello, but more said hello to him than to her, and most of the ones who spoke to him were beautiful girls.

"I'd be jealous," Kate said.

"Huh?"

"If I were going with you and all those women said hello to you, I'd be jealous."

"What would you do?" he asked, sounding pleased and amused. "Would you give me a karate chop?"

She laughed. "Karate isn't for jealous lovers, it's serious business."

They finally sat at a small table at the back of the room and ordered draft beer. Daniel got up and put some money in the jukebox. Kate looked around the room, quite sure neither Robbie nor Jay Jay would be there, but hoping anyway that they were not. If they were, they would come over to the table and sit down. This was the first time she'd had a chance to find out what Daniel was really like, and she intended to find out as much as she could. They'd become friends through the game, and had spent all that time together, but really each knew very little about the other's private thoughts, until tonight. He came back to the table.

"Would you think it was terribly corny if I asked you to tell me your life story?" Kate said.

"It's not as corny as my life story," Daniel said. "But since it's also luckily very short and dull, I'd be glad to."

She found his life immensely reassuring. It was so normal, so nice. Robbie's life had been sad, and Jay Jay's bizarre, and even her own had been disillusioning, but Daniel had a real life, the kind people wished they had. She could see him in her mind: the loved child growing up surrounded by the encouragement of his family, and she wondered, as she often had before, why he had chosen to bury himself at a university like Grant. Nothing is ever like it seems, Kate thought. This was turning out to be one of her favorite evenings.

"Why did you pick this school?" she asked.

"It's what I wanted."

"But you could have gone to M.I.T.," Kate said.

"That's what my parents wanted."

"You didn't do it to spite them—I can't imagine that."

"No, I came here because I really don't think I'm

ambitious or competitive. I want to make up games for computers and have a quiet life with a lot of fun in it. I guess if I were growing up in the Sixties I'd be a dropout. This is sort of my compromise. And besides, Grant isn't a bad school. Why did you come here?"

"It's where I got in," Kate said. "Grant isn't Ivy League, but as you say, it isn't a bad school either. It has a good creative writing department. I can go out for honors and write a novel as my thesis. You can't do that at every college."

"I wish I could make up a computer game for my thesis," Daniel said.

"Why don't you ask them? They might like the idea."

"I think I will," he said, very pleased. "Thank you."

"Any old time." They had another beer. "Let me ask you something," Kate said. "Have you noticed Robbie acting kind of strange lately?"

"What kind of strange?"

"Well, he gave Tony Nelson his shirt just because Tony said it was a great-looking shirt."

Daniel shrugged. "Tony Nelson is on partial scholarship and has a part-time job to help get through college. I think that was a nice thing for Robbie to do."

"And lately he's been paying for everything."

"He probably figures we've been taking advantage of Jay Jay. And I think we have."

Kate sighed. It was so difficult to explain. And now that Daniel put it in this light it seemed so normal. How could she tell him it wasn't one thing or the other but little bits and pieces that added up to a new and different Robbie? "Maybe it's my writer's imagination," she said. "It's like . . . don't laugh . . . it's like Robbie is taking being a Holy Man out of the game and putting it into his life."

He did laugh.

"You're laughing," she said.

"Kate, you're so creative. You're wonderful. I really don't think Robbie is turning into Pardieu, nor are you turning into Glacia, nor am I turning into Nimble. I haven't stolen a thing lately, or even written a bad check. If anything, the game is an outlet for our fantasies. We work out all our problems in the caverns and then we leave them there."

"What problems do you work out?"

"I think I just play the game," Daniel said. "Liking the game more than studying is my problem."

"Mine too," she said. "I guess you're right about Robbie. I'll try not to worry anymore."

When they drove back to the dorm Kate felt happier than she had in a long time. She had always thought of Daniel as her friend, but now he was *really* her friend. For the first time since Robbie had become impotent she didn't feel like there was something wrong with her. She felt just fine.

In the dorm, coming in, she and Daniel passed Robbie in the hall. He smiled at them beatifically, with absolutely no curiosity in his eyes, and they smiled back and said hi. Jay Jay would have asked them where they'd been, afraid he was missing something. Robbie apparently didn't care.

CHAPTER SIX

Jay Jay was happy. Now that Kate and Robbie had broken up he was no longer jealous of Robbie, and had decided good old Robbie was one of the nicest people he'd ever known. Robbie even lent him his car so he could take an extra large prop to the caverns, and didn't try to sneak around to find out what it was. It was a coffin Jay Jay had borrowed from the drama department. He had discovered a veritable treasure trove of props there, and no one seemed to mind that he took things as long as they weren't needed and he brought them back. He'd had to tell two of the drama students about the game in the caverns, but they didn't seem to care and they promised not to tell anyone else. They had all the fantasy they wanted from their plays, and he knew they would never encroach on his game.

Jay Jay had also decided what the treasure would be: an excellent copy of the dull-black steel Porsche watch, which he'd seen during his Christmas shopping in New York. He'd collected money from the others, and when he went home for Spring Vacation he'd pick it up. It was a man's-size watch, but he thought it would look good on Kate if she won it. He was so fond of the watch he thought he might just buy one for himself while he was at it, since he couldn't win it.

He wondered how far into the caverns they would be by the end of the school year when the treasure was finally found. It occurred to him that they were doing an extraordinary thing mapping the caverns this way. It was even a sort of public service. Maybe after they were through, other students could use the caverns for a geological study of some kind. It never occurred to him that this was an inflated and unreal idea. After what he had conceived and done, nothing else could ever be too unreal.

Lately he was hardly ever in the dorm. Besides having to show up at classes, he was either playing the game, getting things he needed for it, or in the caverns setting his scenes. He was always precise and careful about leaving a trail so he wouldn't get lost. They were now far beyond the place where rice would help them get back; by now a trail of rice could take you in circles and you'd never get out. This was just as well, since he had been buying so much rice that the checkout clerks at the supermarket thought he was some kind of health freak. Now Jay Jay spray-painted arrows, codes, and direction symbols on the walls of rooms they had used, and kept his maps with him at all times. He was so busy, as his chores as M.C. became more complicated, that he didn't even have time to go to the movies anymore. That was the one thing he regretted. But one had to have priorities, and since he had to make the choice, Jay Jay chose the game. Watching movies, much as he loved them, was passive.

His fear of the caverns had turned instead into a kind of respect. It was as if he and the maze understood each other. He wondered if that was the way someone felt who trained a huge, dangerous animal. You could never become the master of that animal, but you both agreed to work together. Some nights, after he had finished what he had to do in the caverns, Jay Jay would stay there for a while, surveying this domain that would never be his but would never be anyone else's either. He knew if he ever got lost there was a strong probability no one would be able to find him. He was the only one who understood his direction codes. But somehow that didn't scare him. There was a lure to this dark and deadly place; it drew him, called to him. He knew what that attraction was. It was not death, it was not danger, it was not the excitement of fear and the relief of fear overcome. It was none of these.

It was power.

CHAPTER SEVEN

Robbie thought about the game all the time now. Even when he was doing other things, it was with him. Whenever the Grant swimming team competed against another college and won, the others were jubilant but he only pretended to care. How trivial it seemed, compared to his other world! When the Grant team lost and the others were depressed he pretended to be unhappy too, but losing was just as unimportant as winning. There were no risks, no real excitement, no genuine fellowship. The coach yelled at those swimmers who had not done their best, goaded them to try harder. Robbie could not imagine a Maze Controller behaving in such an irrational way. He thought perhaps next year he would switch to another sport; one that would let him be alone and in peace.

Being Pardieu gave him that peace. He moved through the game in the caverns as if it were a magical dream, and at night his dreams took on the quality of real life. It was hard sometimes to tell what was real and what was not, but this didn't bother him—he rather liked it. At times he felt he had real powers; that his mind could extend far beyond his physical self and create miracles. His new monastic regime of giving up meat, alcohol, and sex made him feel cleansed. He had also given up all sweet and artificial desserts, eating only an occasional piece of fruit. He had lost weight, but that was natural. He felt closer to the purity of his spirit.

The Great Hall came to him almost every night in his dreams now, with such a look of saintly beauty on his face that it made Robbie want to weep with gratitude. In his dreams he was always Pardieu, and he was better, stronger, more worthy than ever before. At last he was ready to receive messages about his mission.

He dreamed about the City of The Two Towers. They rose up out of mist in the pink and blue sky of dawn, gleaming white and tall. Pardieu was walking along in this mist as though he were in heaven, and The Great Hall was walking beside him.

"That is where you must go," The Great Hall said.

"Where is it."

"Underground."

What did that mean? A secret city under the earth? "Where?" he asked.

"When you are ready it will be so easy."

"How will I know?"

"You will."

"When?"

"Soon."

The graven Eye of Timor was always with him now, and often Pardieu patted the pouch where he kept it, or sometimes took it out to look at it for reassurance. He kept his possession of it a secret. Someone might try to steal it—perhaps Nimble the Charlatan, for Charlatans were never to be trusted.

Now when he awoke from his travels through the

streets of his dreams Robbie began to make a map of them so he would remember. They looked just like a maze, but they were a different maze from the one in the caverns, which he had already mapped. He knew he had secret knowlege of the future in this new maze, and almost every day he was able to add something to it. He reread Tolkien and Castaneda, and sought out books on the occult, but none of them seemed to apply. The Great Hall was displeased.

"Books will not give you the answers," The Great Hall said. "Only I can. Why are you so impatient?"

"Because I love you," Pardieu answered respectfully.

"Yes, I have seen that. You have purified your body, now you must purify your mind. You must seek the way to clarity."

"How must I do that?"

"Trust me. Remember what you see."

"I am making a map."

"If it pleases you."

"But does it please *you*?" Pardieu asked.

The Great Hall gave him a kindly smile. "When you are truly ready you will not need maps. You will know everything."

Everything! By day Robbie drew his map, intricately, carefully. Sometimes he looked at it and wondered how he could ever have been wise enough to draw such a marvelous maze. He never had before. He drew it on the palest blue paper, the color of the sky in his dreams, and on the edges of the paper he drew the tall white towers and the clouds below them. In the most beautiful illuminated letters that Pardieu could make he wrote THE GREAT HALL. Then he wrote THE TWO TOWERS. He surveyed his handi-work and thought that something was still missing.

Then one day he realized what it should be. It was the mark of his love and respect for The Great Hall and for Pardieu's sacred mission. Precisely, neatly, with red ink, Robbie drew a tiny heart hidden in the center of his maze.

No one came into his monastic room anymore, so it was not necessary to hide any of this. Besides, even if someone saw all these things he had drawn, that person would have no idea what they were.

CHAPTER EIGHT

For the first time in his life Daniel felt a new and surprising emotion: he was genuinely jealous of Jay Jay's ingenuity. Sometimes he thought it was really himself he was annoyed at, not Jay Jay, because he hadn't thought of playing the game in the caverns even though he'd run past them and wondered about them, and because he'd never had the inspiration of using real props. A long time ago, when Daniel had bought his first beginner's Mazes and Monsters rule book, the introduction had said this was a game where nobody ever lost. But that wasn't true. If you got killed you lost. You could create a new character and start again, and you could even use the same character you had become attached to, but that character was a neophyte, a newborn. Having to start all over from nothing when success was so tantalizingly close was certainly losing.

He had lost control of his own game, he had lost his position of power as M.C., and now he had watched his self-respect dwindling as Jay Jay constantly amazed them all with his brilliant imagination. If only Jay Jay hadn't been such a genius in what was supposed to be Daniel's chosen field for life after college . . .

Daniel realized there was really only one way he could get his pride back. He had to outwit Jay Jay and win the treasure. He would never go into Jay Jay's room and steal a look at his maps; the idea was repellent. But he wanted to be ahead, to know what was planned, and thus keep out of trouble and make the right decision. You never knew what the throw of the dice would determine, but if you knew where the dangers were in the caverns and what to stay away from, you had a much better chance of winning. Daniel decided what he had to do. He didn't like it—it was dangerous and pretty dishonest—but something beyond his control kept nagging at him to do it until he felt he would never be able to concentrate on anything again, not even schoolwork, unless he did it.

He had to sneak into the caverns alone and find out what Jay Jay had planned.

First, though, he had to get rid of Jay Jay. The fanatic was in the caverns every night. Daniel couldn't go in the daytime because he needed his bicycle to carry his equipment, and someone might see it. What could entice Jay Jay away from a night in the maze without arousing his suspicions?

Daniel went in search of Glenna, the girl Jay Jay had taken to the Fifties Prom and hadn't seen since. Maybe this wasn't a very nice thing to do, but on the other hand, the worst thing that could happen would be that she and Jay Jay would have a date, and the best thing would be that they might even have a little romance. He found her in her room studying.

"May I come in?" Daniel asked pleasantly.

"Sure," she said.

He sat down on the edge of her bed, since she was in the desk chair. "How've you been?" he asked.

"Fine. How's Jay Jay?"

"It's funny you should ask. He was just mentioning you the other day."

"He was?" She looked pleased. "What did he say?"

"Oh, something about you being a very interesting person and he really wanted to see you again but . . . Jay Jay's very shy, you know."

"Oh, he is not."

"When he's planning a party he's not shy," Daniel said. "But he's much too timid to invite you to the movies, for instance."

"Did he say that?"

"I know Jay Jay very well. He's one of my closest friends."

"I'd ask *him* to the movies," Glenna said. "I'm not scared of him. I think he's cute."

Sitting duck.

Jay Jay and Glenna went off to Pequod to the movies the following Tuesday night. She rode behind him on his motorbike, screaming with fear and pleasure. "She's too young for me," Jay Jay had said. "But I don't want to hurt her feelings." He had seemed quite flattered at the thought that any girl, even Glenna, had had a secret crush on him all this time.

Two sitting ducks.

As soon as they were safely gone Daniel got his things together: his flashlight, the map of the maze, fresh graph paper and pencils, an enormous roll of twine, his knife to cut it with, chalk to mark the walls as he entered rooms, a sponge and a plastic bottle of water to wash the chalk marks off when he left the rooms on his way back to safety, and the all-important compass. He would take the large lantern Jay

Jay had left in the caverns. He was a little nervous, not about being caught, but about getting lost. He reminded himself that Jay Jay had gone alone into those caverns almost every night for nearly three months now, and nothing had happened to him. Jay Jay hadn't been afraid, and he was only sixteen.

Daniel put his paper bag of equipment into his bicycle basket and rode away into the dark evening, as if he were just going into town. But where the road branched to the east, toward the caverns, he turned off to where they beckoned him.

CHAPTER NINE

Kate was driving back to the dorm from town, where she'd been to the drugstore to pick up some things. She'd bought three different kinds of shampoo when she needed only one; anything for the hair was her weakness. And she'd bought a new kind of conditioner, and something she'd never tried before called a Finishing Rinse. She hoped it wasn't a rip-off. Coming toward her, on his way to town, she saw someone on a bicycle who she could swear was Daniel. She thought of honking at him, but it was too dark to be sure, and if it wasn't Daniel she didn't want to scare him. She looked into her rearview mirror after she passed him and then she noticed that he turned at the turnoff that led to the caverns and disappeared.

That was odd. Why would Daniel—if it was Daniel—be going to the caverns? That road led to a lot of other places too, but they were all too far away to get to on a bike. Even if he were a commuter coming back from the library, he wouldn't live there. He'd live in Pequod, or in the suburbs, not east of here. Besides, she was sure now that it had been Daniel. She turned her car around and went back, and drove to the caverns to find out.

She parked in the clump of trees where they always

parked when they played the game. She left her headlights on so she could see, and walked around. The
night was clear and still, with a light wind rising and
the moon and stars very bright. The ground was still
muddy and oozy from the week of rain that had followed the spring thaw. Whoever had come here must
have wanted very badly to be here.

Then she saw Daniel's bike, hidden in the bushes.
She knew it was his because he was the only one at
school who had a bicycle with a sticker on it that
said: NEVER HIT ANYONE SMALLER THAN YOU. Her heart
lurched with fear. He had hidden his bike and gone
into the caverns alone and she didn't know why, but
she knew he was in terrible danger.

Kate went back to her car and got her flashlight
out of the glove compartment. She turned off the
headlights so she wouldn't run down her battery—or
be caught—and walked to the caverns guided by the
wavering beam of light in her hand and the moonlight.

She paused at the chain and felt as if she were
choking. She couldn't go in there alone, not in the
dark, not for anyone . . . she was too afraid. She
took another step and ducked under the chain, moving the flashlight up and down and around the now
familiar black stone walls.

"Daniel!" she screamed. "Daniel!"

Silence. Maybe he wasn't in there. She went back
outside and ran around in the mud calling his name,
but he never answered and she knew he was in the
caverns and that she had to go in. Maybe he was
hurt, or lost. He'd probably gone in to play some sort
of practical joke on the rest of them, put in some

scary prop for the next session, and she was sure he had his map. She didn't have hers; why would she?

"Daniel!"

She ran into the caverns quickly, like someone terrified of water jumping in for the first time.

"Daniel!" Her voice echoed off the vaulted walls as if it were mocking her. Daniel, Daniel . . . *Yell, Yell.*

The darkness of the laundry room flashed through her mind, and she could almost hear the insane whispery breathing of that man. But there was no rapist-murderer here now, only the pitch dark that frightened her so much she felt icy cold and sweating at the same time . . . and the real dangers of the caverns . . . and Daniel. The thought of never seeing Daniel again made her start to cry. She suddenly remembered how last Christmas she had thought if you really loved someone you had to be willing to die for him, and she realized she felt that way about Daniel and always had, but she'd been afraid to admit it to herself because she thought he would leave her. I love him, Kate thought.

She walked slowly, cautiously, to the room she remembered contained their lanterns, and with a gasp of relief saw them in the corner. There was the tin box of safety matches too. Kate lit one of the lanterns. It was better than the flashlight, but she was still in the dark and still in danger. She walked through the part of the maze she remembered, more quickly now, avoiding the bottomless pool, calling out Daniel's name until she was hoarse. Jay Jay had painted all kinds of graffiti on the walls so he wouldn't get lost, but she had no way of deciphering it. If Daniel's nearby he has a light with him, she thought, and I'll see it. She had forgotten to count the lanterns, but she hadn't seen the large battery-powered campsite lamp anywhere and she realized Daniel had taken it. Maybe the batteries had gone out . . . when had Jay Jay changed them?

"Daniel!" He'll hear me, even in the dark, and see my light. Maybe he fell and he's unconscious, or . . . No, she wouldn't let herself think "dead."

Now there were only the new uncharted places, the maze only Jay Jay knew, and parts no one knew yet at all. She suddenly realized she wasn't afraid of the dark anymore, hadn't been for almost five minutes, and was only afraid of what could happen to her if she took a false step. I won! she thought. I conquered the dark! She entered a small passageway and went through it to another room. Her light shone off the ghostly shapes of the stalactites and stalagmites—what were they anyway, petrified water?—and the damp cold walls. Nothing in this room, back again to another . . . and Kate realized she was lost.

Lost.

At first she ran in circles, frantically, like a panicked animal. Then she forced herself to stop and think. She was crying again, little gasps of grief and fear. Somewhere she could hear the sound of water dripping, and she wondered if that was the earlier room with the bottomless pool in it or another new one. At least sound would be a help. But then she realized that it didn't matter: the caverns branched off endlessly, repeating their patterns—you could wander here forever and ever and not know the difference. But of course it wouldn't be forever; it would only be until you were dead.

She remembered something she'd read about being

able to live for a month without food, but only two days without water. Was that right? Maybe she should find a pool of water and drink from it. At least that way she wouldn't die in agony; she'd just faint and slip away. *She didn't want to die here!* It couldn't be possible—she had to find her way out.

And yet she knew it was quite possible. All of them had always known that.

Part of a poem by Edna St. Vincent Millay went through her mind:

Alone, alone, in a terrible place,
In utter dark without a face,
With only the dripping of the water on the stone,
And the sound of your tears, and the taste of my
*   own.*

She thought of the education she had thrown away; the things she hadn't done or tried to do. Now she never would. She would never know the mysteries of growing older and finding out about life. She would never write her book. She thought about Daniel, how she loved him, and wondered if he could have loved her and if they could have been together if not for tonight. Her parents would be brokenhearted to lose her, and her sister . . . Who would have dreamed she would be destined to die in a cave?

She kept moving on as she thought all these things, simply because she could never just lie down and wait for it to be over. Small rooms and large ones, tiny passageways . . . trying to find something familiar. She prayed. It was the first time since she was a little girl and had said her prayers by rote in Sunday school, but they said it was never too late.

And then she realized that when the kerosene in her lantern was gone she would be left alone in total darkness.

"Help!" she screamed. "Help, help, help, help!" The walls mocked her with their echo. *Elp, elp, elp* . . .

She would watch the level of oil in the lantern, keep walking, and find a room to die in.

She kept walking and screaming, her throat sore, shivering now in the dampness, hating the echo that reminded her how helpless she really was. She began to think she was losing her mind. The echo had changed, and now it wasn't saying "elp," but "Hey."

Hey, hey, hey . . .

Daniel!

Kate waved her lamp in wide arcs, shouting his name. "Daniel, it's me, Kate! Here, I'm here!"

"Stay where you are," he called. His voice was faint and far away, but she heard him. "Keep calling so I can find you."

She suddenly felt warm, as if the blood was returning to her numb body. He would find her. She would live. She kept crying out hoarsely, and after what seemed a very long time she saw the reflection of his light against the black glittering wall, and then she saw the light itself. And then she saw him. No one had ever looked so wonderful to her in her life. She flung herself into his arms.

"What are you doing here?" he said.

"Me? What are you doing here?"

"My God," he said, "you don't even have a compass."

"Don't let go of me," she said. She burrowed into the safety of his body, his arms around her, her face against the reassuring scratchiness of his sweater. She kept her arms locked around his waist so he wouldn't stop holding her.

"Why are you here all alone?" he said.

"I came after you, you dummy. I thought you were going to get lost, and then I did."

"You came after me alone in the dark?" he said, sounding amazed. His voice was soft, and he seemed very touched. "That was . . ."

"Was what—crazy?"

"Was heroic . . . and . . . the most caring thing anyone ever did for me."

"I love you," she said. It slipped out before she could stop the words. Now she'd ruined it and he wouldn't be her friend anymore. She felt the tears start again, and knew she was only making it worse by crying in front of him, making a fool of herself.

He drew back and looked at her, his eyes wide with tenderness and surprise. "I love you," he said.

He kissed her, and they clung together, kissing. That sensual mouth—she couldn't believe how good it felt, better than anything she had ever let herself imagine.

"Let's get out of here," Daniel said.

He took her hand and led her to the passageway he had just entered. She followed him then, holding her lantern in one hand and the edge of his jacket in the other. She saw he had been marking the walls, and now he stopped quickly to wash off the markings as they left each room, and to recheck his map.

"What are you doing?" Kate asked.

"I'll tell you later. Let's just get out. You've had enough of this place for one night."

When they reached the familiar room where the

lanterns were stored they put them down and turned out their lights. Now they had their flashlights and Daniel was holding her hand again. Kate felt as if she had been in this place all night. She had no idea what time it was. They ran the last few steps to the safety of the outside world and stood there under the stars, breathing the clear, fresh air.

"I saw your bike," she said.

"Why don't I drive your car? I'll come back to get my bike tomorrow."

"Let's put it on my ski rack," Kate said. "Somebody might steal it, or see it, which would be bad enough." Why was she being so logical, when all she wanted was for him to make love to her? But she wouldn't ask him; he'd have to make the first move.

Daniel put his bicycle on top of her car, and then they got in. He tossed his bag of equipment into the backseat. While he drove she leaned back against her seat, too excited to be tired, thinking she might never be tired again. He was so beautiful she couldn't stop looking at him. He loved her . . . she was so happy she could hardly believe it.

"I'll tell you why I was in the caverns," he said. "Maybe you won't love me so much anymore."

"You were burying a body?"

"I was cheating. I wanted to find out what Jay Jay had planned so I could stay ahead of him and win the game."

"I didn't think you cared about winning," Kate said, surprised.

"I didn't think so either. You know how I always said I wasn't competitive. Well, it seems I am." He looked at her. "I risked my life and I cheated, just to win a game. I, the guy who claimed to be a happy dropout, am probably the most competitive person I know. The midnight revelation of the caverns."

"That's not so bad," Kate said.

"What isn't?"

"Being competitive."

"I don't mind finding out I'm competitive," Daniel said. "I'm sort of glad and relieved. But what about that crazy thing I just did?"

"I know you wouldn't cheat on something that mattered," Kate said. "Like an exam or something. This is just a game."

"But it got to be more."

"You're not going to tell Jay Jay, are you?" she said.

"No. He'd be too flattered." They both laughed. He told her how he had tricked Jay Jay into having a date, and Kate was delighted. She felt stoned: comfortable, happy, safe. The lights of the huge dorms swam before her eyes.

He took his bike off her car and locked it to the iron bike rack in the parking lot. "Are you hungry?" he asked.

"Uh-uh."

"Do you want a drink?"

"Do you?"

He didn't answer. He didn't need to. He put his arms around her again and ran his lips across her hair. "Will you stay with me tonight?" he asked. He sounded almost shy. Daniel . . . shy?

"Yes," Kate said.

The dorm was quiet when they went up to Daniel's room, and Kate looked at her watch for the first time and realized with surprise that it was two thirty in the morning. She was glad no one had stopped them to say hello. She just wanted to be alone with him.

His skin was like silk, with firm, smooth muscles moving under it. She had always known he would have a beautiful body. But best of all was the way the two of them made love, as if they had each been starving all this time for the touch of the other; and Kate thought perhaps they had. She wanted to bite him, devour him, and at the same time she felt as if she were melting. The pleasure was so total she had never felt this way before, never even come near it. Don't stop, she thought, don't stop, don't ever stop.

He didn't seem to want to stop either. They made love all night, over and over, desperately and intensely. There was nothing but the world of their bodies. The waves of feeling left them surprised and insatiable. When they finally did have to stop they still clung together, looking at each other and kissing.

"I love you so much I can't believe it," he said.

"I bet I love you more."

"I bet you don't."

"Good," Kate said. They both laughed with happiness.

"I always thought I was Mr. Spock," Daniel said quietly. "I thought I had no feelings, like a Vulcan. I never thought I could fall in love, even though I really wanted to."

"You aren't Mr. Spock," Kate said. "You're the Tin Man. You know, from *The Wizard of Oz*. He thought he had no heart and all along he had the biggest, most loving heart of all."

"I just feel like a totally different person," he said. "I mean, it's weird. Before, I felt like I was dead."

"Raising the dead," Kate said. "Like in the game."

"Oh, wow, the game! I've mapped it almost as far

as Jay Jay got, and I know where the good stuff is, although he'll probably put in more."

"Are you going to play it anyway?"

"Are you kidding? Of course I am."

"Well don't tell me anything," Kate said. "I want to be surprised. It's no fun if I know in advance."

"I just thought of something really disgusting," Daniel said. "I am destined to be a rich, successful captain of industry. Work in computers and make up games on the side for fun."

"You don't sound too depressed about it."

"I'm a little stunned, but not depressed. It's my destiny."

"Good," Kate said. "Jay Jay and I plan to be famous, so you have to be too."

"And you and I will always be in love," Daniel said.

"Oh, I hope so," Kate said. "Please, let's."

"We will."

She knew it might really be possible. A feeling of peacefulness and bliss came over her, and she kissed him. Then she fell asleep in his arms, so exhausted that for the first time the narrow dormitory bed didn't seem too small for two people.

The next day neither of them went to classes. They slept until noon and appeared at lunch holding hands. After lunch they went back to Daniel's room and made love all afternoon. They had to get up for dinner because that night they were scheduled to play the game.

"I really don't want to go in those caverns tonight," Kate told Daniel. "Last night is still too close."

"But this time you have *two* people who know the caverns," Daniel said.

She forced herself to go in there and the game quickly took over, as she had hoped it would, and then everything was all right. After the game, when they all went back to the dorm, Kate brought her pillow into Daniel's room, where she was going to spend the night. They hadn't had to discuss it; they both simply knew that they were going to be together as much as possible. When Jay Jay saw her going into Daniel's room with the pillow, in her bathrobe, Kate thought she caught him looking sad. He's jealous, she thought. Poor Jay Jay.

She was relieved that Robbie didn't seem jealous at all. He didn't even seem to notice. And anyway, they were good friends now, nothing more.

The next day Kate and Daniel went to the shopping mall after classes and bought a king-size mattress and sheets and a blanket, all of which they brought back to the dorm. The purchase would leave both of them broke for months, but it was worth it. They were dragging the mattress up the stairs when Robbie appeared. Kate had a feeling of déjà vu about that mattress number.

"Oh, let me help you," Robbie said pleasantly.

He not only helped them with the mattress, but he helped them drag Kate's bed into Daniel's room and put the two beds together with the king-size mattress on top. They had to take the desk out and put it into Kate's room.

"This looks really decadent," Daniel said, surveying their huge bed with pleasure.

"Perfectly suitable for a future captain of industry," Kate said. They both laughed.

"Captain of industry?" Robbie said. "I don't understand."

"I changed my mind about being a dilettante," Daniel said.

"Oh," Robbie said. Then he smiled and raised his hand in a benediction. "Bless you, my children," he said.

CHAPTER TEN

A long time afterward Daniel would look back and think that he should have noticed what was happening, should have anticipated it—he who was so bright, observant, and logical. But he had been in love, and the amazement and joy of this unexpected miracle was the focus of his attention. Besides, perhaps logic had been his downfall. To have been able to anticipate something so mad and strange took a mind that was open to anything.

But it was now; the end of winter, the beginning of love. Kate was everything he had ever wanted. He knew that things between them would keep getting better and better. They planned for her to come home to Brookline with him for the Spring Break. He had told his parents he was bringing a girl who was important to him and they were pleased. His mother said she would have a good excuse to fix up the guest room, a chore she had been putting off. Daniel felt too sanguine to argue with her about sleeping quarters, although he knew that Kate's mother, from what Kate had told him, would probably have let them stay in the same room.

He hoped Kate wasn't jealous about all the girls who had been before her. She saw them everywhere;

in the dorm, on the campus, at classes. And that was just some of them! None of them had been in this new bed with him though—this was for the two of them and their new life. Those girls had only been physical attraction. He would have had more cause to be jealous—if he were a jealous person—of guys Kate had actually *loved*. He wanted her to love him more than she had ever loved them, and she assured him she did.

He didn't want to rush things, but at the back of his mind was the idea that if their relationship kept getting better, after they graduated they would live together, and then they might get married. Why not? He wanted to marry, and have children, and he knew he would be perfectly happy to spend the rest of his life with Kate. He couldn't say anything to her though, because ambitious women panicked if they thought you were trying to tie them down or interfere with their lives. He would have to live where the best job was, and maybe Kate would want to go to New York and get a job in publishing. She worried so much about her writer's block that if she couldn't write that novel she was dreaming of, then she would want to go to work in a field where she could learn more about writing. Daniel wondered if the best job offer for him would come from a firm in New York, and then everything would be solved. There was no point in worrying this far in advance. He was astonished at how much he had changed already—he who never wanted to plan for the future was now filled with plans.

She told him one night about the man in the laundry room who had tried to rape her, and Daniel wished he could kill him.

"Why didn't you tell the school authorities?" he said angrily. "You should have demanded they hire a security guard."

"Ha," Kate said. "Somebody has to get raped or killed first, and then all the future victims have to make a petition . . . guards cost money, you know. People don't care about other people in this world. You have to take care of yourself."

He had never heard her sound so bitter. He held her. "I'll take care of you."

"I know," she said. "But I hardly knew you then."

"I wish I could do something to make it never have happened."

"It helped a lot that I was able to tell you," she said. "I never could tell anyone before—at least, no one who mattered to me—and I had to pretend I didn't care. It was the only way I could handle it. I do feel better now, really."

He and Kate talked about going to Europe for the summer. They could figure out a really cheap way to go, and maybe their parents would give them the money. Or maybe they could go to San Francisco, stay at Kate's house, get jobs, and earn enough to go for the last three weeks.

"My father's going to have an expensive new baby by then," Kate said. "He might say he can't afford to send me to Europe, or, on the other hand, he might feel guilty enough to say yes."

"It would be nice if we could go in June, after my brother's wedding."

"But whatever we do," Kate said, "you and I will do it together, and it will be fun."

She wrote a poem for him. "It's kind of dumb," she said, embarrassed. He didn't think it was dumb at all.

He thought it was marvelous and he kept it in his wallet.

With his life so full now, a life that had been almost too full before with all the things they continued to do, how could he have noticed anything? Even Kate, wary as a rabbit, didn't notice anything either.

CHAPTER ELEVEN

Jay Jay knew that the Kate-Daniel romance was for real, and it made him feel alone again. He couldn't even fantasize that Kate was giving each one of them a chance and his would be next. He hated being so young. He never wanted the girls who wanted him; they were always little kids. It was March. The grim hateful weather had started to grow softer, but he knew it was tricky. Tomorrow it might snow. April was when everything got better and you knew there was some hope you would see spring again. The Spring Break started the first week in April, and Jay Jay thought that to cheer himself up he might as well give an April Fools' Day party, to end the Winter Semester properly and send everyone off on their way with a nice hangover.

He made a list of everyone he liked or wanted to know better. The four of them, of course; Perry and his medical friends, Glenna, Tina, the twins . . . he would invite all of Daniel's former girl friends just to stir up a little mischief. He had saved his old party lists so he wouldn't forget anybody. Everyone who was invited could bring friends, so it ought to be big and noisy, just the way he liked parties to be. It would be a normal party—no tricks or gimmicks. He had used up all his tricks on the game. The only thing he did to make the occasion special was teach Merlin to say "April fool," a whimsical little touch, Jay Jay thought. He would start the party in the afternoon. If it was like all his others it would last far into the night.

Jay Jay was rather looking forward to Spring Vacation this year because his mother, when he phoned to tell her when he'd be home, informed him that she was going to Key West to decorate the house of a new client. She was all excited. Jay Jay didn't dare ask her if she'd touched *his* room, and she didn't say anything, but of course she never did. It would be fun to have the whole apartment to himself. He thought of inviting Kate and Daniel and Robbie to visit him, but the thought of having Kate and Daniel behaving like a honeymoon couple in his own apartment was too much; he'd have to be a masochist to inflict that on himself. Besides, his mother was always afraid his friends would scratch some of her precious furniture, or make cigarette burns or spill something, if they stayed over when she wasn't there. It was tempting to invite them just to bug her, but the pleasure of upsetting her wasn't worth the other thing. Anyhow, Kate was going to Daniel's house. Meet the folks. Yuck.

Jay Jay mailed out fifty formal invitations. He would probably ask about a dozen other people when he ran into them—anyone who looked like a good addition to his life. Fifty was the perfect core number for a party.

"Do you need any decorations?" Perry asked him. "A nice pickled embryo?"

"I want them to have a good time, not get sick," Jay Jay said.

They played the last game of the Winter Semester in the caverns on Saturday night. It was a particularly long session; they were all reluctant to leave things unfinished. But, of course, things were always left unfinished in the game. . . that was one of the things that was so good about it. You were always in suspense, wanting to go further.

April Fools' Day was clear and not too cold. By the time the sun disappeared everyone was well into the planned evening of merrymaking in Jay Jay's room and the hall. Jay Jay was wearing a red cashmere sweater, immaculately pressed jeans, and his World War I German helmet with the spike on top. Daniel and Robbie took turns as disc jockey. The music was loud, the guests were making rash promises they would later regret or forget, and Merlin's raspy voice seemed to have the authority of a Greek chorus.

"I love you," Perry said to Tina, whom he had just met.

"April fool!" Merlin said.

Tina laughed. She had metamorphosed into Kim Novak now, and was wearing a plain silk shirt and a tight skirt with a slit. Tiny pearls replaced the safety pins that used to be in her earlobes. Jay Jay decided he was definitely destined to become a starmaker.

"Kate," Jay Jay demanded, "take pictures!" He had a beautiful twin on either side of him, and he thought he might send the photo in to *The Grant Gazette*. It was the sort of thing they liked: a record of happy college days. Kate ran to get her Polaroid camera, and Cindy and Lyndy smiled their dazzling smiles for publicity.

Jay Jay's favorite joyful records were blaring from his stereo, a glass of his favorite white wine was in his hand, sexy women were making a fuss over him, and he was in charge of this entire event. He had made all these people happy, enlivened their lives, brought them another terrific evening they would talk about for weeks. He was the instigator, the leader. He felt wonderful. The great Jay Jay had done it again.

"April fool!" Merlin said.

A Greek chorus is more than a commentator on events or an indicator of splendid ironies. Sometimes it also foretells the future.

Often it warns.

CHAPTER TWELVE

Robbie lay on his bed in the dark, listening to the party guests making noise downstairs, the music playing. Moonlight was shining in through his bedroom window. He was thirteen again, and he had gone upstairs to be alone for a while. None of the people down there were his friends, and he couldn't connect with them at all. He was still dressed because he might want to go back to the party anyway, and he wondered if everyone would be so glad to see him back if he had run away.

He was the Robbie then and the Robbie now, waiting for Hall to come in. Part of it was like a dream, seeing the past and the future—knowing Hall would come in although it had not yet happened, feeling his throat close with the pain of tears because he knew what would happen, needing to see Hall. It was Hall's sixteenth birthday party, April first, and soon he would come to say good-bye and then he would disappear. It hurt so much to know all of this that he couldn't bear it.

Pardieu's hand reached out again to touch the little pouch of spells he always wore tied to his belt. He took out The graven Eye of Timor that had the power to raise the dead, and he stroked it like a touchstone. Every indentation of it was familiar to his fingers so often had he felt it, waiting for the time that he could use it. He waited for The Great Hall, and then he appeared, slipping through the wall, standing all pale and shimmering in the moonlight.

"Now, Pardieu," The Great Hall said. "You are worthy. You know how to find me."

The tension flowed out of Pardieu's body and he sighed with gratitude. "At last . . ." he whispered.

The Great Hall seemed to dissolve just as he stood there in Pardieu's sight, but Pardieu was neither afraid nor sad because he knew that soon he would be with The Great Hall again, this time forever. He rose from his bed. He had his sword, his coins, and all of his charms, and he would use these and his wits to be safe from evil. He was worthy. He knew his mission. He would bring back The Great Hall and then everything would be right again.

He slipped out into the dark, away from all Humans and Sprites and other beings who wasted their time with frivolity, and walked along the road, heading east. The landscape was changing with the beginning of spring. Pardieu could smell the flowers under the ground, feel the dampness of the unborn green shoots, all of nature waiting to be reborn. He was a part of this now, and of all things unseen and unknown: the highest level of Holy Man after so long a time of waiting and trial . . . at last.

On a quiet weekday night nobody paid any attention to the clean-cut college student walking down the dark road in jeans and Windbreaker. He walked so steadily, with such an obvious sense of his destination, that anyone who saw him would simply not notice him at all.

PART FOUR:

THE MAZE

CHAPTER ONE

The day after Jay Jay's party everyone started to leave for home. Daniel and Kate went together on the train to stay with his parents. Jay Jay had planned to ride to New York with Robbie, in Robbie's car, but Robbie's door was open, his bed hadn't been slept in, and his things were still there, so Jay Jay figured he had struck it lucky at the party and found love. If he was shacked up in another dorm, who knew when he would decide to get his act together for going home? It might be tomorrow. Jay Jay didn't plan to hang around this dreary campus till then. A couple of people had asked him at the party if he needed a ride to New York, so he put a note on Robbie's bed and left with a congenial group who had plenty of room in their large car for him and Merlin. It was typical of Robbie, Jay Jay thought, not to bother to lock his door. He didn't worry that someone might steal his stereo or records, or make long-distance calls on his phone. Not that a person who wanted to pick those flimsy dorm room locks couldn't anyway, but you didn't put temptation in the way of the greedy. Jay Jay had his own lock: a dead bolt. His insecurity probably came from having his mother redecorating his room all the time, but it also came from practicality. He owned a lot of expensive things.

On the drive to New York Jay Jay did something unusual for him—he took down the phone numbers of everyone in the car and gave them his. He said maybe he'd have a small cocktail party during the two-week vacation, and invite them. The euphoria of his successful April Fools' Day party was still with him. He didn't mention that he had no other friends in New York to invite.

He entered his apartment with the same mixed feelings he always had, but this time they were a little different. His mother wouldn't be there, elusive and unloving, but on the other hand, if she had changed his room he wouldn't have the outlet of yelling at her. His fists clenched. If she had touched his room he'd call her in Key West, embarrass her right in front of her client. That would fix her.

He drew a deep breath and went into his room. It was fabulous! He couldn't believe it! She'd done it like a Sydney Greenstreet movie, complete with mosquito netting, a ceiling fan, and palm trees. His beloved old movie posters were on the sisal-covered walls. It was the tropics; glamorous and sleazy. There should be a bar down the street, with Rita Hayworth in it, or Ingrid Bergman, or spies and writers. And the nicest thing of all—almost a loving touch if he didn't know his mother better—was a beautiful brass stand with a hook for him to hang up Merlin's cage.

"I love it, I love it, I love it!" he sang. "Don't you love it, Merlin?"

Merlin blinked in surprise.

"Hey, Merlin? What do you think? Should we write her a thank you note?"

"Birds can't talk," Merlin said.

He would definitely have to invite those people over for a drink, just to see this.

Kate got along with Daniel's parents immediately, and knew they liked her too. She was crazy about his brother and future sister-in-law, and thought the only thing that was missing to make this a perfect family environment was a couple of animals like she had at home. She had never seen so many books in anyone's house; they were even piled up on the floor. She was touched that Daniel's mother had fixed up the guest room specially for her. It had formerly been his brother's room. There were brand-new sheets, still stiff from just being taken out of the package and not laundered yet; new carpeting and towels in the bathroom, and a new shower curtain. There was even pretty guest soap and cologne. Daniel had rented bikes for them both, since he'd left his locked in their room at college (Kate thought of it as "their" room already, although hers was still hers), and she and Daniel rode into town where she bought a plant and candy and a bottle of wine for his parents. She would have bought them the world if she could afford it. They made it so obvious they were glad she was making their son happy.

His parents went out with their friends or visiting or to meetings quite a few evenings, and Kate and Daniel were able to be together for a while in Daniel's bed. She wondered if his parents had any idea. She thought they did; they just didn't want to be confronted with what was happening.

Kate loved his childhood room, filled with souvenirs and memories. She made him show her his yearbooks from high school, and pictures of when he was a little boy. She looked through his old, discarded records, and the books he'd loved as a child, and they compared tastes. All of these things had helped make him the person he was today, and she felt sentimental about them. She even loved the low mirror in his bathroom, picturing him when he was short.

They rode their bikes all over Brookline, and he showed her where he'd gone to school. He took her into Cambridge and Boston in his father's car, and he showed her Harvard, where his father taught, and all the historic sights. They went to movies and out to eat with a lot of his old friends. It was probably the best vacation Kate had ever had in her life.

Daniel was worried his parents might say something to him about Kate's not being Jewish. He knew his mother. Sure enough, one morning when Kate was upstairs taking a shower, his mother approached him, a cup of coffee in her hand, a nervous look on her face.

"I like Kate," his mother said.

"I'm glad. She likes you too."

"She's not Jewish."

"I know."

"Do you think she might convert?"

"*Convert?* Mom, I just started going with her—we haven't talked about getting married."

"I know what will happen," his mother said. "You'll go with her for a couple of years, you'll probably live together like your brother and Beth, and then you'll get married. You won't discuss religion. Then you'll have children and what will they be?"

"Boys or girls," Daniel said.

"Very funny. What about her parents? Do you think they'll like you?"

He shrugged. "Kate says they'll love me."

"I just don't want you to get hurt," his mother said.

"I don't intend to."

"I think it would be nice to have Jewish grand-children," his mother said. "Not half-and-half. Not let-them-decide-later. Not atheists. It's important to me. They have to know who they are."

"They'll know," Daniel said. He didn't like having this discussion. The way he dealt with things was first things first, and there were so many things that had to happen before he and Kate even planned marriage that it was frightening to think of all of them at once. He was trying to plan the next couple of years, and his mother wanted him to arrange the lives of people who didn't even exist yet. Why did her generation worry so much?

"I know the two of you never discussed it," his mother said.

"No, we didn't. We're still getting to know each other."

"That's a good subject for getting to know each other," his mother said. "Just ask her."

Kate came downstairs then and saved him.

CHAPTER TWO

Cat Wheeling felt right away that something was wrong when Robbie didn't come home for Spring Vacation the day they were expecting him. The next day she was sure of it. She tried to keep from getting hysterical; telling herself that boys his age got caught up in their social life and forgot to make phone calls. But Robbie had always been a responsible person. She telephoned him at school, but the phone in his room rang and rang and no one ever answered. She thought of him in a car wreck somewhere on the highway and felt sick with fear.

His father started calling the hospitals. No eighteen-year-old student named Robert Wheeling had been admitted for any reason. Was there some hospital they had forgotten? But Robbie had identification, and someone would have called his family. If he hadn't been taken to a hospital . . . if he were dead . . . the police would have called.

Cat drank steadily, to keep sane, and her husband looked at her with such hatred she wanted to throw the glass at him. "Can't you even stay sober for this?" he said.

Her knuckles on the glass were white. "Call his friends," she said.

"No wonder he doesn't want to come home."

"That was a vile thing to say to me. You are a disgusting man. Call them!" Her words came out with a hiss from behind clenched teeth. She would have called them herself, but she knew how drunk she would sound.

Hall sighed. "If Robbie were with a friend he'd phone us," he said. "Robbie never just disappeared. He knew how much it meant to us to know he was safe."

Neither of them said: *Because he's the only one we have now.* But they were both thinking it. They could not believe it could happen all over again. It would be too unbearable.

"What about his friends from school?" Cat said. "What if he decided to visit one of them?"

"He'd have called. Besides, we don't know who his friends at school are."

No, they didn't. Not even a first name. He'd always said school was fine, his classes were interesting, he was still swimming on the team. But no names, no anecdotes. How could they know, when no one ever had a real conversation with him? Robbie was so well adjusted, so polite and helpful and *nice*. He always wanted to know what he could do for you. It was as if he were trying to deflect attention from himself and keep his secrets. Could that be possible? Robbie with secrets?

"Robbie never took drugs," she said.

"No."

"He was happy," she said. "Wasn't he?"

"Happy?"

"Wasn't he happy? Did he seem unhappy to you?"

"No, he . . . he . . . seemed fine."

"He wouldn't," she said. "Would he?"

"Wouldn't what?"

"You know."

"Run away? You think Robbie would run away?"

No, not Robbie. Never. Cat poured herself another glass of vodka, spilling some. For once Hall didn't say anything about it, and she wanted to give him something in return, some gesture of trust. They could not afford to hate each other now. "I think something happened to him," she said. "I think we should call the police."

The next day he called the police in Pequod, where Robbie had last been seen. But this time it was different—it was not the way it had been with Hall junior.

"You're talking about an adult," the officer said.

"He's eighteen."

"That's an adult. He has legal rights. He can just walk away if he wants to. Eighteen-year-olds disappear all the time; younger ones too. They come back after a few days, a few weeks. Wait till vacation's over. He'll turn up at school."

"Our son wouldn't just disappear and then turn up again."

"Were there any circumstances indicating involuntary disappearance?"

"That's what I'm trying to find out," Hall snapped.

"Did he talk about suicide?"

"Robbie? Never."

"Was he mentally or physically incapable?"

"No, of course not."

"Why don't you talk to his friends," the police officer said. "I bet he told some of them where he was going."

"His friends have scattered for vacation."

"Then give it some time. First of all, you'd have to come here to make a report in person, and from what you've told me there's no reason to. He just took off. Don't worry about it."

Hall hung up and turned to look at Cat. She had been listening on the extension and came back into the room, feeling like a sleepwalker.

"When that little bastard comes back," Hall said, "unless there's a damn good reason, I'm going to take away his car."

"He's an adult," Cat said in a dead voice. "Can you take away an adult's car?" She started to cry.

He made a move as if to comfort her, and then drew back. He was not quite sure if she was being ironic or taking one of her customary digs at him. She wished he had put his arm around her so she would not feel so alone, but it was probably too late. She wasn't even sure if what she'd said had been her usual angry reaction to his narrow-minded stubbornness, or if she had been voicing aloud something she had just discovered that shocked her and made her cry. Robbie was their child, no matter whether or not the law said he was never to be considered a child anymore. What was wrong with their home that they had existed all this year treating Robbie as if he were a little boy, a "teen-ager," when in reality he could do anything the law said she and his father could do and no one could stop him? He could get married. He could leave college. He could move away. It was no longer called running away. He belonged to himself.

Cat realized then that their other son—the Hall junior they remembered—had vanished forever. They remembered the sixteen-year-old. If Hall was still alive he was an adult too, and would never again belong to any of them. When she had been growing up she had been taught that families were forever, but that had only been another of the world's lies. Now she was forty-three years old, her family had fallen apart, and she of all of them was the only one who still felt like a child. She was the only one who could not take off, run away, do what she wanted. The law might allow her to, but nothing in her conscience or upbringing would. She would worry too much about the others.

"Don't drink any more," he said. "It makes you depressed."

"Drinking is the only thing that makes me able to *survive,*" Cat said.

"Well, at least you admit how much you drink."

"So what? I admit it." She took a big swallow of her vodka. It went down comfortingly.

"That's the first step in being able to stop," he said.

"I don't want to stop."

"But maybe someday you will."

"Mmm." She looked at the colorless liquid in her glass. It was kinder to her than anyone she knew.

"When Robbie comes back," he said. "When this tension is over. Maybe then you will."

"When I *want* to is when I will," Cat said. "Not when you want me to."

"That's all right," he said.

But the days went by and Robbie neither came home nor called. His friends phoned often, none of them aware that he wasn't there where he was supposed to be. He's away, Cat would say—a half lie—didn't he tell you his plans?

His friends were all disappointed. They had parties to invite him to, or just wanted to see him. No, Robbie hadn't told them he had decided not to come to Greenwich for Spring Break. Cat didn't tell them Robbie hadn't told his parents either.

She couldn't bear to think that people would be talking about her, saying it had happened all over again with the younger son. No matter what the law or the police called him, her friends didn't think Robbie was an "adult" who could just walk away, and neither did she.

All the students but one came back to Grant after Spring Break. At first it simply looked as if Robbie had returned with the rest of them. His door was open, his room was neat—with the exception of his desk, which was covered with the customary student clutter—his clothes were in the closet, and his stereo was gone. If anyone had wondered where he was it would appear he had taken the stereo into Pequod to be repaired. It would not occur to anyone immediately that he had gone away leaving his door unlocked and therefore someone had stolen it. It was extraordinary that the thief had not taken his records too, but whoever it was had been in a hurry.

Kate was happy to be back in her cozy nest with Daniel. They unpacked quickly so they could find Robbie and Jay Jay. Daniel was so neat. Kate knew if she hadn't been living with him she would have tossed everything on her bed and gone to find her friends first. But trying to be less sloppy was a small price to pay for all the sweet things he did for her. They were back and forth from their two rooms (she had decided to think of her room as theirs too, this term) when Jay Jay came running down the hall waving a piece of paper in his hand.

"Something's happened to Robbie," Jay Jay said. "I left this note on his bed three weeks ago and it was still lying in the same place when I went in. I'm worried."

"You mean he left school with his door open?" Daniel said. He shook his head. "Even Robbie wouldn't do that. He's around somewhere."

"I asked everybody on his floor," Jay Jay said. "His car is in the parking lot but nobody's seen him all day."

"What's unusual about that?" Daniel said.

"He didn't come to see us," Kate said. "Were his clothes and everything there?"

"Yes," Jay Jay said. "When I put the note on his bed there were wrinkles like he'd been lying down, and they're still there."

"Ah," said Daniel pleasantly in a gypsy accent, "the famous wrinkle reader."

Kate felt uneasy. "Maybe he went home before you left the note, and when he came back he just didn't notice it."

"A weak excuse," Jay Jay said. "Robbie's bed was always so perfectly made it looked like he was in the Army. He would have seen my note the minute he came back and he would have felt bad for abandoning me, and he'd have come to find me and apologize. You know that's what Robbie would do."

"He would," Kate said. "What do you mean he abandoned you?"

"He promised me a ride to New York and then I couldn't find him."

"Then you abandoned him," Daniel said lightly.

"Well," Jay Jay said, "maybe he had something

more important to do and he was going to find me later. I'll put the note back so he remembers."

But they didn't see Robbie that night in the dining room, nor the next morning at breakfast. After breakfast the three of them went to Robbie's room. The bed hadn't been slept in and Jay Jay's note was still there. Robbie's car was still in the parking lot.

"I think maybe we should call his family in Greenwich," Kate said. "If he was going somewhere, he'd have told them."

"Where would he go without his car and his clothes?" Daniel asked.

She looked up Robbie's number in her little address book and dialed it right from his room. Now she was sure something very bad had happened, and she was afraid to even begin to think what it might be.

His mother answered.

"Is Robbie there?" Kate asked pleasantly.

"No." How nervous the woman sounded! Kate could hear it vibrating down her own body. "Who is this?"

"This is Kate Finch, a friend of his from Grant. Did he go home for vacation?"

"No. Didn't he tell you his plans?"

"No," Kate said. "When is he coming back to school, do you know?"

"Don't you know?" his mother said. Her voice cracked.

"Don't I know *what?*"

"What? What?" Jay Jay hissed, poking her. She glared at him.

"Don't you know where he is either?" his mother said.

"Don't *you* know?" Kate asked.

"He never came home," his mother said. "Are you a very good friend of his?"

"Yes. But we all thought he was going home."

"Oh, no . . ." From the pain in that woman's voice Kate knew exactly what she was thinking. Robbie's older brother had run away and now his mother thought Robbie had gone off too.

"I'm sure he's all right," Kate lied.

"What makes you so sure?"

"Well . . ." What was the point in lying when it might hurt Robbie if something awful had really happened to him? "We'll ask around, okay? I'll call you if I find out anything."

Kate hung up and looked at Daniel and Jay Jay. "Robbie's vanished into thin air," she said.

Daniel started looking through the papers on Robbie's desk. Kate and Jay Jay joined him. There was some homework, but mostly maps and mazes; the ones they had used for the caverns and one they had never seen before. It was on pale blue paper, intricately worked out, with a tiny red heart in the center of it. Around it was a beautiful drawing of two white towers set in the clouds in a striated pastel sky.

"I didn't know Robbie could draw," Kate said. "And look at the gorgeous lettering."

"*The Two Towers*," Jay Jay said. "That's the book by Tolkien."

"Where's 'The Great Hall'?" Daniel asked.

"In some book, I guess," Jay Jay said. "Or maybe in the game. It looks like he was working on a new one."

None of it made sense. There were all sorts of books in Robbie's bookshelf; many of them dealing with the occult and other mystical things. That part made sense, in view of Robbie's new religious kick, but none of it gave any explanation of where he could have gone or why.

"Maybe he went on a retreat or something," Jay Jay said hopefully. "You know, with one of those cult groups."

"He would have told us," Daniel said. "Those people are always telling you how great it is and how it's changed their lives. Robbie never proselytized about anything."

Robbie's room made them all feel uncomfortable. It was such a normal room: normal furniture, normal possessions, a few maps and things pertaining to a special hobby. Jay Jay picked up the note he had left on Robbie's bed and started to crumple it up.

"Don't!" Kate said. "That's evidence."

"Yeah," Jay Jay said worriedly. He smoothed out the note and put it back. Then they trooped despondently into Jay Jay's room, where he opened his closet and brought out a bottle of red wine that was left over from his party, and a box of Oreo cookies.

"Hi, Merlin," Kate said. "Say hello."

"Birds can't talk," Merlin said.

They sat down and drank and munched. The sky darkened outside their window as the sun set. Daniel sighed. "Do you think some maniac got him? Like the Freeway Murders in California?"

"Robbie wouldn't hitchhike," Jay Jay said. "He had the car."

"April fool," Merlin said.

April fool . . . why was that somehow so important?

"Wait . . ." Kate said. She started to think out

loud. "Those maps Robbie made . . . The Great Hall . . . Robbie's brother's name was Hall. The one who ran away. It's not a place, it's a person."

"He had a brother who ran away?" Jay Jay said. "He never told anybody."

"He told me," Kate said. "And April first, April Fools' Day, was the night his brother left . . . at his own birthday party. We all saw Robbie at Jay Jay's party, and then we never saw him again."

"You mean he went off to look for his brother?" Daniel said.

"Oh, my God!" Kate said. Now she knew: she was right, she had always been right. She should have listened to her instincts.

"What? What?" Daniel and Jay Jay clamored.

"Robbie's gone into the game," she said. "He's become Pardieu."

"The caves!" Daniel said.

"We have to go get him," Jay Jay said. He grabbed all his equipment—the maps, the spray paint, the compass; the safeguards that had lulled them in the real world, the magic that had gone awry in the fantasy one—and they ran down to Kate's car.

They knew at once she was right.

"It's my fault," Jay Jay kept saying all the way to the caverns. "It's my fault."

"No," Daniel said. "It's mine. Kate suspected it, and I talked her out of it. She saw him becoming Pardieu. Now when I look back it was all so obvious, but I ignored it because it was so *unreal*. Who could have dreamed of such a thing?"

"It's not anybody's fault," Kate said. "It's the game's fault."

"Oh, who cares anyway who's to blame?" Jay Jay

said finally, as the red Rabbit skidded into the safety of the clump of trees outside the forbidden caverns. "Just let him be all right."

The dark rooms of their maze looked different now, and the pleasure was gone. A decomposing body could be real. There were no monsters; only the reality of death. They held their lanterns high and searched carefully, calling for Pardieu because they knew Robbie would not answer, and each of them felt an icy terror far beyond anything they had conjured up in their make believe. For the first time they were playing the game as they would have liked to play it—to the limit of danger and fear, and with a true yearning for the reward—but now there was nothing in it at all of fun or adventure. There was no sign anywhere that Robbie had passed by, but if he had believed himself to be Pardieu then he would have gone off with nothing. The dripping of the water on the stone reminded them all that he could have drowned.

Finally they stopped to rest in a small room of the maze. "We can't do this alone," Daniel said.

Jay Jay was hunched in the corner looking very small and frightened. "His map was different," he said softly. "I don't understand his map."

"He invented his own caverns," Kate said. "A Holy Man can see things that aren't there. Don't you remember?"

"What are we going to do?" Jay Jay said.

Daniel sighed. "We have to go to the police."

"And tell about the *game*?" Jay Jay squeaked.

"No, no," Daniel said. "Leave it to me."

They made their way out of the caverns and drove to the Pequod police station. They identified themselves as Robbie Wheeling's friends and said they had reason to believe he was missing. They described how punctual and responsible Robbie was, and said they were sure he had come to some harm. Robbie always had a lot of money with him, they said, and now he had disappeared after promising a ride home to his friend Jay Jay, over three weeks ago, and they were very concerned. His car was still in the parking lot and his clothes in his room. He had apparently never left Pequod. He was a person who trusted strangers. Perhaps he had been murdered and the body hidden in some . . . place. His parents had not heard a word from him either, and were worried too.

"There is one other strong possibility," Daniel said. "Robbie was very interested in those caverns near the campus. He had been talking about going into them. We think he did."

"You think he went into the caverns over three weeks ago?"

"Right."

"Without water that length of time he'd be dead," the police officer said.

Kate could hardly catch her breath. A vision of the caverns as they had been that terrible night she was lost in them flashed through her mind: the blackness and the power of them. She could see Robbie in there alone. "Maybe there's water in the caverns," she said. "But you have to look for him either way, don't you?"

"Oh, of course. Dead or alive."

Dead or alive. She felt her world falling all around her. She couldn't look at the others; she knew they felt the same way she did.

CHAPTER FOUR

As soon as they got back to the dorm from the police station, the three of them—in confusion and desperation and guilty fear—removed every trace of the game from their rooms and locked all of it in a locker at the bus station. They had left everything in Robbie's room untouched. They wanted to go back to the caverns to take away their costumes and wipe their fingerprints off the lanterns, but they didn't dare. Someone would see them now. They tried to reassure themselves that since this wasn't a murder the police would be more concerned with finding Robbie than in finding out who had played the game with him. But they were so furtive they each felt as if they were really covering up a crime of violence, not just a prank that would get them expelled. If Robbie had gone into the game and died because of it, he had done so because of them. Part of their minds said logically that wasn't true, but the pain of having been responsible remained. The worst was knowing they had done this to someone they cared about so much.

The Pequod police department sent a detective to the dorm where Robbie had lived, to find out who his other friends were and question them, and particularly to get more information from Daniel and Kate and Jay Jay. None of the three of them had expected that. They had thought the cops would just go into the caverns. The detective's name was Lieutenant Jerry Martini. He seemed like a nice enough man; he told them he had two kids of his own in high school, that he worried about secret depression in young adults, and the risks young people took because they thought they were immortal. Martini was so devious he insisted on talking to each of them separately, leaving them totally unprotected and frightened. He went into Jay Jay's room first.

Jay Jay put his hands into his pockets so the cop wouldn't notice that his palms were wet. He was sure police detectives looked for things like that. He hoped he looked so preppie and wholesome that no one would think he himself went lurking around in forbidden caverns.

"You were a good friend of Robbie Wheeling's, right?"

Jay Jay nodded. "He was a . . . why are you saying I *was* his friend, like you think he's dead?"

"Sorry. What were you going to say?"

"That he's a really terrific guy. Everybody likes Robbie."

"When you last saw him, was he depressed? Moody?"

"I don't think I ever saw Robbie depressed," Jay Jay said. "He was kind of into mystical things . . . spiritual things."

"Like Mazes and Monsters?"

Here came the big stuff. Jay Jay's heart began to pound. "You mean the game?"

"Yes. He was into the game, we could see that."

"Oh, yeah," Jay Jay said. "He was really involved with it."

"Did you play it too?"

Jay Jay thought fast. Give him just enough so he doesn't catch you in a lie. "I used to. But it takes up a lot of time, and I'm a straight-A student, so I can't afford to take too much time off anymore."

"What about the caverns?"

"What about them?"

"We heard some of the students were playing Mazes and Monsters in the caverns," Martini said.

Jay Jay's stomach pitched. Who had told? Perry? Somebody in the drama department? He tried to look pensive. "I heard that rumor too," he said in his most ingenuous way.

"Did you ever ask him?"

Think fast, Jay Jay thought. Say yes so they'll go in and find him. Say no—they'll go in anyway. No, you have to say yes. "Not exactly," he compromised. "He did say he thought it would be a lot of fun to play the game in the caverns. He really seemed interested in those caverns."

I blew it, he thought. Did I blow it? I should have said, *Yes he did!* Now I can't go back and say he did; he'll know I lied. Jay Jay was starting to feel really sick. His skin was prickling all over. What had happened to the great Jay Jay, the future actor and star?

The cop walked over and looked at Merlin. "What kind of bird is that?" he asked in a friendly voice.

"A mynah bird."

"Does it talk?"

"Birds can't talk," Merlin said.

The cop laughed. "Funny. You teach him that?"

"Yes," Jay Jay said. "A smart mynah bird can have

a vocabulary of several hundred words. Speaking is a conditioned reflex with them though—they don't reason the same way we do."

"What's his name?"

"Merlin," Jay Jay said. His skin wasn't prickling quite so much. He tried to decide if Martini was playing Good Cop to disarm him, or if he really was interested. He supposed a mynah bird was something Martini didn't see very often, even in his line of work.

"Does Merlin bite?"

"All birds bite," Jay Jay said.

"Fecalite," Merlin said.

"Oh, shut up," Jay Jay said to him.

"Who else was playing Mazes and Monsters in the caverns?" Martini asked.

Wham! There it came. "I don't know," Jay Jay said.

"But you were his friend."

"He didn't tell me *everything*."

"Did he have a girl friend?"

"He used to go with Kate, but they broke up."

"Was he upset about that?"

"You mean, like suicidal?"

"Yes."

You just told him Robbie was never depressed, Jay Jay reminded himself. But depressed is different from upset over a broken love affair. He thought of saying yes, and the caverns would be a good place to end it all; but he knew the cop would question Kate too, and less information was always better than a clash of wits. On the other hand, Robbie could have hidden his unhappiness from Kate but told his friends . . .

"Was he upset or not?" Martini asked.

"I think he got lost in the caverns," Jay Jay said.

Martini raised his eyebrows. "Why would he go in during vacation?"

"Maybe Robbie and his friends were playing the night of my party," Jay Jay said. "That was the last time I ever saw him."

That is the first intelligent thing I've said this whole time, Jay Jay thought. He felt a sudden rush of relief. In a funny way, it was also a kind of alibi.

Kate had been psyching herself out the entire time the cop was questioning Jay Jay, and by the time it was her turn she had almost convinced herself that what she was about to say was all true. She felt calm, detached, almost schizophrenic. She had always been able to close herself off from dangerous situations and too-painful ones; and now she was ready for something that was both.

"Robbie was really getting to act peculiar," she told Lieutenant Martini. "He was more interested in the game than in me. When he started spending all his free evenings playing the game instead of with me, I realized we had no relationship anymore."

"The game has that kind of influence?"

"Oh, it can become obsessive to some people. You know—all games have a possibility of becoming too important. Gambling, for instance."

"Apparently he was playing the game in the caverns with a group of people. Who were they?"

The important thing, she told herself firmly, is to make them go into the caverns after Robbie as quickly as possible, and not to incriminate any of us. When they find him safe and alive—not *if*, but *when*—everyone will be so relieved they'll probably drop the rest of it.

"I don't know," Kate said. "People wouldn't talk about that sort of thing. It's against college rules, you know. I was so scared for Robbie that I just had to get out of his life at that point. It was too painful to see him taking those risks. He really didn't understand how dangerous it was. A lot of people don't."

"So you think he went into the caverns alone and got lost?"

"I'm sure of it," Kate said.

Daniel couldn't understand why the cops were wasting all this precious time asking questions in the dorm when they should be out in the caverns with a search team. He was frightened for himself and Kate and Jay Jay, but much more frightened for Robbie. Daniel's whole future in the outside world depended on not getting expelled, on being able to have that good job after graduation and build his life. But right now Robbie could be minutes away from no future at all.

"You and Kate Finch are going together?" Lieutenant Martini said to Daniel. It was more a statement than a question. He glanced at the king-size bed in Daniel's room. Daniel didn't like that each of them was being questioned separately. It was as if they were being blamed for a crime. Why didn't Martini just go get Robbie out?

"Yes," Daniel said.

"But you were still friendly with Robbie?"

"Oh, sure. I didn't take her away from him. It was all over when I came along."

"He was playing the game in the caverns. Do you know who else he played with?"

"No. But I don't see how that matters."

"It matters very much," Martini said. "Or not at all. You yourselves suggested Robbie might have been murdered. Suppose someone who was playing the game with him got carried away and killed him?"

Daniel tried to control the queasy feeling that started in his stomach and ended as his whole body shaking. "That's kind of far-out," he said.

"Mazes and Monsters is a far-out game," Martini said. "Swords, poison, spells, battles, killing, maiming . . . a lot of violence there, wouldn't you say?"

"It's imaginary violence," Daniel said.

"We may be dealing with a sick mind."

We are! Daniel wanted to shout. All that time, all that precious time, already wasted! Robbie was in the caverns—why couldn't the cops get him out and then look for their alleged perpetrators, or whatever their dismal jargon called it?

By the time Martini was finished with him Daniel was bathed in sweat. He knew it made him look guilty as hell, but that didn't matter now. All that mattered was to get out of here and be of some real help to Robbie. He had to get Jay Jay's map to the police—the M.C.'s map that went further than Robbie's did. They should have thought of that earlier.

But if Robbie was really lost, the maps wouldn't help. And if Robbie hadn't taken a map then he was certainly lost. All that precious time . . .

Lieutenant Martini was busy with people on Robbie's floor. Daniel rode his bike through the dark to the bus station and chained it outside. He took Jay Jay's map out of the locker, wiped off the fingerprints, and wearing gloves, he addressed the envelope, trying to keep his trembling hand steady as he made neat block letters. He was still shaking all over, as if he had the flu. There wasn't time to send it by mail. He couldn't just walk up to the police station and hand it to them; they knew him. Throw it through the window wrapped around a rock? No, that was some sort of crime, and they were being blamed for enough.

He pedaled as fast as he could back to the dorm. Lieutenant Martini's car was still parked in front. Daniel placed the envelope containing the map carefully under the windshield wiper blade on the driver's side, and then rode away.

He was too nervous to hang around and wait for Martini to be finished and come out. Right now he didn't even want to be with Kate. He didn't know what he wanted to do. He rode his bike back along the road until he came to the detour that led to the caverns, and turned down it, drawn again to the place that had been so destructive to his kind and innocent friend. A searchlight had been set up, and there were some cars and a van nearby; curiosity-seekers. The news had traveled fast. And then he saw the police cars, and for the first time that whole evening the awful shaking stopped. The cops were looking for Robbie anyway.

At least that was a start.

CHAPTER FIVE

The days dragged by. The police were still looking in the caverns and questioning students. The Pequod newspaper picked up the story of the missing student, and of course *The Grant Gazette* did, and then the wire services got hold of it. Suddenly the press was fascinated by the game. The idea that a game that was supposed to be a fantasy could have taken on such reality as to cause the disappearance—and possible death—of a player was thrilling. Sales of Mazes and Monsters soared. It was inevitable that someone would finally advance the theory that the game had caused Robbie to flip out. But it was all conjecture. The fact that Robbie had been so normal: an athlete, good grades, popular, friendly, pleasant, attractive, made the story even more intriguing to the press. It seemed as if reporters were interviewing everyone on the campus.

"Life for most people is boring," a psychologist said. "There's not much excitement. We've run out of frontiers. The only frontiers we have left are in our minds. Testing yourself becomes the challenge. If a person isn't too well put together to begin with, it's not going to be good for him."

Jay Jay threw the paper across the room in disgust.

"Boring?" he said to Kate and Daniel. "He should see our lives. Life is far from boring—it's *terrifying*. Look what's out there. Is he kidding?"

"I don't know what world he's talking about," Kate said.

"When we find out," Daniel said, "let's go there."

The three of them spent most of their time together now, holding on to each other's presence for moral support. They couldn't even think of playing the game, and wondered if they would ever want to again. When they passed rooms where other students were still playing it, they couldn't stand to look. The heartless cries of enthusiasm, the click of the dice, were like laughter at a funeral. There was a lot of free time now without the game. Time to study, to do class assignments, to participate in real life—but they couldn't concentrate. Daniel was lucky that he could run in the mornings to work off some of his nervous energy. But for Kate and Jay Jay, karate and fencing weren't enough. They all tried to keep each other distracted, but it was hopeless.

Naturally some of the students who were interviewed defended the game, because they were still playing it. "It's a perfectly harmless game," one was quoted. "I mean, people who think that stuff is real are just nuts."

Kate, Daniel, and Jay Jay refused to be interviewed. They had discussed it and decided whatever they said could be held against them in some way, at some future time. Besides, they couldn't tell anyone they thought Robbie had become Pardieu. You didn't tell the world your friend was crazy. That would be the ultimate betrayal.

In the midst of all this horrible tension, the amazing thing was that Perry, who had lent Jay Jay the bones, and the people in the drama department who had let him borrow other props, never told anyone. It was, of course, partly their own fear of being expelled for having been part of this madness. But it was also out of loyalty. Nothing they had to contribute would bring Robbie back any faster, so why would they hurt their friend Jay Jay and his friends?

It was spring. The weather had turned soft overnight, and green buds began to appear on the spindly trees around the campus. The days grew longer. Soon it would be Reading Period, and then Final Exams. They had to study—the three of them who had been so worried they would be expelled were now in danger of flunking out because of grief. They began to force themselves to work, and finally it became a relief to lose themselves in their responsibilities.

Still, there were the newspapers to remind them. The police were receiving hundreds of calls and letters; hints of some of them were in the papers. There was a demand for ransom to be left at a motel in the next town, where someone claimed to know that Robbie had been kidnapped. The "kidnapping" turned out to be a hoax. Only Kate, Daniel, and Jay Jay had been sure from the start that it was. They believed nothing else but that Robbie was in the caverns—Pardieu on his quest.

Lieutenant Martini wasn't bothering them anymore. They decided to bother him. They went to the police station three times before they found him in.

"We want to know what's happening," Kate said.

Martini looked genuinely sorry. "Not much luck," he said. "Lots of psychics are coming out of the woodwork. They've got him here, there and everywhere. Most of that stuff is garbage."

"Did any of them say he's in the caverns?" Jay Jay asked.

"Sure. And we looked. But you don't think they'd pinpoint a place, do you? They *describe* a place. That could be anywhere. We still haven't a clue where the body is."

The body? They looked at each other aghast. Robbie was not just "a body." They refused to believe it.

"I thought psychics helped the police," Jay Jay said.

"We use them sometimes," Martini said. "But you only hear about their successes. They never tell the public about their failures. I heard a funny line from one of the officers—he said we ought to give a dinner dance and invite all the psychics, but not tell them where it is. Then we'll see how many of them find it." He waited for them to laugh, or at least smile. They didn't. "One of them sent me a map of New York," he went on. "Can you imagine—New York? Where are we supposed to start looking in a place as big as that?"

"New York State or New York City?" Jay Jay asked.

"The whole state," Martini said. He chuckled. "Big deal."

"What did you do about it?" Kate asked.

"Filed it with the rest of the crank letters," Martini said. "What do you think?"

CHAPTER SIX

Underneath Grand Central Station, in the middle of New York City, there is a maze of steam tunnels that snake around for several miles, supplying steam to the large office buildings and hotels nearby. Not many people know about them, or would have any interest in them. They are the home for drifters, street people; homeless men and women who have no other place they want to go, or can think of to go, or have the energy and hope to go. They carry their belongings with them, and sleep lightly, lying on newspapers, watchful that their meager possessions are not stolen. They eat what little they can get. They cook, talk, make friends. Some of them have been there for years. In the morning the rumbling of the trains overhead awakens them, and many of them leave for the day, to wander the streets. But at night they come back to sleep. This is their home.

There are many ways to enter the underground tunnels from the street, if you know where they are. A polished brass door at the side of the famous Waldorf-Astoria Hotel, emergency exits in Grand Central Station itself, a doorless opening near the lower level that has the words BURMA ROAD handwritten over it. Burma Road is the main tunnel. It is easy to get lost there if you are unfamiliar with the winding passages. It is, of course, a maze.

It had taken Pardieu a long time to find this maze, and now he was resting here before continuing on his journey. He had known from the first moment he set out that he was blessed, but also that he would have to be very careful. A kindly stranger had given him transportation, and after passing through what seemed to be an endless tunnel they had emerged at last into a great city filled with noise and lights and all kinds of beings, mostly Human. Tall towers rose everywhere, but as he scanned the landscape Pardieu saw The Two Towers in the distance and knew he had found the right place. He walked through the streets, watching everything, looking into the eyes of the inhabitants and finding them full of anger and fear. He realized these people did not want to be looked at—they felt it was an assault. And yet some of them had dressed in such gaudy clothing that he knew they wanted to be noticed. It was their souls they were trying to hide. They knew he was a Holy Man and could see within their souls, and so they glared at him. Pardieu looked away, not wanting to incite them to a fight.

Not everyone in this city was unkind. Some smiled at him, returned his glance, and wanted to join him. But Pardieu had to journey on alone. He would smile back and bless them, and walk away.

Whenever he was hungry or thirsty there were places to buy food. He ate simply, buying from vendors who cooked in the open air. At night he would rent a small room in some unsavory inn where he could bathe and sleep, not wishing to sleep in the street. Only Trolls slept in the streets of this city; squat, waddling wanderers carrying bags of plunder and speaking in their own tongue. But even staying at the cheapest places he could find, Pardieu was growing short of coins. Soon he would have to beg.

Everywhere he trudged he looked for some sign that he was closer to the place where he would find the underground maze. "Do you know The Great Hall?" he would sometimes ask passersby, and often they would look bewildered, but occasionally they would point out some way, giving him instructions. He realized they had no idea who he was talking about. They thought he was looking for a building. They were only Men—how could they have heard of The Great Hall?

He tried to recall the map he had drawn, remembering that The Great Hall had told him not to take it because it was unnecessary. Where was he to go? What was the next step? Such an endless city, teeming with people! He waited for night, and his dreams.

Then one night Pardieu had the dream he sought. In it he saw a great door made of gold, as one might find in a castle, and he knew. The next morning he went forth to find it.

He saw it on the second day, set in the side of a fine castle that was guarded by a man in regalia. When the guard turned away, Pardieu pushed the door open and entered.

All mazes are different, and yet they are the same. This one was warm, dimly lit, and pervaded by the strange smell of ancient air. Pardieu longed to be back in the freshness of nature, as he remembered it fondly from so long ago, but he knew he had to go on for he was almost there. He touched his pouch of magic spells, cupping his hand gently over The Eye of Timor, and with the other hand he grasped his sword, in case any monster should appear. Then suddenly, from above, he heard a terrible roaring and screeching that shook the very walls. He knew it was the dragon of the hill, and from the sound it had to be the greatest and most ancient of any dragon he had ever encountered. He stopped, waiting motionless and silent, until the dragon stopped its outcry and was still. Was this to be the final test The Great Hall had set for him—to kill this dragon? In spite of everything—his faith and his magic and the battles he had already won—Pardieu was afraid.

He walked on, careful and alert for danger. Here and there he saw signs that others had been in this place before him. Food had been eaten, bottles of wine drunk and tossed away empty. There were runes written on the walls; names perhaps of other searchers for the treasure. Surely that dragon above had the greatest treasure in all the world. A treasure such as his would feed and clothe many of the poor and needy. As for himself, Pardieu had no money left. He had spent his last coin yesterday, and if he had not had the fortune to have found this place at last he would be sleeping on the street with the evil Trolls, or begging, which he was loath to do. A Holy Man should beg for the unfortunates, not for himself. Still, he was hungry and thirsty, and he hoped he would come upon some other wanderer who might share his provisions with him.

He turned a corner and found himself in front of a cozy little nest made of paper and rags. A Man was sitting there, looking at him curiously. He was a distinguished-looking man—tall and thin with an aesthetic face and silver hair. He did not look like an enemy.

"Who are you?" the man asked.

"I am Pardieu the Holy Man," Pardieu said.

"I'm the King of France."

"Why, may I ask, are you here?" Pardieu asked respectfully.

"There are worse places," the King of France said. "What are you doing here?"

"I am on a quest."

"Aren't we all. I'm making some coffee. Care to have some?"

"Thank you," Pardieu said gratefully. "I would."

The King of France had set up some cooking things in his little corner, and he and Pardieu drank coffee together and talked. He also gave Pardieu some small cakes. "One of these days," the King of France said, "I'm going to leave this place. I say that every day. But then I don't go. Maybe tomorrow."

"Have you been here long?"

"Years."

"Have you ever seen the dragon?" Pardieu asked.

"Seen lots of them. Seen some you'll never see."

"The one above . . ." Pardieu asked. "Tell me of him."

"Stay away from up there," the King of France said. "They catch you, they throw you out. It's safe down here."

"But the dragon guards the treasure."

"Depends on how you feel about money."

"It's not for me," Pardieu said quickly. "It is for the poor."

"Then forget it. Why don't you go home?"

"I can't."

The King of France nodded understandingly.

That night some other wanderers began to come by, carrying bundles of provisions, and each went to a place which seemed to belong to him or her and prepared a nest to sleep in. Pardieu noticed they all slept very cautiously, trusting none of the others. He realized this was a kind of central meeting place, but no one discussed their plans or their quest even though they knew each other. Perhaps they had no quest. They were subterranean dwellers, that was all. He sighed. They might give him food or drink or company if he gained their trust, but they would never come along to aid him. They could not. He was destined to be alone . . . and perhaps that was as it should be.

The King of France was asleep, snoring softly. Pardieu rose to his feet and quietly slipped away. He remembered that the others had entered from a different branch of the maze than he had, and he thought there might be a way to the dragon's lair. All the pathways were dimly lit, and in some of them he came upon other wanderers, also asleep. It must be very late. The dragon was silent. Dragons slept too.

He found a door, and touched it carefully, listening to hear what might be on the other side. He was sure now that this was what The Great Hall wanted of him: to find the dragon where it lay and to enchant it and take the treasure. The dragon was evil, as all dragons were. Perhaps there were slaves that had to be freed. Pardieu kept his hand on his sword. He fervently prayed that he would not be forced to kill anyone or anything ever again, but if he had to kill the dragon he knew he would be forgiven. He opened the door and gasped.

There was a huge, beautiful room with a vaulted ceiling, like a room in a castle. It was empty. Long hallways led into dank tunnels that had the metallic smell of dragon's breath, and Pardieu knew the dragon was somewhere near. He walked down one of these, listening and sniffing, and then jumped lightly into a long narrow ditch that wound deeper into the dragon's lair. He was walking along a kind of metal track that seemed to go on forever. He suddenly realized that he had been walking ever since early that morning, with the exception of the short time he had stopped to rest and take refreshment with the King of France, and he was very tired. It was dark here, and quiet. He could take just a short rest, perhaps sleep. When the dragon awoke Pardieu would surely hear him. It was more prudent to deal with a dragon when you were not so exhausted as he felt now.

To be sure he was perfectly safe, Pardieu opened his vial that held his potion of invisibility. He drank half. That would ensure his invisibility for six hours, which was enough. He curled up next to the wall with his cloak around him, his head resting on one of the tracks, and was instantly and deeply asleep.

In his dream Pardieu heard the rumbling of the dragon, far away. He felt vibrating along the track where he had laid his head. Then he awoke and knew this was no longer the dream—the dragon was awake too, and nearby. Pardieu could hear him, coming closer.

He stood up, peering into the dark. Then he saw the great bright eyes of the monster, like lights, sweeping ahead to find danger. What a fearful racket! Pardieu rushed to the side of the tunnel and pressed himself against the wall as the dragon came thundering past him, screeching and clattering his iron scales, breathing great showers of fiery sparks. Never in his life had Pardieu seen a dragon as immense as this. He was terrified. It would take an army to kill this dragon; it would take a war. How vainglorious he had been to think he could do anything.

When the monster was gone Parideu climbed out of the ditch and ran on shaky legs back to the door that led to the safety of his underground maze. He felt sad and ashamed. He would stay here for a while and live like the others, sleeping underground in the quiet nights and begging on the streets during the day so he would not starve. And every day he would walk and look, waiting for The Great Hall to forgive him for the presumption of going out to kill the dragon unprepared—waiting for his next instructions. He knew that the next time he would be sent to do something that was possible.

CHAPTER SEVEN

It was May. In Greenwich everything was blooming with fresh new lushness. The sky was a clear sapphire-blue. People who had boats began taking them out on the water, white sails snapping smartly in the warm breeze. Robbie had been gone a month.

His absence had not brought his parents closer. Cat knew that happened in nice novels but not in real life. She and Hall had made tentative attempts to be kind to each other, because they had no one else now, but there was still too much blame between them. She wondered if stopping drinking would make her stop blaming Hall for her life, and him stop blaming her for the loss of his children. She doubted it. Not drinking would only make her stop talking about her pain, not stop thinking about it. The only difference was that Hall spent more time at home now, waiting for a phone call from Robbie that never came, and thus Cat was able to talk to him more. She wondered if he really listened.

Most of the time she talked to herself. Sometimes she spoke to the absent Robbie, the way she wished she could do if he were there. "I wanted you to be able to listen to music and look at the sunset," she

said to him. "I wanted you to do all the silly, romantic, quiet things I did when I was young. But you
don't have sunsets—you have war and riots and terror-
ists and threats of nuclear poisoning. You have crime
and drugs. We had implicit faith in money and the
future, and you have only fear. I couldn't keep the
world away from you . . . maybe I made it worse.
Did you hate coming home? Did you hate me? Did
you hate your father? I wasn't angry at you, just the
world. It wasn't your fault, Robbie. Did you think I
didn't love you?"

Now she had no doubt that Robbie had run away,
not been murdered. It still didn't mean that she
would ever see him again. Now that she knew from
the newspapers about the game he had been playing
with his friends she realized Robbie had run away
long before he actually disappeared physically. She
wondered who the other players had been. What kind
of families did they have? Was it their parents' fault,
or life's fault that they had to escape into a fantasy
world of invented terrors?

She and Hall subscribed to the New York, the
Greenwich, and the Pequod and Philadelphia papers.
Except for a few locally written articles expressing
new opinions about motivation, most of the news was
from the wire services and concerned the police inves-
tigation. It was fairly scanty now. Most of the leads
led to nothing. The only thing of significance was
that a truck driver named William Hansen saw Robbie's picture in the newspaper and told the police he
was sure that was the kid he had given a lift to on the
highway outside of Pequod, near the university. The
kid had been going east, so since Hansen was on his

way to New York he had dropped him off after the Holland Tunnel. So now the New York police were in on the case, and there was hope that Robbie hadn't gone into the caverns after all.

Reporters still phoned and came to the house to badger them. Cat and Hall always told them the same thing. "He was under pressure because of his grades. It was near final exam time. He had his extra-curricular activities—the swimming team and that game he liked to play with his friends—and he probably just wanted to get away for a while, somewhere quiet, to reevaluate his priorities."

Weren't they worried, the reporters asked. "Of course. What parents wouldn't be? We wish he would call us. We wish he would come home. We tried not to put pressure on him to get good marks. There is so much pressure today for young people anyway. We always thought he liked Grant."

That girl, Robbie's friend who had telephoned, never called again. Cat had forgotten her name. When the girl had called, Cat had been a bit drunk. If she could remember her name, she would call her . . . but what good would it do? The girl apparently hadn't even been able to tell much to the police.

The police said that if Robbie had gone into the caverns he most certainly would be dead by now. Cat had to believe he was somewhere in New York. Robbie knew New York, and liked it. He could get a menial job, dye his hair, and disappear. Cat refused to believe Robbie would take drugs or live on the street, any more than she could believe he had gone into the caverns to commit suicide. Self-destructiveness was not in Robbie's nature. Hall junior had been self-destructive. But not Robbie.

Robbie was normal. Cat had to believe that. Robbie was just upset.

CHAPTER EIGHT

Every day Pardieu walked the streets of the great city, searching, making his way back at night to the underground maze where he slept. His companions there had told him of a place where he could bathe, so he had no need of an inn. Other travelers refreshed themselves at that communal bathing place too, and it did not seem to frighten them when the dragon roared nearby. Sometimes they even rushed out to be eaten, as if they were under a spell. He remembered an adventure from long ago, when he had traveled to the kingdom of the evil Voracians, where Ak-Oga had eaten the flesh of his slaves, as this dragon-god did. Pardieu feared that in spite of his magic powers he too might fall under the same spell, and was relieved to learn from his new friends in the maze that there were other places where he could bathe where there were no dragons. After he had been walking the streets of the city for a while he even found some of these places himself. He was glad there were so many of them, for he disliked being dirty and unkempt. His beard and hair had grown longer now, and his face looked very thin. The people he passed on the street never gave him food, and hardly ever gave him coins, so he was often hungry. But he had enough food to

live, and that was all that mattered. Fasting was bene-
ficial for the spirit. Soon he would find The Great
Hall.

This was a city of strange contrasts. Pardieu passed
many places of sin, where voluptuous women danced
naked and men shrieked with lecherous glee to see
them. There was garbage tossed in the street, and
beggars rummaged through it for scraps of food. He
saw people in rags, and people in fine clothing.
There were many mutated Half-humans with vacant
eyes, singing in strange tongues or screaming in anger
at things only they could see. You could turn a corner
and find a street filled with horrors, and then turn
again and find quiet and peace, especially in the evening. Pardieu was often lonely, for no one he spoke
to seemed able to understand him, and often they appeared afraid of him, as if he would not forgive them
for their sins. At night he still dreamed of The Great
Hall, and that sustained him through his days of iso-
lation in the midst of dense, unfriendly crowds. All
this suffering was still part of his quest.

He had found a street where young boys and girls
waited until older men came to speak to them, and
then the older man and the young person would go
off together. It was the Street of Messages. Pardieu
took to waiting on that street at night, until his own
messenger would come. Sometimes a man would stop
to speak to him, but whenever Pardieu asked him if
he was his messenger at last the man would look at
him oddly and go away. Pardieu realized finally that
these exchanges took place in some kind of code, and
that he would have to learn it.

There was a lovely young Sprite who came to the
Street of Messages every night and who was the only

one who did not seem to fear him. She would look at him and laugh. Her laughter was like the sound of bells, her hair was long, blond, and silky, and she often wore trousers of velvet and shirts of gauze. She looked like a Princess of the Sprites. She was about thirteen years old in appearance, which meant she could be over a hundred in the Sprite world. That was not old for a Sprite. One night he approached her, praying she would not run away.

"I am Pardieu the Holy Man," he said.

She laughed. "I've been watching you," she said. "You're never going to get a john when you're stoned like that."

"I cannot speak your tongue," Pardieu said, confused and apologetic.

"Hey, man, don't shit me. You're ripped out of your head."

"What are these terrors you warn me of?"

She laughed again. "You're cute, and I have a weak spot for losers. Come on, I'll buy you a cup of coffee."

She took him into a brightly lit eating place where she bought him coffee and small cakes, and some for herself. She was beautiful and kind; the first who had befriended him in the city.

"Now listen," she said, leaning forward over the table that separated them. "There are leather queens and piss freaks and S and M's, but unless you get a real masochist weirdo nobody's going to want you like this. They think you've been smoking angel dust."

"Angel dust . . ." Pardieu said. "How beautiful that sounds."

"Yeah, well, smoke it after, not before. I'm not afraid of you, but I've got friends on this street and

I'm not going anywhere alone with you. Besides, I think you're harmless."

"I am harmless," Pardieu said, grateful to understand at least a small amount of what she was saying. "I am the highest level of Holy Man, and I would harm no one who is not evil."

"This is what you do," she said. "The john comes up and he says something like how much and you tell him, and keep your mouth shut from then on. If he asks your name or tries to make conversation, make up some name. Don't give him that Holy Man shit. How much do you get?"

"How much what?"

"How much money?"

"Very little," Pardieu said sadly.

"I noticed." She surveyed him carefully. "You're kind of old for these chicken hawks, but you *are* cute. Ask him for twenty."

"Twenty coins?"

"Twenty bucks, Par-doo. And don't tell him your name is Par-doo. Say you're Paul."

"Paul," Pardieu said. He nodded. "My name is Paul. Do I ask first or does he offer first?"

"Usually he asks." She laughed. "The small talk is not terrific on this street. Hey, did you ever read *Catcher in the Rye*?"

"No," Pardieu said.

"That was the last book I read before I left home. I loved it. This guy wants to stand in a field full of rye and catch little kids before they fall off a cliff. His only friend is a little girl. At the end he goes crazy and they put him away, but it's really kind of the world that's crazy. I don't know why being with you reminded me of that book just now. Oh, well."

"That was a fine tale," Pardieu said politely. "Thank you."

"Sure."

They went back to the Street of Messages and waited, several feet apart from each other, as was everyone, and soon her messenger came and she went away with him. As she walked away she tossed Pardieu an encouraging glance. He smiled back at her, filled with fellowship and pure love. He knew tonight was the night he would find his answer.

His messenger was an ordinary-looking, respectably dressed man. Pardieu was relieved to see that the look in his dark eyes was not of fear but only of discomfort and a kind of desperate nervousness. It was not Pardieu the messenger was afraid of.

"How much?" the messenger asked.

"Twenty bucks," Pardieu said.

The man nodded and began to walk. Pardieu walked along beside him. His heart was pounding with excitement and he longed to ask many questions, but he remembered he was to say nothing. Are we going to The Great Hall, he thought; at last? Are we?

"What's your name?" the messenger said, finally.

"Paul."

The messenger nodded again and did not reply. They walked to an old and very unpleasant-looking inn, dimly lit and grimy, where the man led the way up a flight of stairs and unlocked the door to a small room. In this room was a bed, a wooden chest, and a chair. It was lit from the outside by the brightly colored lamps that glittered in the street.

"I like it dark," the man said.

Pardieu waited.

The man began to disrobe then, removing his respectable clothing, and Pardieu wondered if underneath this disguise there would be armor or perhaps the raiment of some superior being. "Hurry up," the man said.

"Hurry up what?"

"Take your clothes off."

Why? Pardieu did not understand why he suddenly felt afraid. Where were they going with no clothing? He would not give up his pouch of magic spells, nor his sword, for without them he was helpless. He stood there, thinking perhaps he should obey, for he had waited so long for this messenger, and yet . . .

The messenger was almost naked now, and he only looked like a mortal man. In two swift steps he was across the room facing Pardieu, and he took hold of his robe. "Come on!" he said in a rough voice. Then, with no warning, he placed frantic hands on Pardieu's most private place, and when Pardieu looked at him in panic he saw that the man was fully aroused.

He had been tricked! This was no man, but a succubus, intent on rape. Pardieu knew of such things, and once a succubus entered your body you were in its power. He flung the spell of paralyzation, heart beating wildly now with fear. *The spell did not work!* How could this be possible? This was a most powerful demon indeed, but Pardieu had other charms, other spells. He gulped down the remainder of his potion of invisibility. The dragon had not seen him—nor would this succubus now. The succubus was holding him tightly, trying to place its mouth on him, determined to rape what it could feel but could not see. Pardieu was terrified. He twisted to get away from the demon's grasp, but the strength of his adver-

sary was greater than his own. Fasting and privation
had made him weak, and a succubus was a hundred
times stronger than even a healthy mortal.

Pardieu unsheathed his sword, and with a last
mighty rush of strength he pushed the sword into the
monster's chest.

He was let loose. The succubus's face distorted with
slack-mouthed fear, then pain, and then finally it
sank silently to the floor. It was dead. Pardieu turned
and ran away, out of that room, out of that vile inn,
out to the street, and as far as his shaking legs could
carry him.

Robbie found himself on the street—a strange
street, in a strange city, at night—and he did not
remember how he had gotten there. He caught a
glimpse of himself in a store window as he passed,
and he gasped. He had a little beard and mustache,
his hair was longer than usual, and his face was ema-
ciated. His eyes looked enormous. His jeans and
Windbreaker were filthy, and he could see that he
had tightened his belt to the tightest hold to keep his
jeans up. How long had he been out of it? Weeks?
Months? Where was he?

He looked at his watch. It was midnight. This was
the underbelly of some city: porno flicks, hookers,
junkies, everything garish and dirty. Then he recognized it. He was in New York. All the taxis had New
York license plates. He was on West Forty-second
Street, and he had had amnesia, and he was so
frightened he could not bear it.

He looked wildly for a phone. There was a pay
phone a few blocks on, and he looked through his
pockets for change. God, he didn't even have any

money, just a dime and a quarter. There was nothing in his wallet but his identification. He wondered if he had been robbed. There was blood all over his sleeve and the front of his jacket, as if it had spurted there, and it was still wet. Robbie touched himself gingerly, but nothing hurt, and he realized it was not his blood but someone else's. He had not thought the fear he felt could grow worse, but it did.

His fingers closed on the Boy Scout knife his father had given him years ago, which he always carried out of habit, and he drew it out of his pocket. He opened it. He didn't even have to open it to know. The handle as well as the blade was covered with blood.

Robbie closed his eyes and leaned against the side of the pay phone, feeling faint. He was starving; his stomach hurt. And he had stabbed somebody. Maybe he had even killed someone—he was out of breath as if he had been running. He knew he was crazy, and he began to cry.

In the booth he called Kate collect at college, unable to stop his convulsive sobs. Crazy, crazy, and maybe a murderer too . . .

She never answered. He looked up Daniel's number in his pocket address book and called him collect. He remembered now that Kate and Daniel were living together in Daniel's room. Why couldn't he remember what had happened to him since he left Grant? The last thing he remembered was Jay Jay's party.

"Hello?" Kate said. Her voice was soft with sleep.

"It's Robbie," Robbie said, still crying. The sound of her familiar voice wrenched his heart. He held on to the side of the pay phone so he wouldn't fall. "I'm in New York, and I think I killed somebody."

CHAPTER NINE

"Oh, Robbie!" Kate cried, holding the phone receiver tightly. "Are you all right?" She was completely awake immediately, but the joy of knowing he was alive blotted out—for an instant—the rest of what he had just said.

"Robbie?" Daniel asked excitedly.

She nodded. "Robbie, Robbie, speak to me! How are you? What happened?"

"I don't know how I am," Robbie said. "I don't remember anything. How long was I gone?"

"Almost . . ." She was going to say "almost six weeks," but then she realized it would scare him too much. "Almost a month," she said.

"I don't know why I can't remember," Robbie said. "There's blood all over my knife."

"What knife?" Kate asked. It occurred to her that he might be thinking of the sword in the game, and perhaps there was no bloody weapon at all.

"My Boy Scout knife," Robbie said. "And there's blood on my clothes, but it isn't mine."

"Go get Jay Jay, quick," Kate whispered to Daniel. "Robbie, where in New York are you?"

"In a phone booth on Eighth Avenue," Robbie

said. "I don't even have any money. Kate, I can't remember . . ."

"Did you call your parents?"

"I can't," Robbie said. "What am I going to tell them? They'll have questions and I don't have answers."

"Tell them you're alive and safe," Kate said. "They're so worried about you. We all were. The police in Pequod searched the caverns—they thought somebody murdered you."

"Do you think someone tried to kill me?" Robbie asked. "Is that why I had to stab him?"

Jay Jay came running into the room with Daniel, wearing his bathrobe. "Robbie!" he said, all excited. "Is he all right?"

Kate shook her head. "We'll come and get you," she said to Robbie. "Unless you want your parents—"

"No!" Robbie said, frightened. "Not my parents. I have to get my head together. I can't handle this."

Jay Jay and Daniel were listening, close together with Kate as she held the receiver so they could hear.

"I look like a seedy bum," Robbie went on. "Like I've been sleeping in the street. I don't even know what else I've done. I could have done anything."

"Keep calm," Kate said. She had the awful feeling she would lose him any minute, that he might hang up and vanish again. "It's all right, Robbie. We're here." She turned to Jay Jay. "Where can he go until we get there?"

"Covenant House," Jay Jay said, grabbing the receiver. "Look in the phone book and go to Covenant House. I know all about it because it's one of my mother's charities. They won't ask you any questions;

just if you're all right. They'll give you food and clothes and let you take a shower, and they'll let you sleep there free."

"Are the police after me?" Robbie asked. He sounded as timid and desperate as a lost child, and Kate wanted to put her arms around him and protect him from any more harm.

"Just for disappearing," she said, taking the receiver from Jay Jay. "Nobody's after you for anything bad. There's nothing to be afraid of."

"How do I know?" Robbie said.

Jay Jay took the receiver. "Listen, Robbie," he said. "When you get to Covenant House, tell them your name is Lionel Stander. That's so we'll know who to ask for when we come."

"Who's Lionel Stander?" Robbie asked.

"An old movie star. Okay?"

"Okay," Robbie said tentatively. "Kate?"

"I'm here," Kate said. She took the receiver.

"Kate . . ."

"What, Robbie?"

"Will you come get me?"

"Of course. We'll be there bright and early in the morning."

"Will you help me remember?"

"Yes," she said. What else could she say? She groped for something that would reassure him. "When you have a good meal and a night's sleep you'll feel a lot better."

"Maybe I shouldn't remember," Robbie said.

"Everything's going to be all right now, Robbie," Kate said. "You have us, and we'll stick together. You remember how we always used to do that?"

"Yes."

"Now you go where Jay Jay told you to, okay?"

"Okay."

"And then we'll come get you, okay?"

"Okay."

"And when you get there, you call your mother and say you're safe, and then you can just hang up. She won't know where you are. Okay?"

"Okay."

"Daniel says hello, and the three of us will help you through this, whatever it is. I promise. Everything's going to be all right."

"You won't tell the police?" Robbie asked, sounding panicked.

"No, don't worry. You can trust us."

"I'll see you tomorrow," Robbie said. "I have to get out of here now."

"We all love you, Robbie," Kate said. But he had hung up, and she wasn't even sure he had heard her.

Daniel looked at the clock next to the bed. "We should leave in an hour," he said. "We'll take your car. Where should we bring Robbie when we've gotten him?"

"My apartment," Jay Jay said. "My mother won't care. We have lots of room."

"And then what?" Daniel said.

"Then we find out if he really killed somebody," Kate said. She sat down on the bed, suddenly very sad. "I was so glad he was safe, but he really isn't safe at all, is he?"

"We'll have to take him to his family and they can get a psychiatrist," Daniel said. "It's not murder if he thought he was playing the game."

"Maybe we don't have to tell," Jay Jay said. "Maybe he's all right now."

Kate looked at him in surprise. "But the police will find out."

"People get killed every day in New York," Jay Jay said. "You never hear about it unless it's some kind of human interest story, or a famous person. Maybe it will be an unsolved crime."

"We can't just cover it up," she said.

"Why not? Nobody knows but us. Robbie doesn't even remember. He was supposed to be the victim in this affair."

"You're crazier than he is," Daniel said.

They argued about it all the way to New York in Kate's car. Jay Jay had insisted on taking Merlin, who hopped around in his cage looking very nervous. Jay Jay had abruptly gotten it into his head that if he left Merlin with his friend Perry, Perry would hurt him. The events of the night were getting to all of them.

"This could be the end of Robbie's whole life," Jay Jay said. "He won't be allowed back at school—he might even get put away in one of those places for the criminally insane."

"They'd never . . ." Kate said.

"It's a crime to cover up a crime, you know," Daniel said. "That's us."

"Suppose there isn't any crime," Kate kept saying.

"But suppose there is," Jay Jay would answer back.

"It wasn't his fault," Daniel said.

"Everything's always somebody's fault," Jay Jay said morosely.

"They'll kick us out of school too," Kate said.

"We're not going to tell them we know," Jay Jay said.

"I think everybody needs some sleep," Daniel said.

By the time the sun was up over the skyline of New York the three of them had arrived exhausted. They stopped to look up the address of Covenant House, and then they drove there and parked in a lot nearby, hoping no one would steal their suitcases out of the trunk. They had packed enough things for a few days, not knowing what they were going to do. The neighborhood was part lots, part slums. The large tan brick building looked like a prison, but there was a dove of peace painted on the side, which was reassuring. Jay Jay took Merlin with him.

They walked into a reception room with a few large chairs in it, and a gray-haired woman sitting behind a desk. Through a glass wall they could see a sort of lounge, with brightly patterned carpeting, leather sofas and chairs, and a color television set. There were a lot of kids sleeping on the sofas and chairs, and on the carpet, but none of them was Robbie. Most of them were black. They were all neatly dressed, in pressed jeans, T-shirts, and sneakers. Kate, Daniel, and Jay Jay marched up to the receptionist.

"We're here to see out friend Lionel Stander," Jay Jay said.

"This is the wrong entrance," the woman said. "You have to go around the block."

They went around the block to another reception room. This one had no lounge, and no residents were to be seen. The receptionist was much younger. "I'll have to get someone to find out," she said.

They waited. Finally a young woman came out of a

locked door and looked at them noncommittally. "I
don't know if he's here," she said. "Who should I tell
him wants to see him?"

"Kate, Daniel, and Jay Jay," Kate said. "He's expecting us."

"Wait here, please," the woman said, and went
away.

They waited for what seemed forever, but it was
only about twenty minutes. The woman returned.
"He's not here," she said.

"He might have said his name was Robbie
Wheeling," Kate said. Jay Jay glared at her warningly
and she glared back. She did not think this woman
was going to turn Robbie in to anybody like the cops.

"I'm sorry," the woman said. She really did seem
sorry. "He did come in . . . Lionel, that is . . .
and he said his friends were coming for him. But he
must have left. Maybe he'll come back."

Kate felt the fear begin again. "Did he say anything when he went away?" she asked. Don't let him
be Pardieu again . . . please!

"The last time I saw him he'd had a big meal and
taken a shower," the woman said kindly. "We gave
him some clothes, and he asked for a toothbrush and
we gave it to him. He was tired and he didn't want to
talk, so then he went to bed. I guess he got up very
early."

Holy Men get up very early, Kate thought. They
have to say their morning prayers. Robbie would
have been tired; Robbie would have slept. Pardieu
would have gotten up.

"How could he just go?" Kate asked desperately.

"The kids go and come all the time," the woman
said. "Maybe he forgot you were coming."

"He would never forget," Kate said.

He's Pardieu, she thought. He's Pardieu again and he's gone. She knew Daniel and Jay Jay were thinking the same thing.

"We'll come back later," Daniel said. "Please tell him we were here and we'll come again this afternoon."

Jay Jay wrote down his home number. "Please give him this," he said, and handed it to the woman.

"I'm sorry you missed your friend," she said kindly, as if she thought Robbie was perfectly normal, just like anybody else, or at least as normal as an unreliable street kid could be. She hadn't even been fazed by the presence of Merlin. Kate thought nothing could surprise this woman anymore, and she wondered if even Pardieu could have—but she was not about to ask.

Exhausted and miserable, they went to Jay Jay's apartment. His mother had already gone to work, but the maid seemed pleased to see them and showed Kate and Daniel to the guest room. Kate had never seen such a beautiful apartment, except in magazines. Everything, even the personal objects like a book and some unfinished needlepoint, seemed placed where they were by design, not because anyone actually lived there. If you put people in this apartment, with their everyday mess, it would destroy the whole effect. It was luxurious and glamorous, but entirely without a heart. Jay Jay's room looked like a movie set, but he seemed to like it.

They sat in the kitchen while the cook made French toast and freshly squeezed orange juice for them. They were all too tired to talk, even to think.

"We'll sleep awhile and then we'll go back," Daniel said.

Kate and Jay Jay nodded. They didn't know what they would do if Robbie wasn't there.

CHAPTER TEN

Robbie wasn't there when the three of them went back to Covenant House that afternoon, and although they waited until dinner they realized he might not be coming back for a long time. They would have to take matters into their own hands. Jay Jay automatically took charge of the search. New York was his city—he had lived here all his life—and it belonged to him in much the same limited way the caverns had been his. Daniel and Kate had been here before as tourists, but they didn't know the special places.

He and Kate and Daniel knew now that Robbie was definitely Pardieu again. Jay Jay called the apartment and told the help that if Robbie phoned they should invite him over immediately, not be put off if he looked crummy, and be nice to him. Now it was a question of logic.

They walked down the street, thinking what a big city this was. If someone was wandering aimlessly in New York you couldn't ever find him. He would have to have a pattern, and who knew what Pardieu's mind would choose? Jay Jay stopped at a men's store and bought a Sherlock Holmes hat. Wearing it made him feel a little better.

"If The Great Hall is a person," Jay Jay said, "then The Two Towers is a place. Unless they're two people."

"Robbie only had one brother," Kate said.

"I bet it's the World Trade Center," Jay Jay said. They ran down the street and darted into a cab, leaving two furious shoppers standing on the curb cursing them.

The rush-hour traffic was slow and noisy. The meter kept ticking at an alarming rate. "We should have taken the subway," Daniel said.

"We'd get lost," Jay Jay said. "I never take the subway. I hate the subway."

"We have to get into Pardieu's head," Kate said. "Where would he go when he got to the World Trade Center?"

"Hang around in front and wait for The Great Hall to meet him?" Jay Jay said.

"Let's hope so," Daniel said morosely.

The two towers rose up ahead of them, dwarfing everything else by comparison. They were so enormous the three of them didn't know where to begin to look. They walked around outside and then went in and scrutinized the lobby and restaurants. The hundreds and hundreds of office workers were hurrying home, away, except for people who were meeting for drinks after work. Robbie was nowhere to be seen.

"No one would let him into an office," Daniel said. "Not acting like Pardieu. He has to be in the street somewhere."

They wandered around the nearly empty streets. The sun had set and the arc lights were on. The caverns between the buildings in the downtown business area, now deserted, made Jay Jay feel as if they were sailing between icebergs. What must it seem like to Robbie? They kept turning corners hoping to find him; the tall, lean, familiar figure with blond hair.

"Let's go back to the World Trade Center and go up to the top and have a drink," Jay Jay said finally.

The bar at the top, Windows on the World, was so high up that they might have been in an airplane. It was a large room with windows that reached from floor to ceiling, affording a view of the entire city and the nearby boroughs. Millions of lights twinkled below them—from buildings, on bridges, from street-lights—a veritable maze. How could you even begin to find somebody? They sat at a small table in front of one of the huge windows, and Jay Jay ordered Bellinis for all of them. He had his fake identification at the ready, as always, so he would be served.

"This is champagne and fresh peach juice," he told his guests. "It was invented in Venice, where I plan to go some day before it sinks into the sea."

Kate took a sip. "It's to die," she said rapturously. "And look at that view!" Then she looked sad again. "I shouldn't be sitting here enjoying this while he's out there."

"It's a pit stop," Jay Jay said. "We have to eat and drink, don't we? I, personally, am starving." An Oriental chef was performing flamboyantly at the hors d'oeuvres bar in the corner. Jay Jay ordered sushi for all three of them. He hadn't had sushi in ages.

"I'm not eating that," Kate said.

"Why not?"

"Raw fish?"

"You'll love it," Jay Jay said.

She tasted it gingerly and shrugged. "It's not so terrible."

Daniel was very quiet, deep in thought. "When I was on the subway," he said, "there was a map on the wall of all the routes, and it looked exactly like a maze. What if Robbie's riding the subway?"

"Then we'll have to," Kate said.

"Not at night," Jay Jay said. "We'll get mugged."

"There are less people at night," Daniel said. "He'd be easier to find. Also less trains."

Jay Jay ordered another round and lit one of his thin brown cigarettes. He was terrified of the subway. He would rather go into the caverns alone than have to go there. But at least there were three of them, and Daniel was big. And Kate knew karate. He sighed. He felt like the condemned man eating his last favorite meal.

"We'll protect you," Kate said.

"Thanks a lot."

Jay Jay paid the bill with the credit card his mother had gotten him on the family plan, and they left.

They rode uptown on the subway, walking through the cars, looking for Robbie. Jay Jay kept glancing around looking for potential maniacs. Would Robbie think the graffiti on the walls was familiar? Would he think it was runes? Someone had scrawled in black: MURDER, MURDER, DEATH, DEATH. "Maybe Robbie got mugged on the subway," Jay Jay said. "Maybe that's who he stabbed—the mugger."

They changed trains and kept riding. Now there were very few people, and although most of them looked normal, Jay Jay could hardly wait to get out of there. He kept expecting a gang with switchblades to come rushing on at every stop, like a bunch of Gorvils.

"We'll never find him here," Kate said finally. "This is crazy."

"Let's go home and see if he called," Jay Jay said, relieved.

They went back to the apartment. No one had called, and when they telephoned Covenant House they were told that Lionel Stander a.k.a. Robbie Wheeling had not appeared. The apartment seemed peaceful and safe after the streets. Jay Jay's mother was out, as usual. Jay Jay fed Merlin, and then he and Kate and Daniel went into the kitchen and tried to make Bellinis in the blender. The Bellinis didn't taste bad at all, and they brought a pitcherful of them into his wonderful room while they planned a list of places where they would look for Robbie.

"The Cloisters," Jay Jay said. "It's a former monastery. We have to go there first thing tomorrow."

"On the subway," Daniel said. "It's like roulette—a wild chance but you never know."

To that they added Times Square, because Robbie had been there before; famous churches; and the Lower East Side, because parts of it were right out of another, ancient time, and Jay Jay had an instinct about this. They could stay in New York only ten days, and then they had to go back to school to take their Final Exams.

"I hope he's not sleeping in the street," Kate said. "I can't even stand to think of it."

"Maybe it would be better for him if the police did find him," Daniel said. "At least he'd be—"

"No!" Jay Jay said. "He's ours." He was astonished at the vehemence of his response. He had never admitted closeness with anybody, too afraid of being rejected—*used* to being rejected—and for a moment he was worried that Kate and Daniel might laugh at him. But Kate had tears in her eyes.

"He *is* ours," she said softly. "And when we find him we must never, never play the game again. You realize that, don't you? None of us can. Let's take a vow."

"I don't have to promise," Daniel said. "I don't even want to think about that game after this is over."

"I swear anyway," Jay Jay said. He felt abandoned, as if part of the good luck charm that had made him popular, even loved, with slipping out of his grasp. M & M had been more than a game, it had been his way of having friendships. But he did have friends, didn't he? Kate and Daniel . . . and Robbie when they found him . . . would still like him and want to do things with him, wouldn't they? He wasn't so sure. Their whole friendship was based on the game.

Kate and Daniel got up to go to bed. "See you in the morning," they said to Jay Jay.

"Everybody up at seven," Jay Jay said.

"Fecalite," Merlin said.

"Not you, lazy pig," Jay Jay said to him.

Jay Jay watched Kate and Daniel go down the hall to the guest room, go in, and shut the door. It was a strange feeling. He'd known he wouldn't like it, and he didn't. He wasn't exactly jealous anymore; Kate and Daniel had been living together so long in the dorm, on his very floor, that he was used to it, but . . . this was his apartment, his turf, and his loneliness was more poignant here because it was in his own home. He wondered how many years he would have to wait until he got old enough to be interesting to anybody—not as a trickster or an eccentric, but like Daniel was.

He went into his bathroom and brushed his teeth, and put in his hated dental retainer. It was a good thing he didn't have a girl friend; imagine having to sneak that thing into your mouth at night! That would be the end of romance.

"Good night, beloved Merlin," Jay Jay said. He put the cover on Merlin's cage and went to bed.

The next morning the three of them took the subway uptown and went to The Cloisters, wandering through the beautiful gardens and walking through the old stone halls that monks had trod in silent contemplation so long ago. It seemed such a perfect place for Pardieu that Jay Jay was surprised and disappointed not to see him turning a corner to greet them, complete to his rough brown robe. Instead a group of Japanese tourists came by chattering, taking photographs of each other.

They took the subway back downtown and meandered through the Lower East Side, where everything you could imagine was sold from pushcarts on sidewalks. Old men in long black robes, hats, and full beards and *payess* walked by talking their own language. Would Robbie feel at home here, or out of place? Kate bought a necklace of green glass beads, and then they took the subway back uptown again. Jay Jay was getting more used to the subway and hoped their luck would hold out and no one would attack them. They were very hungry by then, so they stopped at Central Park where they bought shish kebabs and pita bread stuffed with salad from a sidewalk vendor, and went into the park to eat them on a bench. It was a perfect spring day, soft and gentle.

Small children ran around on the paths, and sweaty joggers came puffing through the trees on their way home. People were walking around carrying loud radios playing rock or salsa. It was all so normal. In spite of themselves the three of them were having sort of a good time—it made them feel guilty, but they couldn't help it.

"Let's go to the zoo," Kate said. "Just for a minute. It's right here."

They went to the Central Park Zoo and watched the seals playing. "I love seals," Kate said. "If I had a million dollars and could have any pet I wanted, I'd get a seal."

"He'd be lonely," Daniel said.

"I'd get him a mate."

"What would you get, Daniel?" Jay Jay asked.

"Monkeys," Daniel said. "I love monkeys."

"We don't have to ask Jay Jay what he'd get," Kate said. "He has it."

They went to the monkey house. "That one there looks just like Perry," Jay Jay said.

"Exactly!" Kate squealed. They all laughed.

They went back to the apartment to see if there were any calls, but there weren't. They wanted to have dinner in Chinatown, but they were too tired from all that hiking. They decided to go the next day; in fact, spend the whole afternoon in Chinatown. They added it to their list.

When the week was over they had been everywhere they could think of to go, including the Metropolitan Museum, where they went to see the medieval artifacts, including armor and weapons. It didn't seem any unlikelier a place for Pardieu to be than any other they'd tried. Jay Jay took Kate and Daniel to the Museum of Modern Art to see a couple of old movies he was fond of, and they took him to Times Square to see a really gross porn film because none of them had ever seen one. They made him sit between them because he looked so young they were afraid some pervert might bother him. Jay Jay was rather moved—they really did care about him. In return he took them on the Staten Island Ferry, even though it was corny, and then Daniel insisted on riding on the Roosevelt Island Tramway because it looked interesting. One night they went to a disco.

The three of them were having dinner in a little Italian restaurant they'd found in Greenwich Village, talking and laughing and joking, when Jay Jay realized what had happened. This week was the first time the three of them had done anything together that wasn't in some way connected to the game. Even the parties they'd had, like last Christmas, had been only token celebrations culminating in a game session. They had started the week in New York looking for Robbie, trying even though they knew it was almost definitely hopeless, and they were ending the week as good friends having fun together. They still worried about Robbie and felt heartless and guilty for enjoying themselves . . . but it had happened anyway.

The odyssey they had just been through had been their transition to real life. They didn't need the game to be friends, or for anything else. Maybe they had once, but they didn't need it now.

"Next term," Jay Jay said, "I'm going to join the drama group and direct a play. Something morbid, with lots of props. *Hamlet* maybe, or *Macbeth.*"

"They could really use you," Kate said.

"They sure could," Daniel said.

His friends.

That night when they went back to his apartment and Kate and Daniel went to their room to go to bed, Jay Jay wasn't jealous at all. He could see they really loved each other, and they seemed right for each other. He even hoped it would last forever. If they got married he would give a fantastic bachelor party for both of them.

The phone next to his bed rang sharply in the dark, waking him up. Jay Jay groped for the receiver groggily. "Unhh . . ."

"It's Robbie," Robbie's voice said. "I'm at Covenant House. You said you would come and get me."

"Robbie!" He was wide-awake. "Stay there! Stay there! We're on the way."

When Jay Jay, Kate and Daniel ran into the reception room they were not prepared for what Robbie looked like. No matter what he'd said he had been through, he looked worse. He was skinny, as if he had been starving, and there were sores on his face. He had a scraggly mustache and beard, and his hair hung in his eyes. They could even have walked right past him in the street and not have recognized him. But the sweetness in his face was Robbie's, and the sanity in his eyes was real.

They flung themselves on him, their wounded warrior, and bore him off to Jay Jay's apartment in relief and joy.

"They said I was at that place once before," Robbie said. "Is that true?"

CHAPTER ELEVEN

Robbie stayed with his friends at Jay Jay's New York apartment for three days. He wasn't so frightened anymore about having flipped out, because they kept telling him it was all right. He remembered bits and pieces: Jay Jay's party at school; calling them from Times Square, terrified because he didn't know how he'd gotten there; and waiting for them at the refuge they'd sent him to. He could tell from looking at himself in the mirror that he'd been through a lot, but Kate and Daniel and Jay Jay kept telling him over and over that anyone who'd been living on the streets without money for as long as he had was lucky to be alive at all. He knew that was true, and he began to realize that perhaps Hall was dead. If Hall had taken on another identity and was leading a normal life he would have written or called. No . . . Hall really was gone forever. It was so painful to accept that Robbie felt numb instead of grieved, but he was starting to accept it.

He had called his parents the minute he arrived at Jay Jay's. His father had answered, and had actually begun to cry. Robbie was surprised.

"I didn't do it on purpose," he told his father. "I

didn't want to hurt you and Mom—I just had to take off for a while."

His friends had told him what to say.

"Look," Daniel said, "you were under unbearable pressure at school. It's always hard the first year; college is so different from high school. And you were on the swimming team, and we all played the game too much."

He hadn't told his parents where he was the first time he called. His friends insisted he get his head together first, just in case other people upset him by asking too many questions too fast. Robbie agreed. He didn't want to disappoint his parents any more than he already had. *Pressure* was the operative word. His parents used it to him, and Robbie used it back to them. Demands . . . career choices to be made, schoolwork, and of course the emotional tensions of his broken romance with Kate. He and Kate had been too young and too rushed for big decisions, and Robbie realized that when he mentioned "a difficult love affair" people immediately responded with understanding and sympathy. He didn't feel sorry for himself, and he and Kate were the best of friends now, but it was so easy to say that love had been one of the things that had pushed him over the edge. In fact, she had suggested he might offer it as a contributing factor to his flight from school.

The second day, after spending every waking moment with Kate and Daniel and Jay Jay, Robbie called his parents and told them where he was. They wanted to come to get him immediately, but he told them he was afraid of reporters—it was too soon, and he was so tired. His mother wanted him to see a doctor, but Robbie said there was no need. He felt fine, just tired, and he didn't want to discuss where he'd been and what he'd done. His friends would drive him to Greenwich the next day. That was better, wasn't it? He'd already seen the newspapers, and there was an item about him. It said he'd called his parents and was "safe in an unidentified place." There was also his old high school yearbook picture in the paper, next to the story, and he was afraid his parents would be shocked and upset when they saw how much he had changed. He didn't tell them about the sores on his face, and with good food and a lot of vitamins they were going away.

"Should I leave the beard?" he asked his friends.

"I like it," Kate said. "It's sexy."

"Then I'll definitely keep it," Robbie said, pleased and embarrassed at the compliment. He felt he had been starving for the kindness and love of his friends for such a long time he wondered how he had been able to survive. What could he have expected to find out there on his flight?

"What am I going to do about exams?" Robbie asked, worried.

He wouldn't flunk out or even have to take makeup courses. His parents had called the school, and he could take the exams in the fall. Apparently he hadn't been the first person to panic and run from the pressures.

Pressures.

He would be given another chance.

Daniel and Kate and Jay Jay kept asking him what he remembered from those lost seven weeks. He didn't remember anything. That was the frightening thing—not being able to remember—but they told him over and over that it would be all right. Perhaps,

Daniel suggested, when Robbie was home for the summer he might see a psychiatrist to help him deal with all this. Then when he went back to Grant in the fall he would be stronger, and better able to handle whatever came up. Of course, they all agreed, none of them would ever play the game again.

Yes, Robbie thought, a psychiatrist was a good idea. You couldn't pick up your life after having blanked out and expect everything to be the same. He couldn't imagine what he'd be able to tell a psychiatrist. He didn't even have any interesting dreams. Maybe he could be hypnotized and that would help. It made him feel safer, in any case, to know there would be someone professional to talk to about all this.

He liked Jay Jay's apartment; and Jay Jay's mother, whom he'd seen twice for just a minute each time, was so young and pretty he couldn't believe she had a son in college. When Robbie told her, she had laughed and said she had found Jay Jay on the doorstep.

"She only kept me because I was in a Gucci box," Jay Jay said.

It was strange, Robbie thought, to realize that other people had unhappy home lives too, and never talked about it. For some reason he had supposed he was the only one. Poor Jay Jay. His own childhood had been much better than Jay Jay's, even with the fighting. At least he hadn't been all alone.

"I wish I could make this up to you," Robbie told his friends.

"Make what up?" Jay Jay said.

"I mean, coming to get me, and sticking with me now . . ."

"Robbie," Kate said, "your problem is you never understand your worth. You're a wonderful person.

We care about you. You always do things for everybody, and you never ask for anything for yourself."

"Is that true?" He was so pleased to have all these
compliments that he felt a glow of genuine pleasure.
He'd always thought he was the dull, average one,
tagging along behind them, being allowed to share in
their game and their lives, and it hadn't occurred to
him that his presence actually *added* anything to
their lives.

Jay Jay's mother's apartment was enormous, and
Robbie had his own room, but Jay Jay and Daniel
took turns staying in it with him at night "for company." Robbie knew they were watching him, afraid
he might flip out again. He didn't think he ever
would. The pressures were over, weren't they? College
was over. The game was over. He would have all that
free time this summer, just to recuperate and relax.

But he liked having someone with him at night. It
was cozy. Robbie decided it wasn't too dreadful to be
a little bit selfish just for a few days. After all, he'd
been sick. And sometimes, when he let himself think
about the enormity of having amnesia for such a long
time, it really did terrify him.

The third day, Kate, Daniel, and Jay Jay drove
Robbie up to Greenwich to his parents. His mother
cried, this time, and both his mother and father
hugged and kissed him. His friends stayed for dinner
and then they had to drive back to Grant to take
their Final Exams. They all wished each other luck
and promised to see each other soon. The extraordinary thing was that his mother was hardly drunk at
all.

That night she came into his room and sat on the
foot of his bed. She hadn't done that since he was a

little kid when he'd screamed out after a nightmare.

"I'm so thankful you're back," she said.

"I'm glad to be back," he said. He wasn't sure that was true, but he knew she would like to hear it.

"I won't ask you any questions if you don't want me to," she said. "But there will be reporters. You don't have to talk to them. I'll be here every minute and I'll keep them away."

"Thanks," Robbie said gratefully.

"And . . ." She gave him a wan smile. "I know how much you always hated my drinking. I'm going to stop. I'm going to try to stop—okay?"

He was moved. "That would be . . . that would be really terrific, Mom."

"We'll both get well this summer," she said.

CHAPTER TWELVE

Robbie Wheeling's safe return revived the story of his disappearance, and, as expected, reporters arrived at the Wheeling home to find out what had happened. Robbie's parents spoke for him. He was, they said, having a well-deserved rest after what was naturally an ordeal, and would prefer to let the whole matter vanish into the past. There were tremendous tugs and pulls on any young person starting college—the question of career, the battle for good grades, the search for his own identity, the distractions of romance. He had been upset over the end of a relationship with a girl, his parents said, and he had been worried about Final Exams. He had left school to clear his head, reestablish his priorities. It was much the same thing they had been saying all along.

In the newspaper articles that were written about his escapade, the reporters reminded their readers that what had made the story so interesting at first had been the belief that Robbie had met with foul play because of a game. Mazes and Monsters was a popular game on the Grant campus, as it was in other schools, but one particular group of players had gone too far, taking it from their rooms to the forbidden caverns near the college. All the publicity had done a great deal for sales of the game, but the game had turned out to be a false lead. Mazes and Monsters had nothing to do with Robbie's mysterious adventure—if indeed it had been an adventure at all.

A photographer did manage to take one picture of Robbie, as he was leaving the house to get into a car. You could see how handsome he was, and of course that sold more papers. Robbie's parents said that he was certainly expecting to go back to Grant again in the fall, where his friends would be waiting eagerly to see him.

On the commuter train to New York from a suburb not far from where Robbie and his family lived, a man named James Herman looked at Robbie's picture in the newspaper and his jaw tightened in anger. He felt a little fear too, and a great sense of irony. His shoulder still hurt from where he had been stabbed, and even though the stitches were out there was an ugly fresh red scar. He was lucky he hadn't been killed. It was hard to tell from a newspaper photo, and it had been a while, but he was positive this "nice" Robbie Wheeling was the hustler who'd tried to kill him the night he'd been cruising. No wonder the kid wouldn't talk about where he'd been and what he'd been doing. Wouldn't that be a shock for the parents!

James Herman sighed and tried to relax. Life was shit, and there wasn't much left you could believe in. He had two kids of his own, teen-agers, and he hoped he was bringing them up well. He had a responsible, well-paying job in a big company, a bright wife, a comfortable home complete with swimming pool. There was also a dark side to his nature—the compulsion to seek out young men in degrading places for sex—but no one knew it. No one ever would. He had not gone back to Times Square again, and when the need struck him he would go somewhere safer; perhaps hire a professional call boy.

He didn't know what had turned him into the kind of man he was: a respectable, well-meaning citizen with one fatal flaw. He didn't know what had turned that privileged college student into a knife-wielding junkie. He worried about his own children. He worried about the whole damn world.

The only thing he wasn't worried about was that goddamn Wheeling kid. Robbie Wheeling's secret would stay just that. Let the parents find out for themselves.

CHAPTER THIRTEEN

Kate went home after college was over, to see her family and get ready for the trip to Europe she was going to take with Daniel and Jay Jay at the end of June. The three of them had not only passed their exams but gotten good marks, and her father was in an expansive mood because of his new baby daughter and had agreed right away to pay for Kate's share of the expenses. There were some things she had to sort out in her mind before she left, and she needed this quiet time at home to think.

First of all, there was Daniel, and what would happen after college. He would be a senior next fall, and they had to make plans. He had been the one to bring it up. When he graduated and she was a Senior at Grant he would get a job in the East so they could spend weekends together. Then they would live together, and if it worked out . . .

Marriage. She was still afraid of it. She had seen too many marriages fall apart, especially her own mother's, and there was so much pain. If it was marriage to Daniel she supposed it would have more of a chance than most, but having Daniel and then losing him was too awful to think about. He knew she was afraid of getting married and told her not to be; he wouldn't push it. They could see how things went. Daniel was always so reasonable. Maybe she shouldn't worry about what would happen. Two years was far away. Maybe she should talk to her mother.

Her mother was in her bedroom studying, having decided to take courses right through the summer so she could get her law degree faster. Kate knocked on the door. "Mom? Can I bother you for a minute?"

"You're not bothering me, you're rescuing me," her mother said. "I was getting a headache." She patted the bed. "Sit down."

Kate found a place among the books and papers. "You know I told you all about Daniel."

"The paragon." Her mother smiled. "I can hardly wait till I meet him."

"Well, the problem is," Kate said, "he wants to marry me someday."

"Why is that a problem? You have to marry somebody. It might as well be somebody perfect you adore."

"But I don't *have* to marry somebody. Maybe I'll never get married. Let me ask you a question, and tell me the truth. When Dad left, were you ever sorry you'd gotten involved with him in the first place?"

"I suppose once in a while when I was very angry. But no . . . I wasn't. Whatever we had that was good was worth it. We had you and Belinda. And we had some very happy years."

"When you were my age, if you'd had any idea that things would work out the way they did . . . or that they could . . . would you still have taken the chance?"

Her mother looked at her in surprise. "Of course! You'll never have any life at all if you're always protecting yourself against some future disappointment. Life is risk. Loving somebody makes you vulnerable. That's the way it is. But it also makes you feel alive. If you don't make commitments you'll miss half the fun."

"Commitments can be broken," Kate said glumly.

"And people can die. A lot of things can happen. But you can't hide because the sky might fall down. After all, suppose the sky doesn't fall down? What a waste, huh?"

Kate laughed. "I suppose so."

"There is one thing that's worse than being a romantic," her mother said. "And that's not being one. Believe me, we romantics are not going to become extinct if I have anything to say about it."

"I really love you," Kate said. "Even though you're a nut."

"Yes, well, speaking of nuts, you have to visit your father and see his new baby, and you have to bring a present, so I bought one because I knew you wouldn't. It's a pink bear, and it's on the dresser in that box."

"You bought a present for *his* baby?" Kate said.

"No," her mother said sweetly, "you did."

That was the second thing Kate had to settle—how she would feel about her half sister Laurie. You couldn't dislike a little infant, but her father's sex life had always made her vaguely uncomfortable, and although she had been able to put it out of her mind, seeing the living product of it might be strange. She decided to visit him the next day, to get it over with. Belinda had already been, and he had called twice, and he'd been unexpectedly nice about paying for Europe . . .

The den in her father's house was now a baby's

room. All the paraphernalia of a new life was there: the crib with mobiles dangling over it, the Bathinette, the mountain of soft toys. Kate remembered that for a while she had been afraid her father and Chlorine were going to turn the guest room into the baby's room and push her and Belinda out of his world. Sleeping on the couch in the den was not exactly conducive to frequent overnight visits. She realized she'd been expecting the worst so it wouldn't jump up and surprise her, and she'd been unfair. Her mother was right; sometimes the sky didn't fall. And besides, she hardly ever came to visit anyway, and would even less now that she had her own life.

"I'm nursing," Chlorine said.

Of course you are, Kate thought. It would be a waste of those enormous tits not to. "Can I pick her up?"

"Oh, please do."

Kate reached into the crib and took out the tiny, light creature, protecting the unexpectedly heavy downy head in her hand. The baby opened her eyes and looked at her. "Hi, Laurie," Kate said.

Her sister . . . It was an odd feeling to look at this little thing and realize they were sisters. Kate was old enough to be the baby's mother; she was nineteen now. She would have her own baby with Daniel someday. And maybe when Laurie was older they would all be friends. She suddenly felt a part of the circle of life: someone's child, holding another child, knowing she was finally an adult.

Jay Jay was inspecting his summer wardrobe, trying to decide how much would fit into a backpack, and what he could possibly live without. He decided to take an additional canvas bag in his hand anyway. There would be hats to be bought, and other souvenirs, and he would need something to carry them in. He was so happy about the prospect of his trip to Europe with his friends that he felt stoned. He had arranged to leave Merlin in his mother's apartment in the care of the cook, who was very fond of Merlin and said he was brighter than some people she knew. Jay Jay was sure quite a few of those people had passed through his mother's kitchen.

"Will you miss me, Merlin?" Jay Jay asked. "We've never been separated this long."

"Poor Jay Jay," Merlin said.

"No, lucky Jay Jay. I am going to become a world traveler, and I'll tell you all about it when I come home."

His mother tapped gently at his bedroom door. She was dressed for the evening, in something white and cool. "Darling?"

"Maman! C'est vous."

"If I'm your *maman*, you can call me *tu*," she said. "My little boy! I can't believe you're all grown up, going off to Europe with your friends. I almost feel like a crone. It's a good thing I had you when I was so young. Next thing you know, I'll be ready for some face work. How depressing. Anyway, I brought you a list." She handed him a white envelope.

"What's this?" Jay Jay said.

"Names and addresses of people to call when you're in Europe," she said matter-of-factly. "My friends. Nobody goes to Europe without a list."

Her friends? Jay Jay didn't know whether to be touched or laugh at the irony of it. She had never let him see any of her friends socially here in New York,

but when he went to Venice, Rome, Paris, London
. . . He couldn't imagine what her foreign friends
would be like, but he was sure he didn't want to meet
them. He was going to meet Daniel's friends, and
Kate's friends, who would all be traveling too and
were much more suitable for someone his age with
his life.

"I wrote to them," his mother said.

"You did?"

"I couldn't have you springing on them out of the
blue. They know you might call. You don't have to if
you're too busy, but you might want to."

"Well, thank you," Jay Jay said. He decided to be
touched. He wasn't going to call them anyway. On
the other hand, suppose some of them were really exotic . . . wouldn't it be great to show them off to
Kate and Daniel! "Do any of them have a castle?" he
asked.

"Yes," she said. "Actually, a few of them do." She
looked with disapproval at the clothes he had spread
out on his bed. "And they dress for dinner."

"Oh."

"You still have a week, you can buy something decent." She blew him a kiss and was gone.

Jay Jay opened the envelope and looked at the list,
neatly printed in his mother's perfect hand. He
wished she'd put an asterisk next to the ones who had
castles. He also wished Robbie could have come with
them. That would have made the trip complete. But
Robbie wasn't ready yet for anything that strenuous,
and besides, he was seeing a psychiatrist every day.

A picture flashed into his mind of Robbie's father,
the last day of school when everyone was rushing to
get out and Mr. Wheeling had come up to drive Rob-

bie's car home and to pack his things. Robbie's father had seemed so normal—a typical successful businessman type—not a bit like the fecalite. Mr. Wheeling was exactly what Jay Jay would have pictured to have an all-American son like Robbie, and look what had happened. He looked sad and worn, as if he were still surprised at the unexpected event that had shaken his life. There was only a moment to speak during the end-of-year exodus, but Robbie's father had said to come visit when he was near Greenwich, and Jay Jay had said they all certainly would; he and Kate and Daniel, who would be coming to New York at the end of June.

"Europe will be a good learning experience for you," Daniel's father said. Daniel and his parents were having a leisurely Sunday breakfast in the kitchen of their house in Brookline. Everything in the yard was blooming. You could see it from the kitchen window—what his mother called her "accidental garden"—flowers and vegetables all growing together in a haphazard way. Years ago, when Daniel and Andy were little, they had planted radish and carrot seeds in among her roses, and thus it had remained, with new additions each year.

"And you'll have fun," his mother said. "I think people should do everything they can that's interesting and fun while they still have the chance."

"The chance is never over," his father said.

"Oh, you know what I mean. While he's young and free."

She's talking about Kate and me, Daniel thought. She still likes to think Kate is just a romance that will go away. He didn't tell her that he and Kate had discussed the future: let his mother get used to Kate first. Daniel knew she would. When he'd told his parents that he wanted to go to Europe this summer with Kate and Jay Jay and had asked them for the money, they had agreed right away. He'd gotten three A's and a B plus on his final exams, and his parents were pleased that he had worked so hard. That was another thing they didn't know . . . that he hadn't really worked very hard at all. He thought how many secrets had been kept from them through the years; some the inevitable process of his growing up and separating from them, others through his need to keep the peaceful equilibrium of their home intact. Perhaps if he had told them about the game they would have understood.

"Venice, Rome, Paris, London . . ." his mother said. "Eurail passes, student hostels . . . what energy you three have!"

"We never met Jay Jay," his father said. "He's the gourmet, isn't he?"

"I guess you could call him that," Daniel said. How could he explain Jay Jay? How could anyone explain Jay Jay to someone who hadn't actually met him?

"Wait till you see how expensive Europe is," his father said. "I don't think you'll be doing much three-star dining."

"We don't care," Daniel said cheerfully.

"Of course they don't," his mother said. "Picnics of bread and cheese and wine . . . museums . . . art galleries . . . wait till you really see with your own eyes the streets and buildings you've only seen in photographs. The sense of history is incredible. You'll never be the same again."

"And Andy and Beth will be in Mexico," his father

said. "Ellie, I think you and I should take a trip somewhere."

"I'm game," his mother said cheerfully. "One of the nice things about being the mother of sons is that after a wedding you're not exhausted. I'll go to the travel agent tomorrow and get some brochures. I'd like to go someplace that's not too hot." She gathered up the Sunday papers they had read and began looking for the travel section. "I'm glad that story about that missing Grant boy ended and I don't have to see it anymore. Every time I read about it I felt so upset. You did say you didn't know him, Daniel? I guess you couldn't—it's such a big school—but I'm surprised because he lived right in your own dorm."

"I lied," Daniel said quietly.

He looked at his parents, their faces turned toward him in bewilderment, and he knew he not only wanted but *needed* to tell them the whole story. He'd been so tired when he came home from college that he hadn't been able to face explaining it all and living it over again, but now he was ready.

"Why would you lie?" his mother asked.

"Because I was one of the people who played the game with him in the caves."

"You *what*?"

"In the caves?" his father said. "*You?*"

They both looked stunned; not accusing or angry, simply stunned. "*Why?*" his mother asked.

"That's what I've been trying to figure out," Daniel said.

His father was shaking his head. "Wait," he said. "Please . . . first explain the game to me. I want to know what kind of power a game can have that would make a group of normal, intelligent college students want to risk their lives."

"Oh, yes," his mother said. "Tell us . . ."

So Daniel explained the game, as best he could. It had taken him months to learn how to be a good player, so he obviously couldn't tell them everything in half an hour, but he got across the basics, and more importantly, what the game had meant. His parents nodded; they were really trying to understand.

"I've thought about it a lot lately," Daniel said. "I think the game was psychodrama."

"Working it out," his mother said. She kept nodding. "Yes, yes. But what problem were *you* trying to work out, Daniel?"

"I think the game was my way of competing without getting hurt," Daniel said. "In real life you try difficult things, you win or you lose, and sometimes it hurts too much. We took the game very seriously but it was still a fantasy. Your character could get killed, but it wasn't really you."

"But it could have been!" his mother said.

"I know. And now when I look back I wonder how we could have thought life was scarier than that."

"Who else played?" his father asked.

"Kate, Jay Jay, Robbie, and me. For Kate it was a way of not feeling helpless. For Jay Jay . . . I guess it was the same for different reasons. And they both liked the fantasy. Robbie was the one who needed the fantasy too much."

"I wish you had told us," his father said. "Maybe we could have talked about it, tried to help."

"I didn't even understand it myself," Daniel said.

"And now that you do?" his mother asked.

"I just know I don't need the game anymore."

"And the others? That boy Robbie?"

"We're all going to be fine," Daniel said. He thought about Robbie again, and the stabbing—the part he had kept trying to forget—and he wondered if anyone, even Robbie, would ever find out what had really happened. They all just had to keep believing the "Killing" was part of Robbie's imagination, like the rest of the game. He felt sick.

"Are you okay?" his mother asked, peering at him with a concerned frown.

"Sure. I was just remembering it for a minute. You don't have to worry. We went through a bad experience and came through the other side."

"And you'll never want to do it again?"

"No," Daniel said. "Never." He smiled at her and let the present and future flow into him, and the sick feeling went away. "My life is too full of good things now. I'm not afraid of being afraid, if you know what I mean."

"Oh, yes," his mother said. She looked at his father, and for the first time their faces relaxed. They smiled back at him. "Yes, we do."

EPILOGUE:

HE THAT IS ALONE

Summer 1980

It was a beautiful morning at the end of June when Kate, Daniel, and Jay Jay drove from New York to Greenwich to visit Robbie. There were a few white puffs of clouds in the bright blue sky, and the trees were radiant with fat, green summer leaves. Grass was lush on the sides of the highway, and the air sang with all the life of a summer day: birds, insects, animals, children at play. Kate had never been happier.

She was with the people she loved, and while she was at home she had accidentally solved a problem she had thought was insurmountable. She was going to write her novel at last: she had the story she wanted to tell.

That was the greatest thing of all—her novel! Suddenly she was filled with ideas, her writer's block gone. She would write a book about what had happened to the four of them from playing the game; their fears about life which had been conquered, the terrible thing that had happened to Robbie, and what the game had really meant. Now, at last, she had an experience to tell about, a real story. All her thoughts fell into place so easily. She would simply write about herself and her friends. She would have to reveal her feelings, for the first time—and to strangers—and that would be harder to do than anything she had ever done in her life, but she wanted to. Kate realized that the feelings she'd thought were so shameful, and were so painful, were the same as other people's, and there was nothing wrong with them. Daniel had taught her that. A wave of such tenderness and love for him swept over her that she felt as if she were melting away.

"She's thinking about her book again," Daniel said. "I can always tell when her eyes get glassy."

"You're supposed to be watching the road, not my eyes," Kate said.

"Am I right?" he said. "You're thinking about your book?"

"Maybe," she said. She laughed happily.

"I always said we'd all be famous," Jay Jay said.

"I'll start it next fall at school," she said, thinking out loud. "I'll have to hand in two thousand words a week for my creative writing course, so I can hand in pieces of my novel. If I do more than two thousand words that's all right too. I feel like I could write the whole book in one year."

"You had better make me sophisticated and devastatingly attractive," Jay Jay said.

"Naturally," Daniel said. "It's fiction."

"May your hair fall out when you're twenty-five," Jay Jay said.

"Oh, no!" Kate said. They all laughed.

"And Merlin's going to be in it, isn't he?" Jay Jay asked.

"Of course," she said. She looked out the window at the landscape flashing by; suburbs deepening into country, so close to the city and yet so peaceful and different. This was possibly the most gorgeous day she had ever seen. . . .

"Music!" Daniel commanded. "I want music!" He had given Kate a cassette player for her car for her birthday, and it had become his favorite toy. "It's Jay Jay's turn to pick the tape."

Jay Jay reached over from the backseat and snapped in the score from *Spellbound*. He had given Kate a dozen tapes for her birthday, and nine of them were from old movies. He had told her they were the classical music of tomorrow.

"I wish you'd play *Manhattan*," Kate said.

"You can play it when it's your turn," Jay Jay said.

"How about if I bribe you?"

"There is nothing I want," Jay Jay said. "I have everything."

"Bullshit," Kate said. They all laughed.

"That's a great-looking watch, Jay Jay," Daniel said.

Jay Jay held up his wrist, displaying a dull-black steel watch with a complicated dial. "You know what this was? This was going to be the treasure when we finished the game. Actually, I bought one and hid it in the caverns, and then I bought a duplicate for me. Isn't it great?"

"Yes," Kate said. She felt a small pang. She would have liked to win it. "Where's the other one?"

"In the caverns forever," Jay Jay said.

"And rest in peace," said Daniel.

"Amen," Kate and Jay Jay said.

They turned in at Robbie's family's driveway. There was the big white house, the fruit trees, the rose garden, and down the hill the sweep of manicured grass that ended in a vista of weeping willow trees, a pond with ducks swimming on it, and behind that dark, cool woods. It was all green and peaceful out there, the splash of wild flowers the only other touch of color against the silvery water. Kate felt more aware of colors now than she ever had before, just as her skin was more sensitive to touch and changes of temperature. It was as if, now that she knew for certain she was going to be a writer, everything had to be observed and stored away. Or perhaps it was because she had regained the energies she had given to the game.

Robbie's mother came to the door to greet them. She looked much more rested now, and her skin had the flush of a summer tan. She smiled and drew them into her house.

"I'm so glad to see you," she said. "Robbie will be happy too. It's sad—his friends don't come around anymore. People can be selfish sometimes, can't they? Would you like some coffee? Are you hungry?"

"Coffee would be fine," Kate said. "We just finished breakfast. Where's Robbie?"

"He's up on the hill behind the house," his mother said. "It's his favorite place. The view there is the best one we have, I think." She poured coffee for all of them and handed them a tray with a pitcher of milk and a sugar bowl on it. They were in the kitchen now; she had herded them all in as if they were her Kindergarten class. Kate had the feeling she was going to make them finish their milk and cookies before they went out to play. I must remember that, she thought. Nice line.

"How's Robbie doing?" Daniel asked.

"He's gained back all the weight he lost," his mother said. "I must say it's a relief to look at the

Robbie I remember." She smiled. "I drink a lot of coffee. I'm a recovered alcoholic—that's what they call it. Or 'recovering.' Depends on whom you talk to. Anyway, I do drink a lot of coffee. One vice for another, you might say." She laughed. "But I feel wonderful. I don't know why I have this compulsion to tell you this. I've noticed quite a few of my friends who've licked the alcohol problem tend to announce it to everybody within earshot. I suppose we're proud of it. Maybe it's part of the process. Mea culpa . . . I guess you want to see Robbie."

"We can finish our coffee," Kate said. She didn't understand why she felt so sorry for this woman. Robbie was back home safe and sound, his mother was sober, and yet there was a kind of pathetic, nervous loneliness about Mrs. Wheeling . . . The kitchen was so quiet Kate could hear the clock ticking.

"I know you're the ones who played the game with him," his mother said. Her tone was tense but kind. "I'm his mother, and I can guess these things. But I wanted to tell you that what happened to him wasn't your fault. Robbie was fragile . . . damaged . . . and the game fit his needs. It wasn't your fault."

"Thank you," Daniel said quietly. "I . . . my mother is a psychologist and she uses that word sometimes: 'fragile.' She says some people are more fragile than others. You shouldn't blame yourself either."

She smiled. "Mothers always do. But all right, I won't. I'll just blame the world. Sooner or later that's a good place for the buck to stop, isn't it? Out there in the cosmos?"

I can't stand this conversation, Kate thought. All those undercurrents. I think I'm going to scream.

"Why don't we go see Robbie now?" she said cheerily.

"Of course," his mother said.

They ran out of the house and around to the back where there was an arrangement of white metal chairs and a round table with a flowered umbrella in the middle of it, set out near a huge old tree on top of the hill. It was, as Mrs. Wheeling had told them, the most beautiful view on the property. And best of all, there was Robbie, sitting quietly in one of the chairs, wearing white tennis shorts and a white T-shirt, his face held up to the sun.

"Robbie!" they all yelled joyfully, running. "Hi!"

He turned, and when he saw them his face lit up. He looked wonderful, just like the same old Robbie, and his new sexy beard was neatly trimmed. "My friends!" Robbie said happily. He jumped up and ran to greet them.

"You look terrific," Kate said.

"You certainly do," Jay Jay said.

"Freelik!" Robbie cried. "I thought you were dead. Did you not die when you leaped into the pit? Ah, I know—you are Freelik's son!"

"Cut the crap, Robbie," Jay Jay said pleasantly.

"But no," Robbie went on, as if he hadn't even heard him. "It could not have been so long ago that we had our adventure. You must be Freelik himself. Did someone raise you from the dead? He must have been a great Holy Man, as great as myself. And here is Glacia, and Nimble too! I have been so restless here, planning my next quest, hoping to find companions to venture forth with me."

"Come on," Daniel said. "That's enough. We came all the way from New York to visit you." He sounded nervous, and glanced at Kate.

"You must be tired," Robbie said. "Please sit here and rest."

The three of them sat gingerly on the white metal chairs and Robbie sat down too. "We're going to Europe tomorrow," Jay Jay said.

"Is that very far from here?" Robbie asked.

"Robbie . . ." Kate said, and then she knew. She felt as if something inside her had died.

Robbie wasn't just fooling around, trying to make a joke of the past. He was back in the game.

"I am Pardieu," Robbie said, bewildered. "Don't you remember me? Has someone put a spell of forgetfulness on you, Glacia?"

Kate turned her head away and held back the tears. Oh, Robbie . . .

"I have had so many strange encounters since we last met," Robbie went on. "I saw the greatest dragon that ever existed, and I was almost raped by a succubus. I met the Princess of the Sprites. Ah, Freelik, she was so kind to me. And I met the King of France, who was very hospitable. You must tell me of your adventures too. Did you meet the innkeeper and his wife? It is a good place to stay—very clean, and the food is plentiful."

Oh, Robbie . . . Kate thought.

"I have the Eternally Renewing Coin," Robbie said conspiratorially. "Every night after supper I give it to the innkeeper's wife to pay for my day's lodging, and every morning when I awake it is under my pillow." He reached into the pocket of his tennis shorts and pulled out a coin, and held it up. It was an ordinary quarter.

That's why his mother told us it wasn't our fault, Kate thought. She was preparing us.

"But I need an adventure," Robbie said. "Now that you are here, my loyal friends, let us go forth together." He stood up. "Beyond that stand of trees is an enchanted lake. And beyond that is the great forest. The innkeeper and his wife are afraid of it. They have warned me to stay away. I feel there must be some evil thing within, and if we could rid the forest of it then the innkeeper and his wife could be safe and happy. I would like to do a service for them."

Oh, Pardieu . . . Kate thought.

The four of them walked down the hill toward the lake where white ducks swam. They stopped under the shade of the weeping willow trees, a cave of green lace. Kate looked at Daniel. His eyes were very sad. Then he nodded. "I am the Maze Controller," Daniel said. "This is the . . ." His voice broke.

"The kingdom of the evil Voracians," Jay Jay said. "Ruled by the wicked Ak-Oga. I am Freelik the Frenetic of Glossamir." Jay Jay looked at Daniel, handing him the power.

"There are great dangers within," Daniel said. "But there is also a wondrous treasure. Shall you enter?"

"Yes," they said.

And so they played the game again, for one last time. It did not matter that there were no maps or dice, no rule books, or even that there were no monsters. All of the evil that had ever existed was real again in Robbie's mind, and so when Daniel said there were Gorvils to enchant or kill, Pardieu saw them. The others did not see them. They saw nothing but the death of a hope and the loss of their friend, and they played the game until the sun began to set and long shadows stretched across the lawn. They found the monster in the enchanted forest, and they killed him. The village would be saved, the innkeeper and his wife would be able to live in peace. Pardieu's eyes shone.

"We must go back now and tell them," he said. "But wait—what of the treasure? Would it not be fine to have the treasure, since we have come so far and fought so hard?"

Jay Jay slipped the dull-black steel Porsche watch off his wrist. He held it out to show Robbie, and then he put it around Robbie's wrist. "This is the treasure, Pardieu," he said.

"Ah," Pardieu said in wonder. "Is it magic?"

"Yes," Jay Jay said. "It will always keep you safe." He put his arm around Robbie and kissed him on the cheek.

Then they all linked arms and walked slowly up to the house.

Class Reunion
RONA JAFFE

author of
The Best of Everything

"Reading Rona Jaffe
is like being presented
with a Cartier watch;
you know exactly
what you're getting
and it's just what you
want."—*Cosmopolitan*

Annabel, Chris, Emily and Daphne left Radcliffe in '57 wanting the best of everything. They meet again 20 years later and discover what they actually got. Their story is about love, friendship and secrets that span three decades. It will make you laugh and cry and remember all the things that shaped our lives.

"It will bring back those joyous and miserable memories."
—*The Philadelphia Bulletin*

"Keeps you up all night reading."—*Los Angeles Times*

"Rona Jaffe is in a class by herself."—*The Cleveland Press*

A Dell Book $2.75 (11408-X)